Lizzie's Journey to Yarra Bend

Linley Walker

Lizzie's Journey to Yarra Bend

Dedicated to my great-great-grandmother
Eliza Agnes Merritt (née Dimsey)
(1817–1900)
This is her story.

Royalties from the sale of this book will be donated to Sisters Inside, an independent community organisation which advocates for the human rights of women and girls in Australian prisons.

Lizzie's Journey to Yarra Bend
ISBN 978 1 76109 188 9
Copyright © text Linley Walker 2021
Linleyjoywalker@gmail.com
Cover photo: Darebin Heritage

First published 2021 by
GINNINDERRA PRESS
PO Box 3461 Port Adelaide 5015
www.ginninderrapress.com.au

Contents

Kew, Melbourne, 1900 — 7
England, 1855 — 17
Victoria, Australia, 1855–1900 — 53
Kew, Melbourne, 1921 — 247

Author's Note — 256
Sources — 258
Acknowledgements — 261

But this is not the story of a life.
It is the story of lives, knit together,
overlapping in succession,
rising again from grave after grave.
– Wendell Berry, from 'Rising'

Kew, Melbourne, 1900

Ω

The freshly dug chocolate earth lies in a rough heap waiting to blanket the body of Lizzie; her sullied history an uninvited companion. She will finally come to rest in Boroondara Cemetery on the tenth day of spring in the first year of a new century. The imported pines sigh, as if in sympathy, and the deep, slow, dying groan of a raven expires the family's relief that it's over at last.

The cast-iron sign states 'Presbyterian Compartment', informing the group they are in the correct location. The cemetery has been carved up into the various Christian denominations that have already been established in the colony. The Presbyterians have a prime site – a large parcel of land to the right of the main path, not far from the monumental stone entry gates.

The members of Lizzie's family, those who have become the carriers of the shameful secret, are gathered together for their concluding goodbyes as they await the arrival of the coffin that carries their ancestor to her final resting place. The soughing pine casts a deep shadow on the forlorn little band of secret-keepers. The wind whispers the secret through the trees.

Ern shivers. He moves out of the shade, signalling to the ageing members of the group to join him on the path, where they become bathed in the subdued amber sunlight.

The cemetery in Kew has been named Boroondara, a Woiworung word given by the first people of this land, meaning a place of shade.

Present on this solemn occasion are Lizzie's daughter Eliza and her husband Tom Gardiner; with them is their son Ern. The only other family member present is Lizzie's son Jesse.

'What time did the undertaker say they'd arrive?' Ern asks, retrieving a neatly folded snowy-white handkerchief from his coat pocket, giving his nose a good blow.

'Eleven o'clock.'

'What's that?' asks the softly spoken Ern, cupping his hand to his better ear.

'He said to be here at eleven o'clock.' Tom's voice is raised, deliberate, the words 'eleven o'clock' accentuated.

Tom peers down toward the cemetery gates and signals to the others. They hear the clip clop of horse's hooves, followed by the appearance of the horse-drawn hearse proceeding toward them at a funereal pace. The horses are appropriately black in colour, out of respect for this sacred occasion.

As the driver brings the well-trained horses to a halt on the driveway, the undertaker steps down to greet the mourners.

'I'll go and tell the minister. He'll be waiting in the room they have here for the clergy – shouldn't be long,' announces the undertaker in a reassuring tone. 'There was a bit of a block on Barker's Road just before the bridge – my apologies. That held us up a bit.'

The minister appears, ready to complete the ritual that this family has requested. As he removes his hat in a mark of respect, he quietly suggests they proceed to the graveside. Just three able-bodied men, plus the undertaker, lift the coffin encasing Lizzie's corpse, and carry her to her final destination.

As the small group assembles at the graveside, there is a brief eulogy given by Jesse. He has spent much time agonising over this speech, uncertain about what he should share about his mother's life, and how much should remain unsaid. Uppermost in all their minds is the horrifying impression of Lizzie once she had been officially labelled and judged. They listen to the familiar and comforting words of the minister as he reads from his worn pocket-sized copy of the New Testament.

'I am sure that neither death, nor life, nor angels, nor principalities, nor things present, nor things to come, nor powers, nor height, nor depth, nor anything else in all creation, will be able to separate us from the love of God in Christ Jesus our Lord.' The reverend gentleman closes the book slowly with reverential care.

Eliza clutches the bunch of violets she's picked this morning from beneath the spreading oak tree in Lucy's back garden. They have been bound together with an elastic band and tied with a purple ribbon. She inhales the delicate fragrance before she stoops over the gaping hole and delivers the violets, making the last connection as she sends the simple gift of love to her remembered mother. The formalities are over. Appreciation is expressed to the minister.

'I don't know when the next tram will be arriving, and we don't want to miss it,' says Jesse, proceeding to the path, leading the sombre group.

Tom gently wraps his arm around Eliza's shoulder, aware that this has been a harrowing time for her. 'Now let's get moving. Lucy is expecting us by twelve o'clock, isn't she?' He tries to sound cheerful. He's observed his wife wiping away the tears with the handkerchief she has clutched in her hand throughout the proceedings.

They hasten to the tram terminus just outside the cemetery gates.

After a short wait, the family members detect the horse-drawn tram approaching, as it takes priority amidst the variety of horse-powered transport that meanders down Victoria Street. A scoop boy glides through the traffic to scoop up horse dung left behind by a chestnut mare, upon whose saddle rides a gentleman dressed in a long charcoal-coloured coat and top hat.

This family group comprises the team of secret-keepers, apart from Lizzie's brother William, who is now aged eighty-six and too frail to make the long journey from Ballarat to attend the funeral. In the forefront of their thoughts is the hope that Lizzie's story will be obliterated from the family history and the secret buried with her, never to be exhumed.

Tom guides his wife to her seat, waiting as she positions her small frame, watching as she sedately pats into place the folds of her black mourning dress and crosses her hands neatly on her lap. She made the dress especially for this occasion some years ago, and she's already worn it twice.

The tram trundles along, the family rocking to a sombre silence, each reflecting on their individual memories according to their relationship to their departed family member, until they traverse the Victoria Bridge and alight to change to the cable tram. Ern grasps his mother's elbow, helping her up the steps. He's noticed her being less tolerant in recent months. He puts it down to the grief she suffers since the death of his brother Rob last summer. He knows it's hard for Pattie, his wife, with two small children to care for, living with her mother-in-law, who is so fastidious about the housework. It's not surprising that relationships are often strained.

Once the tram is filled with passengers, it sets off on its route down Barker's Road in the direction of the city.

Passing the cutting in the road with its high ancient sandstone and mudstone cliff faces, which have been there since long before people of the Woiworung nation lived and cared for this place, Ern points upward drawing Jesse's attention to the substantial building high above the road. 'That's the home of the Syme family. You know – the owners of *The Age* newspaper. I prefer *The Argus*, though. You read *The Argus* too, don't you, Uncle?'

In response to Jesse nodding, Ern continues to question his uncle. 'By the way, did you read the article in Saturday's paper about the Aboriginal brothers, the Governors?'

'I didn't see it, no,' he answers, shaking his head. 'A sad case, though, isn't it? I wonder when this bloodshed will come to an end.'

Ern nods. 'I was disappointed with the journalism. The whole tone of the article assumes they should be hunted down and shot, with no mention of capture and a trial,' says Ern, passionately. 'They had been pushed to breaking point. After all, they were only fighting for the land of their ancestors that had been taken from them. Apparently those the Governors killed were all people who had wronged them in some way.'

Jesse is shocked. 'Surely you don't condone killing, Ern!'

'Certainly not. But I do believe that every person, regardless of their skin colour, deserves a fair trial.'

'I hear they're making a big hoo-ha about Jimmy Governor marrying a white woman, too,' comments Jesse.

'Our stop coming up next,' intervenes Tom.

'How long are they going to take to treat these people with the respect they deserve – another century? Surely not.' Ern answers his own question as they prepare to alight and take the couple of blocks walk to Lucy's home in High Street.

Lucy appears through the freshly painted midnight-blue front door, arms extended in an open-hearted gesture, wearing a welcoming smile as she greets the cheerless group. They are all tired from their tedious journeys to Melbourne and the funeral has been an emotional ordeal. Jesse has travelled from Broomfield leaving his wife and family at home; Ern's wife Pattie has remained at Nirranda with their children where they live in the schoolhouse with his parents.

After using the lavatory in the backyard, and freshening up in the bathroom, they move to the dining room, where Lucy's daughter Emily has set six places at the table.

'Just sit wherever you like,' says the accommodating Lucy with a sweeping motion of her arm, and they each move to the places they'd sat several hours earlier for breakfast.

Eliza has always enjoyed visiting Lucy's home, but today she fails to notice the attractive table setting. It is obvious that Lucy has made great effort to make the visit as pleasant as possible.

Emily calls from the kitchen that the meal is ready, soon after emerging and setting a china tureen on the table, then returning to retrieve the other dishes from the kitchen.

'Would you like to say grace, Ern?' Tom asks. He knows how important this ritual is to his son.

Ern proceeds with the words his parents taught him as a child. 'Lord bless this food to our use and us to Thy service, and make us ever mindful of the needs of others.'

Those seated at the table concur with a murmured 'Amen.'

Lucy invites her guests to serve themselves, handing around the dish of sliced roast lamb. The lids of the tureens are removed, revealing their contents of golden roast potatoes, carrots and peas. The meat and vegetables are transferred to their plates, the gravy boat is passed around and they begin to eat.

'Well, how did you find the funeral? Did it all go as planned?' asks Lucy as she unfolds a linen napkin and spreads it carefully over her lap.

Eliza, who strictly adheres to the rule not to eat with her mouth full, nods gently while Tom answers the question.

'Yes, it all went smoothly. Jesse gave a good eulogy.' He nods in his brother-in-law's direction. 'There will be an inquest, I imagine.'

Eliza turns her head towards Tom, giving it a gentle warning shake. She really doesn't want to talk about the condition of her mother now, especially in front of Lucy and her daughter. As they waited for the hearse to arrive, Jesse had given them an account of his viewing of the body the previous day. A look of horror had arisen on his face as he described the state his mother was in.

Tom changes the topic by asking Lucy how her son Frederick's boot-dealing business is going.

'He's doing very well, Tom. He'll be back tomorrow. You can see him then, and he'll tell you all about it.'

Tom has an appointment in the city the following day, and Eliza has decided to return home with Ern, as he needs to be back at the school on Wednesday. The pair board the train in the city, and settle into their seats.

They share the speechless comfort of mother and son for the first hour or so of the journey, until Eliza breaks the silence.

'You know, Ern, I've never talked about my mother very much, have I? You've often asked me questions over the years, but it's been just too hard to talk about. Now she's finally gone, it's a great relief to me. I wouldn't tell anyone else this, but I really did feel ashamed of her. You've no idea how difficult it was growing up with a mother like that. She used to get so angry with me, and it made me feel it was all my fault. I even thought that I might have caused all her problems.'

'Oh, Mother, surely you don't think that? She was suffering from a mental illness, maybe as early as her childhood, I imagine. How can it possibly be your fault?'

'Do you really believe that – that it was an illness?'

'Of course! There's lots of research now on mental illness. There are plans to remove the Lunacy Act so it will no longer be regarded as a crime. And there's talk they're going to change the names of the asylums to hospitals.'

'I know, but it doesn't change the way I feel. People still make jokes about lunatics. You've no idea how it feels hearing them laugh about people like that. That's why I didn't have many friends. I was always afraid people would find out who my mother was, especially when we were living in Ballarat. My only friends were in the church. They seemed to accept me, but I'm sure they must have always thought of me as the daughter of a mad woman.'

'Now, Mother, you have to stop thinking of yourself that way – stop using that language too. You're such a good person and never seem to put a foot wrong. I couldn't wish for a better mother. I often feel you make too much effort to conform and fit in. There really is no room for shame. It's as though the person were to blame. Some even believe that it's God's punishment for something bad that the person or family did. What nonsense!'

'I don't know what I'd have done without you, Ern. I know it's been hard for you keeping the secret. It must have been for Robbie too. Do you remember one day when he was still a boy, he announced to the minister when he was visiting that his grandmother was a lunatic. The minister looked amused. I'm sure he didn't realise that it was true.'

Ern pats her shoulder and mother and son sink back into a comfortable silence, each with their own private thoughts as the train trundles on its westward way.

England, 1855

Eliza

The disorder of boxes and trunks bided their time in the vestibule, testament to Mother's latest grand idea. They awaited the carriage that would deliver them to Liverpool Dock. Treasured and necessary belongings competed for inclusion.

Mother had urged us to make up our minds; each of us was to choose one favourite possession to take with us to the new land. Didn't she realise it might be difficult for us to decide which precious object we treasured above others? After all, she had all her bonnet-making tools and materials, and besides that, the trunk she allowed for her clothes overflowed into the one we girls shared with Jesse.

Jesse had insisted that his sailing boat must make the journey with him. There would surely be lots of ponds in Australia, he assured us.

'It takes up much too much space, Mother,' I'd argued.

She weakened in the end. I could see its mast poking out of one of the boxes that was already crammed beyond its endurance; it looked about to burst its seams.

I wasn't at all surprised when Mary chose Lena. I can still visualise Mary unwrapping the gift from our parents on her second birthday. We were still living with Father then.

Mother's hands were fidgeting with anticipation, her face awash with splendour, eagerly awaiting Mary's reaction. 'Isn't she exquisite!' proclaimed Mother.

I had to admit, exquisite was indeed the appropriate word to describe the face with peach blossom cheeks and glass sapphire eyes – just like the Queen's, said Mother. She declared that the baby doll with its lifelike wax features was a replica of the Queen's newest daughter, Helena. Mary was too young to pronounce the name, so the doll, dressed in frills and flounces worthy of a princess, was known henceforth as Lena. She was now buried deep among our clothes in one of the boxes, soon to be on her way to Australia.

I settled upon the cards Father had sent me each birthday after we moved here from Chelsea. It was either the cards or my sewing box. I knew the sewing kit would be useful, but surely I'd be able to find another in Australia. The cards depicted scenes my father had painted – reminders of carefree times we'd spent together. My favourite was a watercolour of a day at the seaside. The delicate layers of pastel blue sky and ultramarine sea contrasted with the cinnamon sand. Tiny figures of we four Merritt children splashing about in the rippling water completed the spectrum of colours. Our family unblemished. I had six of these cards now, swathed in cloth I'd embroidered with forget-me-nots, especially for the purpose. My father had not forgotten me. I knew that now.

Mother was disorganised as usual. These last few weeks had been a trial for me. I always seemed to have to pick up the slack when she was in one of her moods. Today she was bustling about, agonising over what to take and what not to take. I was surprised we'd got this far.

Jesse was wound up by the thought of travelling on a sailing ship for the first time. Mother found his incessant questions about the journey irritating, and snapped at him. I suspected she had questions of her own that she was unable to answer.

Mary was pursuing Mother around the house, placating; devoting her attention to any inconsequential chore that she believed would help to calm her. I know Mary was feeling apprehensive about leaving our home. She kept it to herself, but I could see that she'd been unhappy since Mother made the announcement. My little sister would miss her small group of friends immensely, and the thought of making new chums in a new land would fill her with dread.

I had tried vehemently to talk Mother out of this one, but as usual I had no success. She would make up her own mind, despite the fact that she seemed to rely on me so much for support.

The previous evening, while we ate our final supper, I resolved to have one last try to avert this latest venture. 'Mother,' I ventured, 'maybe it's not too late to change your mind. Don't you remember that Uncle William wrote back to say he thought it was a bad idea. And Father doesn't even know we're coming, does he?' Little did I know that my disquiet was to become more than a reality.

Mother turned to me, her cheeks creased by her impish smile, her eyes brimming with their twinkle of mischief. 'Oh, darling, it'll be fine. Life in Australia will be an interesting experience. I know you feel sad about leaving your school pals, but I'm sure you'll come to love it over there.'

I gave up then, knowing it best to avoid a confrontation that would be disruptive and cause further anguish for Mary. I decided I'd have to do the best I could to make things work out. After all, our passages on the ship had already been booked and paid for.

The carriage dropped us off at the ship dock on the banks of the Mersey River on the afternoon of a typical wet and windy Liverpool day in the spring of 1855.

I was somewhat embarrassed by Mother's appearance; her costume in vivid colours was guaranteed to attract attention. Its style was distinctly unlike the ones my friends' mothers wore. Her ginger hair bounced around her shoulders in disarray, not tied up neatly like other mothers. I often avoided going out with her, but on this occasion I had no choice.

The hustle and bustle of the pier was indeed an invigorating place to be, and Mother was obviously relishing the atmosphere. I observed an animated sparkle in her eyes as she surveyed the scene before us. We struggled to keep up as she marched ahead jauntily at an energetic pace. It was almost as if she had forgotten that she had us in tow.

I felt sure that Mother had no idea what to expect on this latest venture she was leading us into. I did feel somewhat resentful at the weight of responsibility that always seemed to end up on my shoulders.

Suddenly Mother swung round, and waited for us to catch up with her. She thrust her bag toward me. 'Please take my bag, Eliza,' she said as she grasped the hands of Mary and Jesse, and proceeded to weave her way along the crowded pier.

I followed along behind, while Mary kept glancing back to make sure I was following. I quickened my pace, catching up so that I could get Mother's attention. I pointed in the direction of the multitude streaming toward a huge building that must be the depot we were told to look for. We approached the building and made our way up the steps, staring with astonishment at the spectacle before us. Two or three hundred beds lined the walls of this expansive place, crowded with people like ourselves. The area was a clutter of confusion as everyone experienced the same shocked disbelief with the realisation that they'd all be sleeping together in this vast space with men, women and children that were strangers to us.

As our eyes adjusted to the gloom, most of the people appeared to be cheerful, most likely in optimistic excitement about the changes that the land of promise would deliver for them. Others simply gazed at the spectacle with amusement stamped on their faces. However, some wore expressions of apprehension and a few were crying.

'Oh no!' I thought, as I drank in the scene. 'We'll be sleeping together with all these people. How do we know which beds will be ours? Can all these people be travelling on the *Oliver Lang*?'

Mother broke my thoughts and addressed us in her most assured voice. 'Don't worry, all will be well,' she said as she placed an arm around Mary, whose eyes had begun to water with anxious tears.

Mary brushed away the tears with her bent forefingers.

'Oh, Mary,' said Mother, squeezing her tightly, 'we're all together. We'll find a spot somewhere. It might even be fun!' she smiled. 'Won't it, Eliza,' as she sought my support.

I was pleased that she was showing some concern for us, so I nodded.

'Yes, look!' I said. 'See that man over there. He looks as though he might be an official. We could ask him what we should do, and where we should go.'

Before approaching, we waited until the officious-looking man finished speaking with another family. After finding our names on the passenger list, he directed us to our numbered bunks in the depot. Mother asked lots of questions, firing them one after another, until he turned to greet another group, signifying that this would be the last question he would answer.

'Yes, they're all journeying with you and your family to Melbourne.'

Mother had another thought and turned back, interrupting to ask one further question. 'How long will we have to stay in the depot?'

'Two or three days, I expect. That's the usual. Although sometimes it's a week or two,' he added, as he returned his attention to another group.

We struggled through the confused jostling crowd. I held Mary's hand, giving it a reassuring squeeze now and then, trying to avoid clenching it tightly, lest I might invoke fear in my little sister.

'This looks like our place here,' observed Mother, nodding to the numbered wooden boxes that held the beds with only an arm's length between them.

She heaved the bag carrying our overnight needs, onto the top bunk. We three children were then told to sit along the edge of the bottom bunk while she retrieved the simple meal of bread and cheese she had prepared that morning.

'It's been a long day. The sooner we're all settled for the night, the better. You two sleep down on the bottom bunk,' Mother said to Mary and me, 'and Jesse, you can sleep with me on the top bunk, as you're the smallest.'

Jesse looked pleased, not at being the smallest, but at the rewards that he had become accustomed to by being the youngest. Mary looked longingly at our mother, but she kept silent with her thoughts. After all, we slept together at home, so what else could we expect? Jesse looked as though he was ready for sleep, his eyes drooping sleepily as he leant against Mother.

'Here, get into your pyjamas, Jess,' said Mother as she handed him his warm nightclothes. 'Look, I've brought your favourite blankie, so you can snuggle down and keep warm. You girls can spread your cloaks on the bed if you're cold.'

'How are we to undress in front of all these people, Mother? There's nowhere to change!' I demanded.

'We'll have to manage somehow. Look,' she said, nodding in the direction of other bunks. 'There's a curtain we can pull round, so we can get changed on our beds. Anyway, it's so dark in here, no one will be able to see us,' she added.

Typical, I felt as I sank into a brooding silence, with-holding my frustration.

I woke to the sound of Jesse's piping voice trying to rouse Mother. Shortly after, I heard her trying to shush him up. I snuggled up against Mary, trying to keep warm and listened to the murmuring voices nearby. I began to wonder what the new day would bring.

After a simple breakfast of bread and butter washed down with a cup of tea, we set off to find our baggage.

We approached the pier, where again there was great confusion as people searched through the mass of trunks, cases, baskets and pyramids of boxes, all set to join the voyagers on the ship. It took us more than an hour to locate our boxes and trunks. We had been given two canvas bags each: one for our clothing and personal items and the other to carry the tin plates, mugs, bowls and cutlery we needed for our meals.

Following a medical check by the doctor and considered fit to travel, we squeezed our way through the crowding, pushing assemblage, amid the clutter of other items waiting to be loaded onto the ship: beds, bedding, water cans, pannikins, hook pots, baths, sheep, chickens, a milch cow, pigs, goats, personal furniture and other large items belonging to first-class passengers. The disorder and chaos on the dock was indescribable. I could see Mother was confused and needed some direction, but I wasn't able to help her.

Suddenly a young woman making her way through the disorder turned to us with an engaging smile.

'I'm utterly confused. What do you think we should do now?' Mother shouted to her, trying to be heard above the cacophony.

The young woman gestured as she yelled back, 'I'm heading down here,' her voice barely audible above the din of shouting human voices and the sound of baaing sheep and hissing geese. 'Over here,' signalled our new acquaintance, as she led us to some boxes on the pier where she sat.

Mother positioned herself on a box next to the younger woman, who said, 'I'm Monica, by the way,' heaving with a sigh of relief.

'My name's Lizzie and these are my children,' said Mother, still puffing from the exertion. Eliza, she's the eldest, and this is Mary, she's just turned ten,' she added, tapping Mary's shoulder, 'and Jesse here, he's my baby.'

Jesse had his back to us, absorbed in watching the sailors at their work.

'I'm hoping to get a job as a housemaid in Melbourne. I've heard there's great demand for women to work in the homes of those who have struck it rich at the goldfields. What are your plans?' Monica enquired of Mother. 'I gather you're emigrating too,' she added.

'Well,' Mother hesitated, 'I'm really not at all sure. My husband and son have been out there for a couple of years, and now my brother and his family have gone out. They would have reached Australia about six months ago. We're on our way to join them there. I'll have to wait and see when we get there.'

I wondered if she would have said more if we weren't there.

'Well, all I can say is you're a brave woman to be setting out on such a venture as this with the children and all.'

'Oh, I'm used to it now. I think we'll manage,' Mother said, glancing at me, seeking my assurance.

'I haven't anyone I know going on the ship, so I'm on my own. I hope we can be friends, and I might be able to help you with the children,' said Monica in a comforting tone.

'Well, I do have Eliza. She's a wonderful help with Jesse, and Mary is quite capable too, but of course we would love to have your company,' said Mother with genuine warmth. I could see that she really liked Monica and I hoped the young woman might become a good ally for me, as well.

After we had spent two more nights in the depot, news was broadcast that boarding the *Oliver Lang* would take place the following day.

As we made our way to the pier, we learnt that we were to be the first group to board the ship: the English before the Scots, Welsh, French and Irish. What felt like hours were spent getting organised in preparation for boarding. Monica was unable to accompany us; the Irish were to be the last of the emigrants to board. A man in the queue noticed Mother struggling along encumbered with her brood of children and bags, so he came to the rescue, which meant she now had a free hand to hold on to Jesse, who might be tempted to run off, eager to explore some new adventure. The stream of boarders began to flow slowly toward the great sailing vessel.

We English passengers were marched in an orderly procession until one by one we stepped over the gangway onto the ship at last. We could not help but be impressed by this new clipper, her timbers gleaming in the weak sunshine; the effect of the sun diluted by the chill of the spring morning. Women were adjusting their shawls and caps to fend off the stiff breeze. I was grateful Mother had bought us new warm woolly cloaks especially for the journey. Jesse was wearing his smart new chocolate-brown woollen coat with matching cap.

Amid the chaos, sailors were rushing about. Mother strode ahead of us, clutching Jesse's hand tightly. He seemed to have no difficulty keeping up with her. I held Mary's hand as we hurried to catch up to them. We girls were not dressed for running, and we'd learnt, but not from Mother, that girls of our age needed to act like young ladies.

With excited anticipation, Jesse pleaded with Mother. 'Please, can we have a look around the ship?'

'Yes, let's do that,' she said. 'It will be some time before the others have all boarded.'

Leaving our cumbersome baggage on a corner of the deck, we set off.

Mother showed us the long list of rules that were clearly displayed on a wooden wall. 'Did you hear the captain's rules, Jesse? They're called the standing orders. Remember, he's in charge of the ship, and we need to keep to his rules,' she said, pointing to the long list of 'do nots' that were clearly displayed. 'The poop deck is only for the captain and his assistant, and the first-class passengers, so it's out of bounds for us, unless the captain invites us up,' said Mother.

Nevertheless, I wasn't surprised when she led us up the stairs leading to the pristine deck.

'But Mother, you said we're not allowed up here,' said Mary in an anxious voice.

'Well, I'm sure we're allowed to have a look. The first-class passengers and the captain aren't on board yet, anyway,' she declared, as she dismissed Mary's concern.

'This huge deck is for the use of the first-class passengers. Their private cabins are underneath – and the captain's too. Apparently, most of them are emigrants like us, but are not regarded as such. I guess they think they're better than us just because they can afford to pay for a cabin all to themselves.'

Mary's brow creased into a worried frown. 'Won't we have a cabin of our own then?'

'Oh no! We'll have to share with a lot of other people.'

'What's this down here?' enquired Jesse, as he ran to the rear of the deck.

A uniformed man was there, and he looked up as Jesse approached. 'Slow down, young man. You won't be able to run about like that once we get moving, I can tell you,' he yelled. 'Would you like to have a look?'

Jesse turned to Mother with a questioning expression.

'Hello,' said Mother. 'This is my son Jesse. Please excuse us, won't you.'

'That's okay, ma'am' said the mate as he turned to Jesse. 'I can see he's interested in this equipment, and I've a few minutes to spare, so I can explain how it works if you like. I'm one of the ship's mates, so I help to drive the ship.'

'That's kind of you,' replied Mother as we gathered round to learn about the equipment that would help the ship find its way to Melbourne.

'Here's the wheel and binnacle,' began the mate. 'The case holds the compass – the instrument that helps us to find our way across the sea, as there are no roads marked. This is the place where the helmsmen and the officer of the watch have their stations,' he explained patiently, as he placed his hands on the huge wooden steering wheel. 'By the way, Jesse, my name's Tom. I hope we'll meet up again on the voyage. Now you folks had better go down to the main deck, as it's only the upper crust that are supposed to come up here.'

Lizzie

Returning to the main deck, I was fascinated by the different accents and dialects I heard for the first time; some so strange that I had difficulty working out what they were saying. Their voices were raised as they sought to be heard above the crowd, as they began to forge new friendships; the resonating sound of sailors singing provided an accompaniment to the babble of conversations.

Our names were called and we were led from the sun-bathed deck at the front of the ship to the gloom of the steerage section below. I was deeply disappointed to discover that the cabin was of a similar style to the depot, but on a smaller scale. The wooden double bunks ran lengthwise along the sides and end of the long cabin. Each bed that appeared to be no more than three feet wide would accommodate two adults. As Eliza had turned thirteen the previous year, she would be counted as an adult. Fortunately, she took after me and was still a small person. Each child under thirteen counted as half an adult, so Mary and Jesse were only entitled to half one of the beds. Impossible! By my calculations, our family of four were to sleep in one and a half beds. Amused by the thought, I wondered how that would be managed. I didn't venture to ask the purser if we were entitled to two, and he didn't seem to notice our little family among the chaos.

'Find yourselves a spot, and put your belongings there,' the purser called in a loud voice.

'Well,' I said manoeuvring the bags into a position so I could move along between the table and berths, 'these two bunks down the end will do. Jesse and I will take the top bunk, and you girls can have the bottom one – the same as in the depot.'

I expected Mary to complain, and was relieved when she remained silent. I began to organise our few belongings, trying to create some semblance of domestic comfort, as this would be our home for ten weeks or more.

Down the centre of the rectangular cabin ran a wooden table about two feet wide, with seating benches running the length of the narrow table. There would be little extra room to do anything but eat and sleep in the space provided, I thought, exasperated.

There was no bath or shower on this level of the ship, just a bowl which could be filled with sea water; thus, for the entire voyage, salty sponge baths would be our only option.

We hadn't seen Monica since coming aboard. I'd continued to carry the hope that she might be sharing our cabin. I had asked the purser if he could arrange for Monica to share our space. He became angry when I persisted with my questions as to why it would not be possible. Single women were to be in a separate cabin, he said. I said I was a single woman too, but he just folded his arms, a look of disgust on his face, and stormed off. I shouted at him, saying I'd be speaking with the captain.

As the number of people in the cabin grew to about fifty, the confusion and congestion increased and the later arrivals sought out places that remained. There was little light in the cabin, and with no porthole, the only light came from the hatch above the stairs that led from the main deck.

We were advised that all passengers were to be divided into groups called 'messes', as I was introduced to the people who would be our close companions for the duration. There would be twelve people in our mess, including Lottie and her children, William, aged eight, and two-year-old Louisa; and Martha, a woman who appeared to be a few years older than Lottie, with her daughters Elizabeth and Emily aged ten and twelve. The other two to make up our number were a newly married couple, Joe and Grace.

Lottie was the first to break the ice. 'I'm Lottie – well, Charlotte actually, but everyone calls me Lottie. My husband sailed out last year to get organised with work and to find us a place to live. So now we're on our way to join him in Ballarat.'

Martha chimed in. 'Really! I'm in the same position. My husband has gone ahead too!'

I remained silent regarding the subject of husbands. It was just too complicated to talk about, especially with people I'd just met.

'I hear there's plenty of work out there in the goldfields,' said Joe. 'Many people are going there hoping to make their fortune finding gold. My plan is to try to find work on a farm – that's what I know best.'

I thought I'd contribute to the conversation before anyone asked me a question about Jasey. 'My brother William and his family are in Geelong, as they set sail bound for Corio Bay in September last year, so they should have arrived about five months ago. I haven't heard from him since his arrival, so I don't know what he's doing there, but I'm sure he'll have found something.'

'Do you think he might go to the goldfields?'

'I doubt it. He's not really used to manual work. He's got lots of skills, so he'll probably find something to do other than digging for gold. Anyway, I expect he'll be there to meet us when we arrive, so we'll find out then.'

I was relieved when Joe interrupted our conversation. I was already feeling I'd shared too much, and was afraid questions might arise about our plans on arrival, that I'd find hard to answer. Someone might question why we were landing in Melbourne and not Geelong.

'Well, here we are.' Joe stated the obvious. 'I guess we need to make a few decisions here – get organised, I mean,' as he placed his rough work-worn hands on the end of the long table and leant forward addressing us women and children.

It had been explained how the mess would be organised. Each mess was to appoint a captain, whose role was to collect our weekly provisions. The remaining adults were to prepare the meals and one of their group, usually the man, would take the food to be cooked in the galley.

I felt repulsion at the sight of those grubby hands still gripping the table, and the thought that they'd be handling our food. I was irritated, observing Joe, automatically assuming the role of captain – just because he was the only man – telling us what's to be done. I felt I had to speak up – none of the other women said anything. Someone had to – what's wrong with that? I thought Lottie might have – I had been wondering if she could become a good friend, but observing the expression on her face, it seemed unlikely.

Eliza started doing that thing where she spreads out her fingers with a pressing down action accompanied by that look on her face – the one that says I need to quieten down. She says I babble. Was I babbling or speaking too loudly again? I know my thoughts were competing, jostling for position, as they so often do. No sooner had one thought left before another one took over. It seems to be happening more often these days. Do these jumbled thoughts come out so people can hear them? I noticed our self-appointed captain staring at me, puzzlement on his face.

I had to escape. I should have worn my cloak – but I didn't stop to think; I just needed to get out of there. I couldn't bear the dark down in the hold. I wondered how I would be able to cope in the cramped conditions with all those strange people – too many people; it was simply chaos.

The dark was drawing in when I returned to the cabin to find the children complaining of being hungry. Eliza as usual, had taken over my role. She was probably relieved when I left. I realised by the anxious expression on her face that she needed reassurance – that I wasn't going to cause further disruption. Tea had already been organised, although there was a degree of confusion as people tried to find a place to sit. Joe had been to collect the provisions and the evening meal was to consist of biscuits the size of a dinner plate, rock hard and served with melted suet.

A steward had been down to light the lamps, so there was now a warm glow in the cabin. We discovered during this first disorderly meal-time that there were too many people for us all to sit at once to satisfy our hunger. In future, each mess group would take turns to sit along the table to eat their meals in a rotating system.

My appetite had scampered off at the sight of the suet, but the children were hungry enough to eat, although I noticed Eliza screwing up her face with repugnance. The meal over, everyone began to prepare for the first night aboard. The girls were relieved to find heavy curtains that could be drawn across the ends of their bunks, so once they were in bed they were invisible to their fellow travellers. Jesse was the first to settle, followed about half an hour later by the girls, after which I went to chat with the other women. I'd still not yet found my new friend Monica, and felt the need to get to know Lottie and some of the other women in our cabin.

Excitement rippled through the cabin that tomorrow we were to set sail. I didn't feel the need for sleep and sat talking with Lottie, until she said she must go to bed. I still wasn't sleepy, so I plucked my cape from the end of the bunk and sneaked up on deck, hoping that I'd not be noticed and could spend the rest of the night up there. But a couple of sailors detected me and shooed me away with rum-slurred admonishments, so I had no other option but to stalk off impatiently and return to my cabin bunk, finally falling into a restless sleep.

After our breakfast of porridge without milk or sugar, we made our way to the main deck, where we could hear a band playing on the pier. The musicians played popular tunes which brought an air of celebratory excitement as crowds gathered on the pier to make their final farewells to friends and family. When the band struck up the familiar tune of 'Rule Britannia' I joined in the chorus.

> Rule Britannia! Britannia rules the waves,
> Britons never, never, never shall be slaves.

Eliza looked displeased, pressing her lips into a forced smile, letting me know that she disapproved of my uninhibited behaviour. While there was an air of gaiety, there was also great commotion as officers used vulgar language to express their annoyance with the swarming mass of passengers as they tried to get the ship ready for embarkation.

Assembled on the pier were hundreds of people, family and friends of the voyagers, waiting for their last glimpse of those most dear, many concerned they may never see them again. Passengers struggled to find their way to vantage points, eager to see the faces of loved ones for the last time. We had no one here to wish us farewell, so I moved with the children to the rear of the eager congregation, a feeling of loneliness engulfing me.

'There's Monica,' Eliza said suddenly, as she caught sight of our friend.

With great effort, we struggled through the crowd until we were reunited.

'I'm so glad you've found me,' exclaimed Monica. 'I'd hoped we'd be in the same cabin, but I'm stuck with all the other single women. I've even got to share my bunk with a woman who kept me awake with her snoring. We have a grumpy old matron who's supposed to keep us in order, but there are ructions already, so I expect I'll be on tenterhooks for the whole journey.'

By mid-morning, we noticed the first-class passengers gathering on the pier, preparing to board.

'No lugging canvas bags for them,' I thought, irritated, as we watched the ladies and gentlemen, some with children dressed in their finest clothes, making a grand entrance.

'That's Sir George Stephen and his family,' said a man beside us as he pointed to a refined-looking gentleman wearing a finely cut tailored jacket with tails over his matching vest and bow tie, a top hat covering his greying hair and a walking cane held purposefully in his right hand. 'It might be handy having him on board too, because apparently he trained in medicine for some years before he changed to the law.'

Lady Stephen's hand rested on the arm held out for that purpose, as she completed the semblance of a couple of importance. Five children followed behind as they stepped onto the gangway.

'Look at his wife. Don't she look grand?' admired Monica. 'And all those children decked out like princes and princesses.'

The other first-class passengers proceeded in stately order, as the emigrants surveyed the spectacle. Last to come aboard was the captain himself, Commander Walter Crawford looking very stately in his captain's outfit. His whole demeanour created the impression of a man who would no doubt command respect from the passengers on his ship.

'Aye, aye, sir. All clear!' was heard above the rowdy commotion.

We stood and watched as the anchor was drawn out of the gravelly British sand, and the great vessel left the dock, led on its way by two tugboats, one on either side. Thousands lined the banks of the river, waving handkerchiefs to bid their family members and friends farewell as they set sail for Australia. The sailing vessel was on her way, gliding down the Mersey with the aid of the tugboats, as the crew set to work, unmoved by the passing traffic. Pilot boats hailed them and fishermen yelled good wishes for a safe journey. The seamen aboard, intent on preparing the ship for her voyage, muttered expletives, irritated by passengers getting in their way as they laid out the ropes and prepared the huge canvas sails. Jesse was mesmerised by the sight of the sailors with iron hooks, dragging huge chain cables along the deck.

The *Oliver Lang* drifted out of the Mersey, signifying the last connection with the homeland for most of the emigrants. The ship shuddered from end to end as though it understood the significance of the moment for its human cargo.

Responding to the cry 'Ready about?' the mate called 'Aye, aye, sir!' and the *Oliver Lang* gently entered the sea.

The pilot had been dropped off and the tugs went on their way back up the river.

'Put down your helm's alee!' was the cry. Then finally, 'Raise tacks an' sheets!' and the whole mass of canvas, with its blocks and ropes, was banging flapping and rattling as the huge sails that would transport us to Australia were unfurled.

As the sleepy sun sank beyond the horizon, I realised that for many this would be the last they would see of their homeland and wondered if I'd be one of them.

Once at sea, we retreated to our cabin finding our first meal a mixture of pleasure and pain, fulfilling our appetites on one hand, but creating nausea and vomiting from the rough sway of the ship.

Almost all of the passengers in our cabin who had partaken of breakfast next morning brought up what they had eaten, or felt as though they were about to. I found myself rushing the girls to the water closet only to find a queue and having to find a bucket, which we shared with the family in the bed next to ours. Most were lying on their bunks, afraid to move, lest the disturbance cause them to feel ill again. The constant rolling of the ship, even though the sea was calm, was something we'd have to get used to.

Jesse was the only one of our mess who wasn't sick. He seemed to be taking to sailing like an albatross to the sea. That made it easier for me, as the girls were more capable of looking after themselves, I thought, as we lay listless in our bunks. The only problem would be to keep track of Jesse, who was eager to get up on deck to see what the sailors were up to. I felt that sea sickness could be endured, and that it was the least of my worries.

At dinner time, a steward came and offered some broth, and a little wine for the adults, as no one in the cabin was up to preparing a meal. Jesse, and a few others who still had their appetites intact, were offered some pea soup and biscuits.

The next day, still feeling a little queasy, I decided that the deck above our heads would be a good place to be. The sea air would be refreshing, and it would allow us to escape from the horrible smell of vomit and stale body odour that invaded the closed space. Climbing the ladder up through the hatch proved to be quite a challenge, as the boat rocked continuously. We found ourselves clutching hold of anything within reach, whether it be ship timbers or each other. It felt good to be out of the cabin, breathing the fresh air. As expected, Jesse was off exploring and asking questions of any crewman who would lend him an ear, while the girls and I found a bench to sit on.

A week later, stormy weather blew in with a vengeance. The tossing of the ship by the troubled Atlantic was matched by a restless night for me, and the ringing of the bell to announce rising time was drowned out by the roar of nature from above. Most of the passengers felt ill again, and the pots of tea and coffee were delivered through the hatch with precautions to 'take care lest they spill'. The hot liquid was poured awkwardly with sounds of 'oops,' and 'ouch' and 'whoa' as people tried to manage their hot drinks without spilling them.

In our cabin, breakfast was a chaotic event, with people trying to stay on their feet, dishes and pans sliding about and falling off the shelves, tea and coffee splashing from the mugs and in some cases scalding hot liquid causing minor burns. It was no problem for me as my appetite had not returned. All I dared to consume was an occasional sip of my water ration.

The deck would need to be avoided today, as the galvanising winds of Brazil were causing havoc up there. This was to be expected, according to Jesse. Jesse was always making some discovery and coming out with statements such as 'We're going at six knots today, that's about seven miles an hour,' he'd explain. Usually, I'd try to share his enthusiasm and show some interest in what he had to tell, but I just couldn't seem to muster up the wherewithal in my mixed up mind.

As anticipated, Jesse pleaded with me to take him up to see what was happening on the deck above.

Joe cautioned me. 'I don't think that's a very good idea. She'll be rough up there!'

But I was actually excited at the thought of being on deck. It might help to clear my mind. I'd become sick of being cooped up down in the hold of the ship. 'All right Jesse,' I decided as I gathered a thick shawl and bonnet from where it hung at the end of my bunk. I hurried to tie my fitted bonnet snugly over my unruly hair. 'Let's go, Jesse!' I said, holding out a warm jacket for him.

He thrust his arms into the sleeves and I fastened the buttons for him.

Even making it to the wooden steps was challenging as we struggled to stay steady on our feet. A stifling nauseous feeling suddenly swamped me and I stood for a few moments, clutching Jesse's hand with one of mine and the other the stair rail. We made our way doggedly, struggling to push the heavy wooden hatch open. Eventually Joe, who'd become resigned to my strong independence and disregard of any caution, came to help.

Climbing onto the deck, we were met by a heartless wind delivering a blasting mixture of ocean spray and rain in our faces. I caught Jesse as he almost lost balance on the wet slippery deck, while a sailor who seemed to recognise Jesse, came towards us.

'Over here!' he mouthed, signalling to be heard above the thunderous sounds of the warring elements.

We made our way to the bulwarks on the downward side of the deck while the relentless wind whistled and whined past the ropes above our heads.

We clung tightly to the heavy wooden railing, taking in the turbulence around us; I was consumed by a mixture of terror and exhilaration.

The sky and the sea were indistinguishable, one from the other. The darkened sky melted into the slate-grey ocean, the frothy surface of white foam created a picturesque contrast, but was blurred by the oceanic spray mingling with the rain. The ship was being tossed about among these elements like flotsam.

I pointed up to the poop deck; no use trying to talk. No first-class passengers were promenading up there this morning, but we could see the tarpaulin-clad figures of the helmsmen attending to their duties to keep the vessel, which seemed dwarfed by the vengeful ocean, under control against the raging elements.

We'd have to wait until we were back in the cabin, when I knew that Jesse would have lots to talk about and as many questions following this hazardous ordeal.

The wind and rain whipped around us and my dress was now wet and clinging to my thighs. I lifted my hand to drag away strands of loose hair that had streaked against my face, noticing that the hand had turned a bluey-grey from the icy wind and rain. And yet still I was enthralled by the restlessness of the boiling and churning ocean.

I looked down at Jesse, signalling with my hands and a questioning expression on my face that perhaps it was time to go below to the safety and dryness of the cabin. I could see his little body was shuddering from the biting cold and it seemed he'd had enough. We had ventured cautiously from the safety of the railing that had been supporting us, when a sudden lurch of the ship sent us toppling onto the slimy deck. A sailor came to our assistance, enveloping us with his powerful body, and carried us to the hatch, where he lifted the heavy wooden structure with his strong arms and deposited us in the cabin below in a wet soggy heap.

Emerging below, we found the cabin in a state of utter disorder. We'd found nature dark on deck, but the dark down here was even darker. We had difficulty seeing, our eyes gradually adjusting to the gloom. We'd been ordered to put out all lamps lest they tip over and cause a fire. There had been a couple of fires already, which had led to Sir George enlisting a team of volunteers to take turns on a night patrol, checking that all lamps had been extinguished, and to look out for fires that had the potential to destroy the wooden vessel and its canvas sails.

Fortunately, I had become familiar with the confined space that had become our home for the voyage, and was able to locate our berth without too much difficulty, although we stumbled over things that had been displaced by the tossing of the ship. There were spills from breakfast, and even some of the ocean waves had poured down into the cabin. Everyone in the crowded cabin was sitting or lying on their bunks, as there was little else they could do while nature's war continued to wreak its vengeance above.

Four days after the rough weather began, we were startled awake by the sudden sound of the ship's brass bell signalling that the storm was over. 'Seven bells and all's well!' came the cry from above, in the quiet stillness of the morning.

I was relieved to discover the storm in my mind had abated as well.

Emerging back on deck, there was great relief and the hope that we would not encounter further stormy weather. Once again, routine was restored. Today was a Sunday and, as requested, Sir George led prayers and hymn singing for the passengers who felt thanks to God was due. All first-class passengers attended the weekly church service, dressing up in their finery as though it was a fashion parade. I didn't attend the services. Having questioned religion from an early age, my doubts had been confirmed. How could I believe in a God who would take away my baby?

As we approached the equator, there was considerable excitement among those assembled on deck, about the approaching crossing the line ceremony. The ritual was an old naval tradition from the previous century, where sailors crossing the equator for the first time would undergo an initiation rite. All the ship's crew and some of the passengers who volunteered would be involved. With a pang of resentment, I knew very well that women would not be involved in the performance but would be required to view the proceedings from a respectable distance.

The day of festivities arrived. I'd had little sleep over the past weeks, and had fallen asleep instantly the previous night despite the oppressive heat of the cabin. I awoke to the sound of Monica's voice. A shaft of light bore into the cabin from the open hatch. I lifted my heavy lids, but could not find the energy to rouse myself further. I noticed that the children were dressed, the girls in their cotton dresses.

'Aren't you coming up to see the performance with King Neptune?' Monica asked.

'What?' I asked, still half awake.

'The performance – I thought you were looking forward to it. Everyone's up there. You don't want it miss it, do you?'

'I can't,' I murmured.

'Come on, Mother,' urged Jesse.

I lay there, wishing they'd all just go away and leave me to sleep.

I heard Monica's gentle voice. 'I'll take the children up. When you're ready to get up, you can come and join us.'

I drew the curtain around the bunk, hiding, escaping reality, avoiding stepping into the world, closing it down. This was something I knew how to do. No effort needed.

When I woke next, negative thoughts were flooding my mind. I lay still, immobile, unable to lift even an arm. It was as though I was paralysed. My eyes travelled around the cabin. Not a soul here. I'd never seen it like this, emptied out of its conglomeration of domestication – living in this small space as one family. How could I ever have imagined it would be like his? As usual, I'd not thought this through.

Jasey used to complain that I never thought things through properly. He was often frustrated with me, telling me to get myself under control.

'What do you mean, "under control"?' I'd argue.

He didn't understand me – no one seems to.

I now realised that I'd never really had to care for the children on my own. Moving to Luton had given me the independence I craved. Yes, it had proved to be a good decision, for I had the support of a whole household. Young Thurza was wonderful with the children, and Elizabeth and Ben had just the one child, a daughter about the same age as Mary. Ben was a quiet man, and patient with Jesse's constant questions. He seemed to enjoy Jesse's company, not having a son of his own.

Elizabeth, Thurza and I worked during the day, sewing straw plait into women's bonnets. All the children were now at school all day, and with Ben away at his work as a blacksmith, we women would gather in the workroom and spend the day sewing straw bonnets, uninterrupted. In warm weather, we would move into the adjoining yard, talking and laughing as we worked to produce the straw hats that Luton was famous for. On Mondays, we would walk the short distance to the marketplace to purchase our supplies of straw plaits. The financial rewards were quite lucrative too; we earned more than most men.

I was glad to find I was able to afford a housemaid. That released me from the cleaning duties and some of the cooking. The job I hated most was emptying the chamber pots into the slop bucket, and I was so relieved when the housemaid I engaged took it for granted that this was to be one of her responsibilities. I had felt a little stab of guilty unease when I used my own freshly cleaned chamber pot during the night.

I guess I was fortunate to have such understanding lodgers, too. The household seemed to run smoothly most of the time, except for when I was in one of my aggravated moods. When I was in a frenzy, I'd take myself out of the house and spend the day outdoors, returning at the end of the day. I would scurry around town, seeking out particular items for my new bonnet designs – dyes for the plaits and ribbons, feathers, bows and lining fabrics – and on return would set to work on my new creations. I had brought with me on the voyage one I'd just completed, made from corn straw plaits, the narrow brim lined with lilac silk. I'd trimmed the crown with orange flowers and dyed the ribbon to match the lining.

That was how I first came up with the idea of travelling to the colony. I knew Jasey had gone because his particular skill was in great demand in Melbourne town, and I was sure there would be opportunities for my skill in the hat making industry. I dreamed of becoming a famous straw bonnet designer. It would secure my independence.

Elizabeth and Thurza seemed to accept my unpredictable behaviour, and were there for the children when they returned from school. Without the need for sleep, I'd catch up on my bonnet piecework into the early hours of the morning. After a week or so, I'd be worn out from the endless activity and sleepless nights, and would find myself in bed much of the time, unable to find the will to do anything but sleep.

What on earth was I doing here? I could hear the merriment of the revellers, but was still reluctant to join them. Anyway, I wasn't able to move, was I, in this paralysed state?

Suddenly, I sensed movement, a form materialising on the stairs. The shape moved across where I could a make out Monica's friendly enquiring stance.

'I was hoping you'd be awake. Won't you come up and join us? Jesse is so excited. The girls seem to be enjoying it to some extent, but Mary is just a little anxious – asking where you are.'

'Oh, Monica, I really can't seem to lift myself off the bed. This heat is paralysing. Do you mind? Can you keep an eye on the children for me – please?'

'Of course I can. I'm enjoying their company – especially Eliza. She's such a sensible girl. You must be very proud of her.'

'Thank you,' I murmured as I closed my eyes.

I began to have second thoughts about my decision to take the journey. It often turned out like this, I agonised. Why hadn't I learnt from previous occasions that my grand schemes failed to turn out as imagined? I should never have been a mother – I'm so hopeless at it. I've been counting on Eliza so much, and now I'm having to rely on Monica as well. It's not fair, though. Jasey should be around to help with the children. I know it was I who decided in the end that we could no longer live together, but why should I have all the responsibility? But now we're stuck in this ship on the ocean, so I'll just have to push myself along until we reach the colony. Surely Jasey will be there to meet me.

I'd spent the day unsure whether my thoughts had been dreams or the other way round.

'We've had a wonderful day,' said Monica, as she sank to the bench in our cabin.

I'd settled myself on the girls' bunk following a visit to the water closet and elbowed myself to a sitting position.

Jesse had already begun to recount the events of the day. 'King Neptune and his wife came aboard mid-morning. They were accompanied by the king's doctor, their barber and assistants. You should have seen them, Mother. They were carried along in a carriage drawn by horses made from things found on the ship. Neptune is the king of the sea, did you know that, Mother? He was wearing a crown and carrying his three-pronged trident and wearing a beard that had been painted with red lead.'

'What did you think of it, Eliza?' I asked. As usual, Jesse was taking over and I'd been feeling guilty about expecting so much from Eliza, and decided to make more effort to be more attentive.

'Oh, Mother. It was awful. Up on the poop, they had a bath made out of canvas and new sailors were arrested and taken before a line of crew members dressed as policemen, who interrogated them. I was horrified by the sight of one young sailor who was being held beneath the surface of stinking brine in a huge bath by four crewmen. I thought he was sure to drown.'

'Was he all right – he didn't drown, did he?' I was alarmed.

'No, but I found the whole performance, apart from the arrival of Neptune and his wife, to be really barbaric!' chimed in Monica.

As we were propelled toward our destination, I realised I was spending far too much time lying on my bunk, overwhelmed by negative thoughts about the future. I decided to make a whole-hearted effort and provide some sort of routine for the children to break the tedium. So I decided that our morning routine would include reading time up on deck. I felt I could manage that. I didn't feel like eating breakfast, so could stay in bed while the children ate, and then take them up on deck. I had to admit that the thought of the fresh sea air beckoning us upward did lift my spirits a little. I soon found that the children seemed to look forward to this part of the day and it proved to be a way to get myself out of bed each morning. If I was reluctant, either Eliza or Jesse would prompt me – Eliza with a firm command, or Jesse, more persuasively, climbing up on the bunk, lifting the blankets and tickling the bottom of my feet.

Time spent on deck provided an opportunity for Jesse to expend some of his energy. He could spend hours watching the sailors, who sometimes let the lad follow them while they undertook their chores. I decided to allow the adventurous boy half an hour each morning before calling him to join us, and then I would begin reading aloud to the children from *David Copperfield*.

While immersed in the first chapter of the novel one morning, I paused for a distracted Jesse, who had sighted an albatross, snowy white with wings dark brown, skimming over the smooth surface of the sea and finally swooping to catch some food scraps being thrown overboard. Returning my attention to the book, I lifted my eyes to find Monica's amber eyes gazing into mine.

'What's your book about?' she ventured.

'*David Copperfield* – it's by Charles Dickens.' I held up the green fabric-covered book with silver title and author embossed on its spine, for Monica to see.

'How I wish I could read!' she exclaimed wistfully. 'Do you mind if I listen for a while?'

'Of course, find yourself a seat.'

We shuffled along to make room for her.

I began to read from the beginning of the first chapter again, in a clear dramatic voice as I heralded the scene: 'I am born. Whether I shall turn out to be the hero of my own life, or whether that station will be held by anybody else, these pages must show.' As I paused to turn the page, I looked up to see some expectant faces around me.

A few other people passing by had paused to listen in to the story, and, encouraged by their interest, I created voices for the characters, engaging my audience as any performer would do. I announced the conclusion of the reading session by slamming the book shut to produce a dramatic ending to the performance.

Once the listeners had moved away, Monica asked tentatively, 'Do you think I could learn to read?'

I was moved at the thought of such a sweet person as Monica being unable to read, and wanted to respond with a determined 'yes', with an offer to teach her, but was thankful later that I'd resisted the impulse, instead answering with a vague 'maybe'.

'I can't even write my own name,' Monica lamented.

'Well, I can show you how to do that!' I was developing a great fondness for my new friend and was pleased that I was able to do something for her. She'd been such a help during those days when I lay on my bunk, nursing my melancholic thoughts.

Thoughts of my father when he was demoted to writing master came to mind. My recollections were interrupted by Monica's enthusiastic voice.

'Thank you, thank you. When can I begin?' Her face beamed the pleasure she obviously felt at the thought of learning to write her name.

'Maybe tomorrow – you'll have to begin by learning the alphabet. I'll need to find a slate and chalk. We should be able to manage with the seas more calm.'

Several days passed that felt like an eternity, when a zephyr breeze drifted in. Jesse returned from one of his adventures announcing that the ship was once again moving – at the rate of four knots per hour. I found it hard to believe that the ship was actually moving again.

As the days passed, the ship was propelled on its southward journey away from the equator by winds of increasing speed. Streams of freezing winds blasted the deck. Warm cloaks were donned before we ventured from our cabin.

There had been several cases of measles reported among those on board. I'd been so distracted that I'd not considered the consequences should one of my own children contract the dreaded illness. Lottie's daughter Louisa caught the disease and, not having fully recovered from her earlier sea sickness, she was now suffering from dysentery. The common disease had already caused the deaths of three passengers, and was spreading throughout the ship like wildfire. The little girl's mother was very concerned. The surgeon and Sir George both came down daily to visit her, along with others who were ill. People in our cabin shared their allocation of drinking water to assist those who were becoming dehydrated due to the illness, but the water now tasted stale and rancid.

As Louisa became weaker, the winds became stronger, bringing on another storm of immense proportions. The huge vessel was buffeted by the mounting wind, its joints creaking and groaning as if in protest as it struggled to conquer the raging sea. Jesse's sailor friend had told him to expect storms greater than the one we'd experienced earlier in the journey. There was also the danger of the ship striking icebergs, and to avoid this fatality, the ship travelled only as far south as was deemed safe.

I began to feel anxious, recalling a story I'd read in a London newspaper before we embarked. A ship named the *Guiding Star* had sailed from Liverpool carrying five hundred and forty-six passengers, just four months before the *Oliver Lang* left the same port. After five weeks at sea, contact was lost with the vessel and no tidings had been heard from her since. It was believed that the ship had collided with ice, but the truth would probably never be known.

Overnight, as the storm became increasingly angry, Louisa died. The surgeon had attended the little girl earlier in the night, and at first light he and Sir George came down to comfort her grieving mother. Without the option of laying out the child on the unstable deck above, her tiny body, already stiffened, was laid on the table. Breakfast would have to be eaten on our bunks. The very thought of having to eat off the table on which had been laid a dead body was offensive. It seemed disrespectful to even consider eating breakfast at all in the presence of Louisa's mother and brother. Poor Lottie, I thought, knowing the feeling of deep grief that the death of a child brings. I wrapped my arms around her, and cried with her, until her sobbing ceased.

'I'll come with you to the burial if you like,' I said, a catch in my voice.

'Thank you,' she murmured.

Eventually, two sailors materialised, bringing with them a length of canvas. They proceeded to sew the child's body into a neat parcel ready for her burial at sea, including some ballast to enable the bundle to be carried to the depths of the ocean. As there was no clergyman aboard, Sir George was given the role of delivering the burial service.

As evening approached, the bell tolled, barely heard above the roaring seas. The tiny human parcel was carried up through the hatch, onto the deck, where the tiger wind was venting its fury. Louisa's body was laid on a plank of sea-bleached wood and covered with a Union Jack, its creases revealing its newness. I joined the sorrowful little group as it processed onto the slippery deck as the wind and rain whipped our mournful bodies. I struggled to keep my emotions under control as Sir George read from the prayer book, struggling to hold onto the rail with one hand as the other held the book. He read with the aid of a lantern while his raised voice was almost drowned out by the roaring of the wind and waves.

It was such a sad and solemn occasion. The only colour in this sorrowful scene was the bright red and blue of the flag. As it was stripped from its resting place, the little body slid from the plank into the angry sea with a barely discernible splash, as the two-year-old was committed to the deep. Lottie leant against me; a low keening wail arose from her convulsing body.

The storm rose to an even higher crescendo as long walls of billowing mountainous waves surrounded the ship on every side.

We returned to our cabin, Lottie struggling to keep strong for the sake of her son. All passengers were firmly battened down beneath the decks, with strict instructions not to raise the hatch, lest the cabin be flooded by a huge wave consuming the deck. Without lamps, it was dark and terrifying. While it had been stifling down here only weeks before, now it was freezing, so we had to pile on all the warm clothing we possessed, trying to keep warm. I spread the girls' cloaks around their shoulders, wrapped Jesse in a rug and the children and I huddled together on the top bunk, while the storm released its revenge on the wooden vessel.

The children were able to snatch a few hours sleep in between deafening sounds including a sail being ripped down, and the vessel hitting the surf as it was flung from the crest of a mountainous wave. Close to morning, there were exclamations as water seeped down into our cabin, splashing those in the lower bunks, as the tormented ship suddenly tipped to one side.

At breakfast time, a crewman appeared at the hatch, passing down supplies of food and water for those who felt they could stomach it. Some were too terrified to consider food at all. Many were wet as well as cold, and looking for dry clothes and bedding. Today was the day we were to have taken our bedding up on deck for its weekly airing, but we would have to wait until the storm abated to dry out our soggy mattresses and blankets.

The storm thundered on for another day, without further disastrous consequences, apart from the breaking of parts of the ship and its contents as they were tossed about. Mothers clung to their children, while others prayed. There had been many accidents, one poor boy breaking his leg from a fall as the ship suddenly lurched. Once the storm was over, we learnt that one of the sailors had lost his life when he was thrown from the ship.

As the storm abated, the *Oliver Lang* was transported by the westerly winds that would carry us across the Atlantic.

I was eager to take the children up to breathe the fresh sea air. The tempestuous sea and sky had been replaced by an ocean so still and flat that the silvery surface glistened with the sparkling reflected sunlight. The horizon that surrounded us on all sides was clearly visible and the brilliant blue of the sky came down to meet the glassy turquoise ocean. What a delight! Everything was unimaginably still and quiet. The deck, washed and belted by the pounding waves, had been scrubbed to a state of pristine cleanliness, unlike the fustiness of the cabin below. I wished I could squirt the hose down there and get it clean like this. The freshness of the air up here too, was the exact opposite to the stench of the cramped living conditions down below. If only we could spend the rest of the voyage up here, I might even be able to enjoy it.

Almost everyone had come up on deck today, so we were fortunate to find a spot against the rail. Several of the first-class passengers were on the poop above – the women wearing the latest London styles, parading sedately beneath their parasols. The girls and I owned parasols too, but they were left behind as unnecessary items. I wished we had them now, not to compete with those on the poop, but to provide some escape from the charring sun.

It was now July and the *Oliver Lang* was slipping along, slicing the waters of the Atlantic at a steady pace, and would be reaching the waters of the Australian continent within a few weeks. My mind played over the possible scenarios of what we might expect on arrival, having been unable to answer the children's constant questioning. 'Will Father be there to meet us? Where will we live? Will we be able to go to school?' I wished I had the answers to those and many other similar ones that had been consuming my thoughts. Would their father be there to meet us? I clung fiercely to that nonsensical notion.

I made a concerted effort to deposit my fears to the back of my mind, stowed away during the remainder of the voyage, where they should not be allowed to venture out until the shores of Australia were reached.

To my great relief and that of my fellow travellers, word came at last that the ship was just days from Melbourne. I felt gratified that we'd be arriving safely, given there had been so much sickness; thirteen people had died during the voyage, including four children from one family.

Our luggage was brought up on deck, so we were able to get clothing and other items we needed for disembarking. I retrieved my reticule containing the money I would need to pay for items on our arrival. I was determined not to rely on William and Jasey, choosing to be independent. It would still be cold we were warned, as it was winter in Melbourne. I put a great deal of thought into what we would wear on arrival. It had been years since I'd seen Jasey, and I wanted to create a good impression; most importantly, one that would create the notion that I was coping. I had fought all my life to be independent, and although deep down I knew that I needed the support of the men, I didn't want them to know how much I needed them at this stage of my life.

Victoria, Australia, 1855–1900

Lizzie

Jesse bounded down the stairs into the cabin. He'd become extremely agile on his feet, moving about the ship on his new-found sea legs. On returning to the cabin following one of his adventures, he'd announced that he intended to be a sailor when he grew up. His round face presented a toothless smile that had arrived during the voyage when his two front baby teeth had finally fallen out. 'Tom says the first sight we'll see of Australia will be Cape Otway. He says they built a new lighthouse there a few years ago, so tonight we might see it!' he announced with bountiful enthusiasm.

'All right then, Jess,' I said, 'We'll come up on deck after tea and look out for it.'

That evening after the sun was swallowed up by the ultramarine sea, one of the crew pointed out a light, barely visible in the far distance.

At first light next morning, the deck was a buzz of expectation as everyone jostled for a good position for their first sighting of the land of promise. Smoke arose from the treed hills that lined the horizon. There was nothing spectacular about the unremarkable landscape, despite the oohs and aahs of excited anticipation coming from a few passengers. However, we were all thankful for the sight of any land at all. As the vessel rounded the cape, it entered the strait, to the great relief of all on board.

Approaching Queenscliff, excitement arose as a boat drew alongside our vessel. We watched as the pilot, clad in an oilskin coat, climbed the rope ladder to board the ship, his purpose to guide the ship through the heads and into the bay. Many rushed to ask him questions about Melbourne, eager to learn all they could before they disembarked.

'There's been a heavy rain over the last couple of days,' informed the pilot. 'You'll need to be prepared. There's much mud underfoot.'

Once inside the bay, the landscape encircled us in a welcoming embrace. It felt like a safe harbour. Around a hundred vessels could be seen anchored in the bay: barques, schooners, brigs and a few steamships as well as a number of clippers similar to the *Oliver Lang*. Being among the friendly sea craft reminded us that we were no longer living in isolation or limbo. We were back among civilisation again, and some semblance of everyday life would hopefully be restored.

It wasn't until late afternoon that the ship cast anchor inside Port Phillip Heads.

'You won't be going ashore until at least tomorrow,' replied the pilot when asked by impatient passengers when we would be disembarking.

As I lay on my bunk next to Jesse, who had finally fallen asleep, my thoughts drifted to the coming days. How I longed for the sight of Jasey's dear face, wearing a welcoming smile. Dared I hope that he'd be there waiting on the dock for us? I'd written to William, informing him of the details of the passage I'd booked to Melbourne. Unaware of his address, I had sent it care of the post office at Geelong, where I knew he had disembarked with his family. Surely one of them – my brother or the children's father – would be there to meet us, for surely the two would be keeping in touch with each other. I hoped against hope that William had informed Jasey of our impending arrival, and that he'd be the one to welcome us to this new land.

At the same time, I faced the possibility that neither of the men would be there to meet us. I immediately shoved that thought to the back of my mind as I tossed and turned on the bed, trying not to disturb Jesse as he slept with the ease of a seven-year-old. I knew how disappointed the children would be if their father wasn't there to meet them, as they'd expected. I'd been trying to jolly them along, endeavouring to raise their hopes, just to prevent them from complaining about this venture. I had to admit, it was more to win Eliza's support than any other reason. I began to feel guilty. Did I really have the best interests of the children in mind? What if I'd made the wrong decision?

The thought was pressing in on me, until I couldn't bear to lie there any longer.

Climbing down from the bunk, I made my way up on deck. I found a seat among the luggage. The chillness of the air coaxed my thoughts back to clarity.

The distant lights of the new town twinkled their welcome. I convinced myself that all would be well, and returned to my bunk, still unable to sleep soundly, but in a state where I felt I could face whatever the new day would bring.

At sunrise, I could hear the sailors busy at work, getting ready to steer the vessel into Hobson's Bay, ready for all passengers to disembark.

Almost everyone was awake early, all eager to be up on deck. Passengers jockeyed for a space to sit among the piles of luggage on the congested deck, sharing their feelings and knowledge of what they could expect once they landed. Apparently, there would be a place to store our luggage on the wharf, so we would have time to find our bearings. I hoped we'd not need to use the storage, imagining that, if not Jasey, William would have a vehicle organised to collect us and our belongings.

The sun had emerged to greet us after the heavy rains of recent days, and even though it was cold and wintry, its rays helped to raise my spirits. By noon, a flat-bottomed boat had drawn up alongside; it began to load passengers together with their luggage to be taken ashore. First-class passengers led the way, the same order for the emigrants being applied as when we boarded at Liverpool.

The day was drawing to a close as we eventually approached the wharf. We had lost sight of Monica, who was one of the last to disembark, and I was deeply disappointed that we'd not been able to say goodbye to our dear friend. She was planning to stay at the Houseless Immigrants' Home in St Kilda Road until she found work.

I watched as other passengers were engulfed into the loving arms of family members, receiving warm hugs from friends eager to greet them. Lottie had broken down as she was embraced by her husband, no doubt at the dreadful news she would need to convey – the death of their daughter Louisa.

I looked out eagerly for Jasey, hoping apprehensively that he would be there to greet us, imagining the feeling of being engulfed into a safe, warm embrace. I led the children around the dock, searching for his familiar face to no avail.

'No sign of your father or uncle yet,' I announced in a jollying voice, not wanting to cause them any alarm. 'We'll need to see that our luggage is stored, and then we'll go looking for them,' I said, trying to reassure myself as much as them that all was as I expected.

It was growing dark and a young man had been along, lighting the oil lamps that hung from the tall lamp posts, shedding a glowing light in the misty evening. After spending fruitless hours waiting, fighting to press down upon the panic that was about to consume me, I decided it best to make our way to the address that Monica had mentioned, thinking at least it would be somewhere safe to stay for the night. The pilot had warned us that it was not safe to be out after dark in Melbourne as there had been lots of 'stick-ups', explaining that many bushrangers had been frequenting Melbourne recently, no doubt due to the knowledge that gold was being transported from the goldfields.

It was frustrating to learn that although there was a new steam train operating, we'd just missed the last one for the day. We'd have to take the nine-mile trip by road. I managed to contrive the motherliness of a hen protecting her chicks, knowing that Monica had a reassuring effect on the children. Telling them that we would join our friend at the Immigrants' Home, I left Eliza clutching the hands of her younger sister and brother as I set out to find transport. Eventually, I managed to engage a horse-drawn carriage to take us to our destination.

Returning to find the little forlorn group waiting anxiously for my return, I led them from the dock and we squeezed into a small covered carriage drawn by two overworked horses. The journey was slow, the horses ploughing along the muddy road at a snail's pace due to the recent heavy rains that the pilot had mentioned. The smell of horse dung as it mingled with mud was familiar to me, a reminder of home. At least we kept moving, unlike some vehicles we saw bogged up to their axles in the heavy Melbourne mud. We passed by a scattered variety of timber buildings that looked as though they'd been recently erected, and canvas tents, some lit by lanterns bestowing a homelike feeling. Near the end of the journey, we observed more substantial stone buildings, many still under construction.

Eventually, the driver shouted, 'The new Princes Bridge – Immigrants' Home coming up!'

The horses led us through the gateway and we observed an assortment of iron and wooden sheds.

Beyond the gate, a porter approached as we climbed down from the carriage. 'Are you looking for accommodation, ma'am?' he asked.

I responded with a profound 'yes' and the burly man responded, 'You'll need to go over to see the clerk at the office – find out if there is or ain't any room.'

My heart sank – please let there be space for us to lie down. Fortunately there was.

'You know we've got rules 'ere. You'll need to abide by them or else,' he added.

I didn't bother to ask what was meant by 'or else', nor did I bother to ask what the rules were. I was simply too tired and just longed for a place to lie down and rest.

We were led to the women's dormitory, where we found Monica and a mixed bunch of people. Some had come from the goldfields, while others like us had found their way here from recently arriving ships. The accommodation wasn't much better than the crowded berth of the ship, but I wasn't concerned about that, just relieved that there was somewhere for the children and me to spend the night. After consuming thick slices of bread and butter and cups of tea that were provided for the new arrivals, we found our beds. Once the children were settled, I lay on my bunk and slept like I hadn't since leaving home.

I awoke to find the dormitory completely empty. I hurried into my clothes and went to seek out the children. They were with Monica in the yard. Jesse said they'd had a yummy breakfast of porridge, fried eggs and toast finished off with glasses of fresh milk. My appetite surfaced as I anticipated the inviting meal, but when I reached the breakfast room, I was disappointed to discover that I was too late. I would have to wait for dinner, which could be purchased in the street. The children were eager to explore what lay beyond the doors of this clean but basic accommodation.

Foremost in my mind was the hope of finding Jasey, so I decided to take the children out to look around, inviting Monica to come with us. It was not far off dinner time and I realised that I was ravenously hungry. There were numerous styles of horse-drawn vehicles traversing Princes Bridge, to and from the town centre. Horses dragged along drays and carts, and horses with single riders churned up the mud along St Kilda Road. There were even carts pushed along by men who struggled and slid on the slippery surface.

As we stood at the edge of the road surveying the scene, I compared it to all that I'd known of my homeland. Wooden cottages with picket fences and a few two-storey brick ones dotted the landscape into the distance. Gentle grassy slopes where groups of people were out walking among the sparsely scattered trees reminded me of an English park.

As we turned to face the river, we saw that thousands of tents had created a canvas town. It had apparently been set up to accommodate the burgeoning population. Billows of musky smoke drifted upward, joining a fog-like haze that drifted northward across the town. A clutch of women could be seen drawing up water-filled buckets from the turbulent river.

We set out to make our way across the new bridge that would take us into the town. It was a difficult task as we tried to find dry ground on the wide road. Horse-drawn vehicles moved along in the miry clay at a sluggish pace, splashing the brown slimy contents of the myriad of puddles as they went. I grasped handfuls of my skirts into bunches, trying to keep the hem of my skirt dry by raising it above my already wet boots. Monica caught on, mimicking my actions. It was not a problem for the girls, as they still wore skirts of a shorter length, and Jesse didn't care.

Glancing downwards, we noted the cloudy brown water of the river below, strewn with sticks and other debris it had picked up following the torrential rain.

'It's the Yarra,' declared Jesse, ever curious.

'It's not surprising he knows,' I smiled. 'Well, the Yarra is surely travelling at a fast pace. It's a pity the ocean doesn't travel like that. We'd have been here a lot sooner if it had,' I mused.

On our right, directly over the bridge, we observed the newly completed St Paul's Church. On the other corner stood the warehouses, recently built to store the boundless goods being imported from England to meet the needs and wants of the colonials, no doubt. Horse-drawn carts were coming and going, bringing in supplies from the berthing ships and carting goods on to the outlying goldfields.

As we continued along the road, a disharmonic symphony could be heard. The orchestral banging and thudding was provided by the workers constructing the buildings that were popping their heads up like mushrooms after rain. These buildings would form the basis of the new city, all built with the proceeds of gold-seeking. There were government buildings, private dwellings, shops, churches and schools, all to accommodate the new society.

The sound of horses neighing and snorting mingled with a collection of conversational snippets in a range of unfamiliar British-speaking dialects. The unrecognisable languages of those such as the Chinese who had come from other kingdoms provided a cosmopolitan atmosphere to the place.

Boys carrying bundles of newspapers were crying out 'Melbourne *Argis*,' and 'get your *'erald* 'ere,' in similar vein to the London cries of '*Morning Post*'. There were shops all along the way, with shopkeepers spruiking their wares as they cried 'hot potatoes', 'ginger beer'. It was a comfort to see and smell the familiar fare.

'I'm hungry,' murmured Mary quietly, as she glancing up at me.

'Me too,' chimed the others as we noticed yet another eating establishment advertising meals for sixpence.

We'd seen a few offering a hot meal for fourpence as well, and decided on the fourpenny meal, as I guessed that Monica did not have money to spare. We entered the establishment and took a seat at a table that gave us a view of the street beyond.

As we waited for our meal, Monica pondered, 'I wonder where all the women are?' as we surveyed the passing human traffic.

'Probably at home, doing all the work,' I said.

'I'm hoping to get a job in one of the nice houses we saw back there,' said Monica, pointing back towards the bridge in the direction we'd come from. 'They must have all the same comforts that the gentry back in England have, I should think.'

Our conversation was interrupted by the arrival of our meals. The children had chosen beefsteak pies, while Monica and I chose the corned beef with mustard sauce and vegetables that came with bread and butter. The meal proved to be quite a treat after the bland fare we'd consumed on board the *Oliver Lang*.

We had a superb view of the street and were able to watch the passing traffic while we ate. Men from all walks of life proceeded along the carriageway, sitting astride horses of all descriptions. The gentry sat upon fine polished leather saddles. Smartly dressed in tailored long coats of fine English cloth, all wore top hats and many carried hunting stock whips in their hands. Mounted on thoroughbred horses, they held their bodies erect with a superior air. They were a contrast to the bushmen and station-keepers, clad in short jackets of rough material and military-style boots covering their knees. Beneath their straw hats, their faces were hidden by bushy beards and moustaches from which, for many, protruded a tobacco pipe. They sat astride shaggy-looking wild horses that I imagined would never see the inside of a stable.

Monica spoke hesitantly. 'I wonder if we should go back after we've eaten. It doesn't seem that women come out in town here.'

'Don't worry, Monica. It's probably because they don't feel safe, but it is quite safe. You saw the policemen we've passed on our way here.'

Monica had indeed noticed them. 'They remind me of the Irish constabulary, dressed as they are in green uniforms and armed to the teeth. It doesn't give me a feeling of safety – in fact, quite the opposite.'

'Don't worry,' I tried to reassure her. 'I'm sure it will be quite safe at this time of day. Besides, we've the children with us. People probably view us as a respectable family – me with my children and their nanny.'

I heard Monica and the girls giggle as we entered the street once more.

Taking in the sights around us, we identified a variety of houses, both dwellings similar to the best and worst of those found in London's streets. A huge mansion may dwarf its neighbour's humble abode as if to say 'I've made it', which probably meant that its owner had struck it rich on the goldfields, while the unfortunate neighbour had not.

Suddenly, I noticed a man casually strolling along the roadway towards us. My heart began to thump. 'It's Jasey,' I thought, but as he came nearer, I realised it was not. Of course Jasey wouldn't be expecting us; otherwise he'd have been there to meet us when we disembarked. William was obviously at Geelong; perhaps he didn't receive my letters. How foolish of me, coming here.

Arriving at Bourke Street, it was obvious it must be the hub for the horse industry, with livery stables and a Cobb and Co. booking office.

Suddenly, an idea popped into my head. 'I think I'll go and book our passages to Geelong. We need to find my brother.'

Eliza's face creased with anxiety. 'But what about Father?'

'Well, Eliza, you tell me how we're going to find him here,' I responded, irritated.

'We haven't really looked much yet,' answered Eliza despondently.

'Anyway, I've written to your uncle at Geelong. It should be easier to find your uncle and aunt there,' I said, adding, 'besides, Geelong's a much smaller town, I believe.'

And with that, it was decided. So tickets for Cobb and Co. passages to Geelong were procured for the following morning. The journey would take the best part of the day, depending on the condition of the road.

We had been told to be at the Cobb & Co. office by nine in the morning, so we were all up and breakfasted by eight o'clock. The coach would be leaving for Geelong as soon as it was fully loaded with its cargo of mail and passengers.

As we were preparing to leave, I realised how much we would all miss Monica. It felt like she was our only friend in this alien place. The children had all become somewhat attached to her; she'd been like an auntie to them, and I so appreciated her company.

'We'll miss you so much, Monica,' was my heartfelt and honest plea. 'I wish you were coming with us,' I said as I embraced my friend with genuine warmth and emotion.

'I wish you were coming with us too, Monica,' said Eliza, who had come to depend on the young woman's reassuring presence.

Monica lent down and gave each of the children a generous hug.

'We will see Monica again, won't we mother?' asked Mary anxiously.

'Of course we will,' was my emphatic reply. Although I doubted the truth of my answer, I genuinely hoped we would see our friend again.

'I'll miss you too, you know,' said Monica with feeling. She had been so grateful to me for teaching her the alphabet. She had been able to sign her own name when she registered at the Immigrants' Home.

'I do hope it all goes well for you, that you find the dream job with people who will love you the way you deserve,' I said.

Knowing that Monica's funds were scarce, I opened my reticule and took out a half sovereign, pressing the coin into the palm of her hand without a word. Monica shook her head, raising her hands in opposition, trying to return the gift, but I clasped the protesting hands, closing them with a confirming gesture.

Monica came and stood outside the establishment, pulling her shawl around her shoulders against the wintry chill, and watched us cross the bridge until we turned for the last wave and sight of each other.

The children and I struggled along the street, carrying the bags containing our basic belongings, much as we had at the beginning of the journey. The girls and I were wrapped in our warm cloaks, and Jesse his coat, on this crisp August morning, but the odour that emanated from the soiled garments was a constant reminder of the ship. I was longing to be parted from my cloak, proposing to buy new ones for myself and the children when we reached Geelong. The bulk of our luggage was in storage at Williamstown, and I wondered nervously when there would be an address permanent enough so we could unpack all that we'd brought from home.

Reaching Bourke Street, we found it already abuzz with pedestrians, horses bearing riders, and horses towing a variety of carts and carriages.

'It looks like our coach is here,' I told the children, as I spotted a red-brown coach with corn-coloured wheels waiting near the booking office.

'I think those horses want to get moving,' shouted Jessie, as he watched them stamping their feet, the air breathed from their nostrils magically turning into puffs of steam as it met the cold air.

'I'd better go and check to make sure this is the coach bound for Geelong.' I watched Eliza reach for the hands of her brother and sister, ensuring that Jesse would not wander off and reassuring Mary. 'She is so responsible,' I thought.

A few minutes later, I returned to find the children where I'd left them. 'No, this one's going to Ballarat. We have to wait here for ours.'

Eventually, our carriage approached, drawn by a team of lively horses that were prancing along and raring to go after a good night's rest.

'We have to wait until it's all loaded up,' I explained to the children as we watched our luggage being hoisted to the top of the carriage.

At last we were invited to climb aboard with the other passengers.

The driver shouted his command, signalling to the horses that it was time to get moving.

The horses pranced at a steady pace, weaving their way through the disorderly traffic on the wide thoroughfare until they reached the outskirts of town. Once the horses were able to gather speed, we found ourselves being tossed about by the movement of the coach on the rough road. It was a different sort of tossing to what we'd experienced on the ocean, as the coach hit humps and bumps along the uneven surface.

A sedate, self-important-looking lady sitting opposite my family addressed the children with what I perceived to be an artificial smile. 'How long have you been in Australia?'

'Two days,' answered Jesse.

'My goodness,' exclaimed the lady in a cultured voice. 'Your father must be waiting for you at Geelong then,' she added, as her curious expression sounded more a statement than a question.

'Their uncle and aunt are there already,' I said, intervening abruptly, trying to send a message to the lady that she should mind her own business.

Suddenly, Mary, whose attention was captured by a child waving a rough stick in his hand as he tried to hunt an uncooperative pig along the road, was tugging at my arm to make sure I saw it too. I was relieved of the need to continue the conversation with the lady who had made assumptions that Jasey would be there to meet us. My disappointment surfaced together with a pang of anxiety as I wondered what we would do if we couldn't find William in Geelong.

For the first few miles of the journey, the road was lined with small wooden cottages. They were so tiny, I thought, barely big enough for maybe one or two rooms at most. Children could be seen running about, so I imagined they must accommodate whole families. 'How would they manage?' I wondered.

Leaving Melbourne town behind, the landscape changed to undulating gentle hills covered in fine fresh grass. Trees with odd-shaped branches and grey-green foliage dotted the landscape; very different from the erect pines and deciduous trees with bright green foliage and straight limbs that were familiar to us.

It was approaching midday as the driver's bugle was heard, signifying we were about to reach the staging post where the horses would be swapped for a fresh team. We entered the staging post to find a blazing fire and the inviting aroma of a hot meal. I led the children to the fire, and we steeped our bodies in the warmth from the leaping amber flames.

The food smelled good.

'Mutton stew, I think,' I said to the children as I held out my hands to the fire to absorb its welcoming warmth.

Generous servings of stew and freshly baked damper spread with golden butter were placed before us as we took seats at a table close to the fire. I set aside the children's bowls to cool as they started on the damper, butter dripping from Jesse's chin as it melted on the crusty treat.

'Now that's enough, Jesse,' I chided, as he reached for his third piece. 'Eat your stew now.'

While we passengers warmed ourselves and ate, our hunger soon satisfied, the groom tended to the horses, hitching a fresh team ready for the onward journey.

Our bodies no longer cold and our hunger satisfied, we all climbed aboard once more. The coach bounced along at a steady pace until the driver sounded his bugle again, signifying that we were approaching our final destination. We peered out the window to catch a first glimpse of Geelong town. It was hard enough for the girls and me to see out the high windows of the coach, so I lifted Jesse onto my lap so he could get a good view, as I had done from time to time throughout the journey.

We could see the bay with its assortment of sailing ships at anchor, which pleased Jesse. There was even a steamship, heading in the direction of Melbourne town.

I began to wonder what we should do when we reached Geelong. Finding somewhere to stay would be the first priority. I was reluctant to ask my fellow travellers for any assistance with this, especially the well-to-do lady and her husband who I felt certain would judge me as irresponsible if they knew the uncertainty of my predicament. I decided that when we arrived in Geelong, I would ask the coach driver. Surely he could make some suggestions regarding accommodation. Then we could set about finding William.

Alighting from the carriage, I approached the driver as he was about to unload the luggage. 'Can you suggest where we might find accommodation?'

'Well, ma'am, it depends. What price do you want to pay? There are plenty of places to stay – flash hotels, boarding houses…' He drifted off as he attended to the task of settling the horses.

'Well, just something basic – clean and warm,' I said as I followed him while he attended to his duties. After the previous accommodation at the depot, on the ship and then the Immigrants' Home in St Kilda Road, I felt nothing could be worse.

'There are a couple of decent hotels in Moorabool Street – not too expensive. One of them is called the Royal Oak. I know that one because I've stayed there myself. It's not far from here,' said the driver, as he waved his arm in an easterly direction. Just cross the road here and then you'll find Moorabool Street – just down there,' he said pointing the way.

Struggling with our luggage, we travelled on foot down the roughly made street in the direction suggested by the coach driver, until we found Moorabool Street.

Before long, Mary spotted the sign for the Royal Oak Hotel. 'There it is, Mother!' she exclaimed, obviously pleased that she'd been able to do something to help.

'Good girl. This looks as though it will do nicely.'

Entering the lobby, I approached the stern-looking woman behind the desk. 'What sort of accommodation do you have that would suit us?'

'Do you all want to be together in the same room? If so, we can give you a room with two large beds. Or would you require two rooms?' asked the officious woman, peering over the top of her glasses.

After enquiring as to the cost, I decided. 'One room will be adequate.'

'How long do you plan to stay?' came a further question that I'd not given thought to.

The woman was obviously growing impatient, so I decided on the answer 'one week', after weighing it up in my mind. Surely it wouldn't take more than a week to locate William.

We found our room more than comfortable after the experiences of the past few months. An open fire was sparking and crackling as we entered, its flames shedding a warming glow to the generous space. The beds were made up with crisp white sheets and topped with fluffy feather quilts in a colourful floral pattern in shades of pink and green.

A simple supper of vegetable soup with fresh crusty bread was served in the dining room, after which the children were happy to settle for the night. I unpacked their night clothes and before they snuggled down beneath the eiderdowns, Eliza reminded her sister and brother to say their prayers.

As Jessie knelt beside the bed, he recited the prayer that provided comfort for childish fears of the dark.

> Jesus tender shepherd hear me,
> Bless thy little child tonight,
> Through the darkness be thou near me,
> Keep me safe till morning light.

But the prayers of his sisters, older now, would begin with 'God bless', followed by a list of all those nearest and dearest to them. Any further prayer would be a private conversation they shared between themselves and God.

The children fell asleep almost instantly, but I was wide awake, turning over in my mind the happenings of the last few days. I'd become resigned to my unrealistic hope that Jasey would be here to meet us. I was beginning to feel really concerned I might never find Jasey or William at all. Finally, I came up with the idea of inserting a notice in the local newspaper in an effort to find William.

Everyone had been exhausted from the long journey of the last three months, sleeping in the cramped conditions below deck on the ship. It was so good to have a room to ourselves and the privacy it afforded.

Eventually, sleep claimed me and I sank into a sound slumber and was surprised to find that the day was well advanced when I awoke. Mary was awake and reading her book, but Eliza and Jesse were still sleeping. Once all were awake, we took the stairs down to the dining room, where roast lamb with gravy and vegetables, followed by apple pie with cream, was being served for dinner.

'How do you plan to find Uncle William, Mother?' asked Eliza as we ate.

'We'll go out and have a look around when we've finished our meal.'

'But didn't you write him a letter, Mother?' Eliza asked hesitantly.

'Yes, in fact, I wrote two letters to let him know we'd be arriving in Melbourne on the *Oliver Lang*, but it seems that he may not have received them. I need to find the office of the local newspaper. I'm going to put in a notice letting him know we've arrived.'

After dinner, I approached the woman at the hotel reception desk and asked for directions to the local newspaper office.

As the girls donned their cloaks and Jesse his coat before heading out into the wintry weather, I noticed how shabby we all looked. We'd all set out on the journey from Liverpool looking resplendent, I thought. I reminded myself to search for a shop where we could purchase some new clothing before the day was out. After all, I wanted us to look presentable when we met William and his family.

Following the instructions given for the office of the newspaper, we soon came across the sign that read *Geelong Advertiser and Intelligencer*. I explained to the man at the counter that I wanted to place a notice in the newspaper for the following day.

'Please write down the wording here,' he said as he handed me a pen, a jar of ink and paper. 'You're in time for tomorrow's edition – that's Saturday 4 August.' After perusing my notice, he suggested a couple of changes.

Satisfied that the message said what I wanted, I paid for the advertisement and then set out to find a shop where we could purchase some new clothes.

The shop assistant in the department store suggested a black finger-tip-length cashmere shawl fringed with elaborate knotting that created a lattice effect for me. 'Here, try it on,' she said.

I wrapped it around my shoulders and paraded before the children. Suddenly my eyes lit upon a shawl in a paisley design. 'Oh, look at this one, girls. It's exquisite!' Once I'd set eyes on the swirling brightly coloured pattern, I had to try it on. The burnt orange, cherry red and deep purple yarn reminded me of a shawl of my mother's. It brought back a rush of fond memories I couldn't afford to indulge. I wished I'd kept some of Mother's things.

'You look simply stunning, Mother,' said Eliza, as she gazed at me draped in the soft woollen shawl.

I realised it would be wiser to choose the black, but I couldn't resist the alternative. Eliza chose a more conservative one, in a soft green shade. Mary decided on one of a similar colour to mine, but a smaller version.

I told the shop assistant to throw away our old cloaks; that the girls and I would wear the new shawls.

The shop assistant sounded shocked. 'Oh, don't do that! Why not get them cleaned? They'll do that at the hotel, I'm sure. Just ask at reception.'

Eliza said sensibly, 'Yes, we must do that, Mother. We might need them. The weather's quite cold today.'

Jesse chimed in expectantly, 'That means I can keep my coat!'

I realised he was looking forward to showing his smart coat and hat off to his father, brother, uncle and cousins.

'That will do for now, girls. We'll pass well enough. No one will notice what we're wearing under our shawls or cloaks. Spring's not far off, so the weather will warm up. Then we can get some new clothes for the summer season. We've got lighter clothes in our luggage at Williamstown too,' I reminded them. 'We'll get your coat cleaned as the shop assistant suggested, Jesse, so you won't need anything new for now.'

The following morning, I was eager to see my advertisement in the newspaper, so I left the children at the hotel while I went out to purchase a copy of the local newspaper in the street. The *Advertiser and Intelligencer*. What a curious name for a newspaper, I mused, as I enquired as to the cost.

'That'll be sixpence, ma'am,' said the paper boy.

I hurried back to the hotel, and searched for the advertisement. Under the heading 'NOTICE', I read aloud to the children,

WILLIAM DIMSEY is requested to communicate with his sister MRS MERRITT, at the Royal Oak Hotel, Moorabool Street, Geelong.

'Let's hope Uncle William buys the paper, Mother. We're here for a week. Surely someone he knows will see it and tell him,' said Eliza with hopefulness in her voice.

'Well, I've just thought of another idea, Eliza. Where do you think your uncle and the rest of the family would be on Sunday morning?'

'At church of course,' said Mary.

'Well, Christ Church is just up the hill, and Sunday is tomorrow, so let's go there in the morning. I'm sure we'll find them there. What a surprise it will be for them!'

I was longing for a bath, and spent the afternoon arranging baths for us all. We hadn't been able to bathe since leaving our home in Luton, having had to suffice with washing in cold seawater. It felt as though salt was ingrained in every crevice of my body; I could still taste it on my skin.

Slipping out of my cumbersome regalia, I tested the water for warmth with my toes, and stepped into the bath gingerly, allowing my body to adjust to the above-body temperature. I sank beneath the surface, soaking my tired muscles in the comforting water. I clasped the oval-shaped translucent bar of Pears, its silkiness caressing my body, relishing the delicate floral perfume of the familiar amber soap as it washed away the accumulated salt from the months on the *Oliver Lang*. Massaging my hair into a lather with the Pears, I lay back, luxuriating in the cleansing ritual. The water had become cool, my skin wrinkled, when I stepped out, dried myself with the voluminous fluffy towel, and dusted my body with the perfumed powder provided. I found the children waiting anxiously. 'Had I been that long?' I wondered.

The next morning we all woke early, the girls and I wearing our new shawls as we prepared to attend the church service.

'It's a pity we haven't our Sunday bonnets. These will have to do,' I told the girls, wishing we had the belongings that were still stored at Williamstown near the ship's dock.

Jesse was still happily wearing his coat that had not yet been cleaned. I'd tried to clean it and mask the smell by rubbing at the spots with soap and water and spraying it with my eau de cologne. Jesse was not bothered, but he objected to the smell of my perfume.

Stepping out into the street, we heard church bells calling the people of the town to worship. Groups of people approached the sandstone edifice that was obviously incomplete, with scaffolding around the rear of the building.

'It's not as grand as the cathedrals at home,' said Eliza. 'The bell tower is not very tall at all.'

Suddenly memories of my childhood came flooding back. St Mary's in Hitchin had been my second home.

'Did I ever tell you about how I climbed the bell tower at Hitchin?' I asked the children.

'No,' said Jesse. 'Please tell us about it.'

'Not now, we don't have time. Remind me tonight and I'll tell you the whole story at bedtime.'

The children loved hearing stories of my childhood.

Standing outside the church, my eyes searched each group of people as they entered the church yard; I longed for one of these family groups approaching to be mine. It was almost time for the service to begin, so I led the children inside. Perhaps William was already seated with his family.

The words of the familiar liturgy flowed over me as I waited impatiently for the final 'Amen' so I could resume my search for William. Proceeding out of the church, I became increasingly apprehensive, as there was still no sighting of the familiar faces I desperately needed to see. Our little family stood about in total isolation. I felt completely alone as I listened to the congregation happily conversing with one another.

'We'll wait until the vicar has finished talking to people, and then ask him if he knows them. Perhaps there's a reason they couldn't come to church today,' I said, clinging to hope.

Finally the vicar appeared to be free. He extended his hand as I approached, saying, 'Hello, I'm the Reverend George Goodman. You're new here, aren't you?' he asked as he smiled and clasped my extended hand with his firm cool one, and leant down to greet the children.

'Yes, I'm looking for my brother. His name is William Dimsey and I'm sure he would be attending here. He arrived from England with his family in December last.'

'Dimsey, you say. I'll need to check my records. I must say it does sound familiar. Could you come to see me at the parsonage tomorrow and I'll see what I can find out for you,' he said, and after a pause continued, 'I do recollect that there was a funeral.'

My heart sank. 'Could it be that William is dead?'

Following dinner, I instructed the children to lie on their beds for a nap but, as Jesse and Eliza began to protest, I said they could read their books, but must lie down. I needed some peace and quiet to rest my troubled mind, which had been swinging back and forth from hope to despair, like a pendulum.

I lay on the bed, encouraging the children, and picked up *David Copperfield*. After reading only a few paragraphs, I dozed off. I awoke with a dream fresh in my mind of my brother as protector. 'What if William is dead? How will I cope?'

After supper, Jesse reminded me of my promise to tell them the story of my climb up St Mary's bell tower. We snuggled up together on the girl's bed for the telling of the tale.

'Once upon a time,' I began – I always began my stories with the children in this manner – 'there was a little girl called Lizzie who was being her most troublesome self. It was the end of a school day, and her parents were consumed with other affairs concerning the school after long hours of teaching their pupils. Her father had bookwork to attend to at the church.'

I was interrupted by Jesse's question, 'Why did your father have to do work at the church?'

'He was the parish clerk. I thought you knew that. He had to or-ganise and record the baptisms, weddings and funerals,' I answered, adding, 'I'll tell you more about that another time,' and I continued the story. 'So the little girl's father offered to take her with him to the church, as he knew she loved to spend time there. She knew every foot of the churchyard and every headstone. Sometimes, she would meet a friend there. They would play hide and seek outside among the tomb-stones; and inside in the chapels and porches, and among the pillars and screens. Alone as she was on this day, she went to have a look at the animal carvings on the front pew desks. One of her favourite things was the angel screen that guarded the entrance to the Guild Chapel. She felt as though she was surrounded by angels when in the cathedral. She would sometimes go around counting how many angels she could see depicted in the carvings and paintings around the walls. There was a section she liked to explore called the Charnel House that was once used as a prison by Cromwell's men.'

Jesse began to ask another question.

'Now please don't ask me about Cromwell. It would take too long to explain that now,' and I continued with my story. 'Time passed slowly and the little girl became bored. She noticed that her father was still engrossed with writing in his books. She'd often wondered what it would be like to be up at the top of the bell tower. She went over to where her father was working and whispered softly, "I'm going up the tower,", hoping he wouldn't hear because she knew he'd stop her, but later she could say that she had told him so. He was so absorbed in his work, she felt certain he hadn't heard her. So off the little girl went, into the vestry. She found the door to the tower open, so off she set, climbing round and round and round the steep stone staircase, until she reached the first level, where she saw thick ropes hanging from above. She tried to give one of the heavy ropes a tug, but it would only budge an inch or two, no matter how hard she tried. She imagined they were the ropes that the bell ringers pulled to make the bells ring.

'Little Lizzie climbed upward once more, circling round and round again. Once up to the next level, she found herself dwarfed by enormous bronze bells – she counted, one, two, three… There were twelve. There was not much room to move in there, so onward and up she wound, round and round the narrow staircase. The little girl had the feeling that she was climbing up to the sky to fly with the birds. When at last she reached her destination, she found herself among the tops of the tall trees in the church yard, their leaves fresh and green with spring growth. She flung her arms wide like this,' as I demonstrated to the children, 'like the wings of a golden eagle, and she glided in circles on top of the turret as though she was about to fly out over the village and beyond, above the rolling hills.

'The parapet was too high for her to see below, so she climbed – I always was a good climber – up on top, enjoying the warmth that the stone surface had soaked up from the sun during the day. She sat surveying the scene below and beyond. She could see the stone monuments on her grandparents' graves near the gate to the churchyard that led to the market square, which had been swarming with people hours earlier for it was a market day. It was quiet now, and the little girl watched as a few people loaded their carts as they packed up the remaining wares from their stalls. The horses skittered as if to say, "Let's get moving, I want to get home to my stable."

'Unaware of the time, little Lizzie sat and watched, enthralled, while the glow of a few oil lamps illuminated the windows of the well to do, and the odd torch on a couple of street corners produced a flaming radiance in the fading light of day. Suddenly, the little girl heard her father's voice coming from the stairwell, unsteady, but controlled, probably so he wouldn't frighten or startle her lest she fall the hundreds of feet to the ground. "Come here," he said, his arms held out invitingly. She ran to be enfolded in his strong arms, soaking up the loving embrace that was a rare treat for her.

'They began the descent in cold silence as they retraced their steps unwinding round and round the three levels in the dim evening light. Once back on the ground in the vestry, her father began his tirade. "You, naughty girl." His voice was filled with anger.'

I paused, discarding my storytelling voice. 'I realise now that he was angry because he knew if I'd fallen, I'd have been killed. I know how worried I'd be if one of you did that.'

I resumed the story. 'The little girl wondered how her father had discovered she was up there. She'd planned to come back down before she was missed. She soon had her answer. William showed up. Of course, she thought – big brother always watching out for me. Mother had sent him to tell us it was teatime. As he'd entered the churchyard, he happened to look upward and caught sight of me sitting on the top of the turrets.'

The story over, I said, 'Now it's well past your bedtime. We need to be up early tomorrow for my meeting with the vicar.'

Jesse was already asleep when I climbed into bed beside him. I lay awake, my mind drifting to thoughts of William. The story had stirred up memories of my big brother as protector, but a righteous one he was. He never misbehaved, or let our parents down. People would say, 'You're Mr Dimsey's son, aren't you?' in a tone that showed he was valued and respected like Father. I, on the other hand, always felt accused of some misdemeanour, and, 'You're Mr Dimsey's daughter, aren't you?' was said in a way that made me feel ashamed.

My first thought on waking next morning was of William, and my need to know that he was alive and well. Finding Jesse already up and clothed, I woke the girls and urged them to get dressed too for my meeting with the vicar. As we negotiated the stairs, the flavoursome aroma of bacon and eggs drifted up to meet us. Eager to be on my way, I urged Eliza to hurry as she rested her knife and fork while she chewed some bacon. Jesse had already finished. So had I. Mary promptly laid her knife and fork on the plate, announcing that she'd had enough.

Stepping onto the busy roadway, we waited as a bullock wagon overloaded with wool lumbered past on its way to the wharf, the driver no longer needing to prod the tired beasts, as they made the downhill run. We could see the wagon's destination lying below – Corio Bay, with hundreds of ships lying at anchor. Our gaze followed the passing coaches laden with miners, merchants and professional men, coming and going between the goldfields and the booming town of Geelong.

We found the parsonage near the church and could hear the builders hammering purposefully as they toiled to complete the extensions to the church following their day of rest.

The Reverend Goodman presented himself in response to the resounding raps of the polished brass knocker on the heavy wooden door. The vicar greeted us, apologising for the noise, as his eyes focused on the construction work. 'The church was only completed eight years ago, but already it's been outgrown. They're adding a transept and sanctuary now.'

Anxious to find answers to my consuming fears, I didn't answer. I was interested in nothing but my brother's welfare and whereabouts.

'Ah yes, following my conversation with you yesterday, I soon found the family. There's only one reference to that name in our records. There were six children, I believe. I remembered the funeral too. The ones for little children always stick in my mind – so sad,' he said in a melancholic voice.

I felt instant relief that my brother must be alive, followed shortly by heartfelt sadness when I realised that one of William's children must have died.

The vicar led us into his office, where a dark green leather-bound burial register lay on his desk. He turned the stiff, grey pages of the book carefully. 'See here,' he said pointing to the entry that read, 'Anna Maria Dimsey, buried Geelong Eastern Cemetery, 31 January 1855, daughter of William and Mary Dimsey.'

'Would this be the family?' enquired the minister as he turned to me with a quizzical expression.

'Yes,' I said. Empathic thoughts of my sister-in-law tugged at me as I remembered the death of my own baby. 'They sailed from England on the *Agra* in September, so would have entered Corio Bay about early December, I expect.'

'Ah, yes. I do recall,' said the vicar. 'Their ship dropped anchor on the day of the Eureka Rebellion – it was the third of December. I distinctly remember your brother explaining how frustrating it had been waiting to come ashore due to the goings on at the diggings. I suppose it's understandable after such a long voyage, and the little one was already unwell when they arrived. I suppose he wanted to get some medical help for his daughter in Geelong.'

'I wouldn't be surprised. The surgeon we had on the ship was thought to be very incompetent, actually,' I said, recalling Sir George's scathing remarks.

The vicar returned the heavy book to its place in his ornate oak bookcase.

'Do you have any idea where the Dimsey family is now?' I ventured.

'I'm not certain,' said the vicar, 'but I believe they may have gone to Ballarat. If you can't find them here, that seems to be the most likely possibility. Many people are heading for the goldfields to take advantage of the opportunities that are arising there.'

As the reverend showed us to the door, I shook his hand as I thanked him for his time.

My hopes of finding William and his family in Geelong continued to fade.

'We'll wait until the week is up, just in case they're still here,' I explained to the children as we retraced our steps down the hill towards the hotel. But if we don't hear from your uncle by then, we'll just have to take the journey to Ballarat.'

The week soon passed as we explored the new town, taking time to rest from our epic journey. The cold weather continued, so I was glad I'd been persuaded by the shop assistant to keep our cloaks and Jesse's coat. I had arranged to have them cleaned at the hotel. Returning from an outing one day, the garments were found hanging in our room, looking like new, but smelling of the chemicals that had been used to clean them. Although the girls complained of the acrid odour, they'd shaken off the putrid smells accumulated on the voyage. Jesse didn't complain; he was just pleased that his new coat had been rescued, no matter how it smelt.

Everywhere we went, I asked the same question of any strangers we met. 'Do you know a man named William Dimsey? He arrived here with his wife Mary and their six children December last.'

Over and over again, I heard the same response – they had not heard of him or his family – each time leaving me with a feeling of disappointment coupled with fear that maybe we would never find them.

Jesse had particularly loved the walk down to the port where we caught sight of ocean vessels of all kinds, including sailing ships similar to the *Oliver Lang*. It brought back memories of the laborious journey still so fresh in our minds.

Walks to the beach were a lot of fun. Although the weather was too cold for swimming, the children were able to paddle in the calm water of the bay. The girls helped Jesse build a sandcastle on the beach, while

I sat close by letting the sand run through my fingers as I watched people passing along the seashore.

I decided to take the children to the new Theatre Royal, where we all enjoyed a pantomime about the gold diggings. It was the children's first visit to the theatre, and although the performance was aimed at an older audience, the children loved the colour and music of the spectacular show.

I struggled to hide the anxious feelings that kept rising up within me. I was determined to find my brother, not only for my own selfish reasons, but for the sake of the children. I now realised I had not considered the children when coming up with my original plan. My quest to find a place in the straw bonnet industry, I now realised, was fanciful. Now there was no turning back, and the children had become the focus for any future plans.

I was grateful and relieved that I'd managed to survive the journey to date without any major mishaps, but knew the day would come again when my anxiety would be so difficult to manage that I'd not be able to cope. I was always worried that my bouts of confusion and relentless activity would return – and the times when I couldn't raise myself from my bed. I now carried the constant fear that if and when it did happen, there would be no family there to help care for the children.

I had to concede that William and his family were no longer in Geelong and must have gone to Ballarat. Leaving the children under the watchful eye of an older woman we'd met at the hotel, I walked to the Black Bull Inn in Malop Street where I'd seen coaches arriving and departing, laden with passengers. I was informed that no booking was needed for the daily coach.

'Just turn up,' was the answer to my enquiry, 'but be here early if you want a seat inside, otherwise you'll have to ride on top, and at this time of the year it gets pretty cold up there. It'll take all day and cost you five pounds,' said the young man behind the counter.

'Five pounds!' I exclaimed, shocked at the exorbitant fare. 'That's ridiculous! I can't possibly afford that. I have three children as well as myself.'

'Yes, and extra if you've got luggage too,' replied the young man in a tone that sounded as though he agreed with me. After glancing around, he leant across the counter so he wouldn't be overheard, and whispered, 'But I hear you can get fares on a coach for as low as ten shillings now. Go down to the port and ask around. I'm sure you'll find a carriage to take you to Ballarat for a great deal less than five pounds.'

I hurried back to the hotel, growing more and more agitated. Dashing along Moorabool Street, I was nearly run down by a stray bullock that had broken loose and was ambling along the road. 'Hells bells,' I exclaimed as I gathered my skirts, and continued rushing along, almost at a run.

I found the children engaged happily in a game of dominoes, as the words tumbled out in a breathless voice, 'I have to go down to the port now. Can the children stay with you while I do that?'

'Certainly,' replied the kindly lady. 'We're fine, aren't we, children?' and the girls nodded, no doubt observing the state I was in.

Safer to stay here, they probably conceded.

Jesse, however, said, 'Can I come with you, Mother?'

'Oh, all right,' I answered impatiently, already on my way. 'Come on then.' I clasped his little hand, yanking his body into action, not slowing my pace until we reached the bottom of the hill.

Down at the port, I approached a man who was loading goods onto a cart and asked, 'Do you know where I can get a cheap coach fare to Ballarat? For four people, that is,' I added.

The man didn't look up as he continued with his task and waved his hand to identify a group of men standing on the wharf. 'Ask over there. Perhaps someone there might know.'

I approached the group, and listened to the accumulated knowledge, finally coming to the conclusion that a passage could be obtained for one pound per person on a coach that left further down Malop Street.

'You'll have to be there early though,' said one man, 'as there's lots of people heading for the goldfields, and the coaches fill up fast.'

'Thank you,' I said, in a hurry to be off, grateful for the advice as I turned to look for Jesse who had wandered off to look at the ships. Catching sight of him, I called, 'Come on, Jesse. It's all right. We'll be on our way to Ballarat tomorrow.'

A slight glow in the sky signalled the day was dawning as we set out for Malop Street. As we made our way along the street, we spotted a dilapidated coach attached to a motley team of horses that looked as though they had seen better days. I approached the driver and enquired if he could take the four of us to Ballarat.

'Yes, indeed: two pounds inside the carriage and one pound on the roof. Which do you prefer?'

'We'll ride on top, thank you.' I rather relished the idea of being out in the open air. It could be an exciting journey. I was in the mood for that, I thought, as the driver helped us climb aboard.

'This will be fun! Much better than travelling in the bottom of the dark and stinking hold of the *Oliver Lang*, don't you think?' I said, trying to enthuse the children.

Before long, a large woman, assisted by the driver, struggled to mount the coach. Panting heavily from the effort, she slumped onto the front seat and set about arranging the various parts of her copious figure into a comfortable position. My attempt at conversation was met with an abrupt 'Hrmph.'

I caught a glimpse of the kindly face of a man as he made the ascent to the top of the coach.

'Hello, there. I'm Daniel Crocker,' he proclaimed with an accent that was recognisably American.

I observed the owner of the voice. His brown, brimmed felt hat was tilted at a jaunty angle. His colour-matched overcoat was of a fine cloth and tailored to fit. He finished off the outfit with a red necktie that gave an individual flourish complementing his self-assured demeanour.

'Surely he could afford the two pounds to ride inside the coach.' My musing was answered by his declaration that he would much prefer to be in the open air than cooped up inside the cramped coach.

'Hello,' I said, as I introduced the children to the American.

The woman remained silent, as she fussed with the contents of her carpet bag.

'Well now, you must all call me Dan,' said the man with a generous gesture of his arms. I had already decided to name him the American. 'Not much room up here. Hardly room for the six of us,' he pronounced.

After some discussion, it was agreed that the woman, who was now already settled on the front seat, should remain undisturbed, and that Mary and Eliza would take up the other two spaces next to her. Jesse would sit between me and the American on the rear seat.

Once the coach was filled, mostly with single men on their way to the goldfields, we heard the driver signalling to the team of horses that the journey was about to begin.

It was still quite early in the morning, long before the sun would push the darkness and cold away. I wrapped my cloak tightly across my chest and put my arm around Jesse, snuggling up close.

The horses slowed as they ascended a hill on the outskirts of town.

'What's that on top of the hill?' asked Jesse.

'I don't know. It looks like a pole with something on top,' I said, straining to see the object of Jesse's enquiry in the pre-dawn light.

'It's a bell,' broke in the American. 'This hill is called Bellpost. The bell is an alarm used to warn the settlers that Aborigines are planning an attack.'

Out in the country, we travelled along the crest of a hill where we had a fine view of homesteads surrounded with grassy rolling hills dotted with flocks of grazing sheep.

'Look, Mother,' said Jesse. 'Lots of sheeps.'

'Yes, I see, Jesse. But it's not sheeps – just sheep.'

'But there's not just one. It must be sheeps,' retorted Jesse.

'It's just the English language, Jesse. I know we say cow and cows, and pig and pigs, but when it comes to more than one sheep we still say sheep. Sheeps isn't a word at all.'

'Well, that's stupid,' said Jesse pausing to think. 'So sheep is the word for one sheep and for hundreds of sheeps like there are here.'

Over Jesse's head, I caught the eyes of our new acquaintance.

He seemed amused. 'Aye, he's a bright little lad,' he said, nudging Jesse with his shoulder.

I was surprised that there didn't appear to be a road at all, just a hotchpotch of tracks that had been made in order to skirt around boggy patches left by earlier traffic heading in both directions. The tracks wound their way around swamps and rocky outcrops, alongside creeks, over hills and down valleys as the driver guided his team of horses through the multitude of eager humanity rushing to the goldfields surrounding Ballarat.

We soon discovered we had a running commentary for the journey. Our American companion was a fount of knowledge as he continued to describe the changing landscape. It was obvious he'd travelled this way on many occasions. 'Perhaps he's a merchant,' I speculated, trying to guess at his occupation, not wanting to be deemed nosy by asking the question.

The woman swivelled in her seat with great effort and leant toward me and whispered loudly. 'I wish he'd shut up. He's such a know-it-all, and his voice is so loud!'

I remained silent. I was actually enjoying the descriptions and explanations of what we were seeing, and it was keeping the children entertained. Jesse was even providing encouragement to the man who'd asked to be known as 'Dan', as the curious boy asked questions for clarification.

As the coach negotiated a steep descent, Dan informed us that the Moorabool Valley lay below.

'Moorabool,' said Jesse. 'We stayed at a hotel in Moorabool Street.'

'It's named after the river,' said Dan. 'We'll be crossing it soon, but we'll be stopping at Batesford first, where the horses will be swapped for fresh ones. You can get breakfast there. There are a couple of hotels, but in my opinion you're better to wait until the next stop, where you can get an excellent breakfast at Dunlop's Inn.'

The horses were drawn to a halt.

The driver, who had climbed down from his seat on the coach, called out to us, 'Fifteen-minute stop. Breakfast here if you like.'

Conscious of my diminishing funds, I had purchased in Geelong the previous day a loaf of bread, half a pound of butter and a jar of strawberry jam for the journey. I found a bench in front of the public house where breakfast was being offered. Tearing off chunks of the crusty loaf, I proceeded to spread them generously with butter and jam with the small knife I carried in my bag. I handed each of the children an appropriately sized piece according to their individual appetites.

When we had finished eating, I led the children into the hotel, where I ordered four cups of tea, adding, 'Three with extra milk and sugar please.'

We had barely finished drinking our tea when people were seen to be climbing back aboard the coach, and we were on our way again. The fresh horses trundled along at a steady pace as the Moorabool River came into view. The driver guided the horses to a walking pace as he steered them across the rickety wooden bridge that sank in the middle from the many burdens that had been carted across its rugged structure. I looked down anxiously, catching sight of the river flowing swiftly below, following rain in the hills above.

Dan entertained us with stories of miners striking it rich at the goldfields. There were a few tales of men who had become instantly wealthy; one story circulating in the goldfield community was of a man who found eight pounds of gold washed from just two dishes of earth. Dan said that he believed the anticipation of instant riches was at fever pitch.

Conversation slowed to a trickle as the coach rocked and jolted over the rough terrain. The sun sent a glowing message that it was about to surface above the hills to the east.

'Next stop coming up,' declared Dan. 'This is the Dunlop Inn, where you can get a breakfast as good as you'd get back in England. That is, if you haven't eaten already,' he added, catching my eye and winking with a nod of his head.

Ignoring him, I asked the children if they were hungry again, but as it was little more than an hour since they'd eaten, they all indicated that their hunger was still satisfied.

'Let's have a look around then,' I said as we paused to watch the team of horses being let to a stable, the sweat dripping from their flanks.

Their nostrils puffed hot clouds of vapour into the chill air; a pungent familiar horsey smell emanated from their spent bodies. We turned to watch as fresh horses were being led out ready to be harnessed to the coach for the onward journey.

The sun at last shimmered above the distant hills as the coach trundled forward. I was grateful to be seated at the rear of the coach top, relishing the warmth of the sun on my back. The human traffic on its way to the diggings was thickening, as those travelling on foot joined the throng. People were seen packing up their hand-made tents. Wisps of smoke identified recent campsites, where the campers had lit fires for warmth, to cook their meals, and to dry out the dampness of the day's journey.

Further on, when we took a detour to avoid a boggy section of the track, we spotted small dwellings in varying shades of brown that blended with the landscape. There was a look of permanence about them, unlike the numerous tents that had been seen all along the way. They were built from poles cut from saplings, the sides made from bark slabs and completed with grasses similar to the roofing thatch of English houses. A small fire accompanied each home, its spiralling smoke blending with the backdrop of grey-green vegetation, curling ghostlike. About a dozen Aborigines were gathered around one of the dwellings; some wearing fur capes. A waterhole was seen through the scattering of gums nearby.

'They're interesting-looking houses. I've never seen any like that before,' I commented.

'They call them mia-mias,' said Dan.

'Mia-mia, that's a lovely name for a home. They look a lot like the tents we've seen, but made of things they've found in the bush,' said Eliza.

I detected an unfamiliar aroma transported on a drift of smoke. 'I wonder what they're cooking?'

'Well, it could be possum or kangaroo, or maybe a lizard or a goanna,' said our American acquaintance.

The hotchpotch of traffic traversing the countryside kept us entertained. Most of those making the journey on foot were men. The belongings they carried either on their backs in a swag or in wheelbarrows or hand-carts, confirmed they were fortune seekers. Those with swags carried extra items in their hands such as a gold-fossicking tool, or a saucepan or frying pan they'd need for cooking the food supplies they carried with them for the journey. The wheelbarrows and carts were laden with picks and shovels, gold pans, cooking utensils, food and other supplies they would need for the expedition, such as canvas to make a tent to give them shelter for the ambitious journey that could take them months. I saw a man pushing a baby's pram, its contents overflowing with his numerous belongings.

Others more prosperous rode horses, some fortunate to have a second horse attached, loaded with their abundant belongings. Heavy drays and lorries were laden with supplies for the thousands of people already living at the diggings.

Most men wore flannel shirts and moleskin trousers. Some wore vests and others were clad in various types of coats. Many wore brimmed hats in a range of styles. Heavy boots appeared to be an essential item, both for the muddy conditions of the rugged terrain on the journey and digging for gold once they reached the goldfields. Some also wore leggings which helped to prevent their trousers from becoming muddied by splashes from passing vehicles. A number of seamen could be seen, identified by their sailor's coats and woollen caps, having jumped ship on hearing the stories of instant riches to be gained. Their voices rang with oaths that were now familiar to us, having first heard them on the ocean voyage. The occasional crack of a gun could be heard; perhaps a traveller shooting a native animal or bird for their dinner.

Hours passed. Regular stops every hour or so to change the horse team broke the monotony. At one stop, mid-morning, I produced oranges, and the children enjoyed the juicy treats. Hours of sitting still required strength of will; fortunately, the interesting sights along the route interspersed with snippets of conversation provided a welcome distraction.

When the sun had moved high above us, Dan spoke. 'A good cheap dinner can be purchased at the next staging post. It shouldn't be far now. The keeper's wife puts on a fine dinner for one shilling – a generous helping, plenty of meat in the stew, and potato mash and damper to go with it. A cup of tea to wash it down is included in the price.'

I had been prepared to purchase one meal along the journey, so I decided it would be wise to take this opportunity.

'How does that sound?' I asked the children. Their murmurs and nods confirmed their agreement.

The journey to Ballarat continued uneventfully as the coach traversed its way through gullies and small streams. From the opposite direction, bullockies drove their teams of up to eight bullocks, cracking their whips to drive forth their cargo bound for the port in Geelong. The wagons were laden with wool which would be loaded onto sailing ships along with gold for the return voyage to England, replacing the human cargo brought to Australia.

Smaller carts and drays were on their way to collect goods shipped from England to supply the rapidly growing population of Ballarat.

I had purchased boiled sweets in Geelong. Noticing the children's energy diminishing, I produced the brown paper bag I'd kept as a surprise until now. Their faces lit up as I produced the striped peppermint humbugs, aniseed and raspberry delights for the first time on the journey. I'd decided to wait until we were well along the way, aware that once the children knew I had them, they'd be constantly asking for more. I expected the bag to be empty by the time we reached Ballarat.

I handed the bag to Jesse first, knowing he would not be fussed regarding choice, as he thrust his little hand into the brown paper bag and popped a sweet morsel into his mouth. The girls will choose the raspberry ones, I guessed as I observed them carefully peruse the contents of the bag. Sure enough, they each held between their forefinger and thumb a transparent ruby globe that shone like a glass bead, before it was placed on their tongue.

'Mmm,' murmured Mary, 'thank you, Mother,' as she sucked on the sweet confection.

I chose a peppermint-flavoured humbug; it reminded me of the rare treats of childhood. After offering the sweets to the other adults, the woman declining my offer and Dan choosing aniseed, I twisted the paper bag closed and returned it to my bag, keeping it within easy reach for the anticipated further requests.

'Will we get there soon?' Jesse enquired.

Overhearing Jesse's plaintive query, Dan replied, 'Sorry, laddie, a fair way to go still. It'll be well after dark when we get there.'

'Do you have any ideas about accommodation?' I asked. I'd been starting to worry about what lay ahead on our arrival.

'I'm staying at the Imperial on Bakery Hill. I always stay there. But there are lots of others,' said Dan as he continued to list numerous hotels. 'There's the Golden Fleece, the Elephant and Castle and the Temperance. There was Bentley's too, but that was burned down in the miners' rebellion last year.' He paused, searching his memory for names of other establishments.

'Tell me about the Temperance Hotel. That sounds like a good place for us to stay,' I told the children. 'I'm sure they'd know of your uncle there. I can't imagine him not being involved in the temperance movement.'

'What's the temperance movement?' asked Mary.

'It's about not drinking rum and other drinks like that. Some people worry when they see people get drunk.'

'Like the sailors on the ship?' asked Jesse.

'Yes.'

'But they seemed happy – just a bit silly.'

'Well, sometimes they get angry too,' I said, unsure about how to explain, not wanting to frighten him, but at the same time hoping he'd grow up with a healthy attitude on the subject. 'Anyway, people like your uncle decide it best never to drink alcohol at all. They're known as total abstainers.'

I knew William's views on alcohol and guessed that it was quite likely that he would be involved in the movement against it. Although I didn't drink alcohol myself, simply because I'd grown up in a family where, apart from my grandmother's occasional brandy for medicinal purposes, the women didn't drink. However, I didn't see any cause to be too concerned about the habits of others.

'Where is the Temperance Hotel? Is it far from where the coach stops?' I asked.

'Most of the hotels are along the main road, but it would be better to ask the coach driver to drop you off near the hotel, as it's not safe to be walking about after dark.'

Darkness fell as the carriage meandered along the well-worn track, the fatigue of the passengers revealed in a number of ways. I found myself snapping in response to the children's questions. The grumpy woman sitting next to Mary had fallen asleep by the sound of the snoring coming from her open mouth. When Mary began to complain, I managed to change places with her at the next stop. I then gave the woman a slight nudge with my elbow whenever she began to lean my way. This caused the woman to give a sudden jolt and a snort, as she became partially awake.

At last the lights scattering the hillsides ahead signalled our destination was not too far away. Our American friend remained silent, the scene conveying the unspoken message that we were approaching the diggings.

Through the darkness of the night, lamps from an occasional passing vehicle could be seen through a film of smoke accumulated from the fires lit by those residing on the goldfields. Those on foot had set up their camps for the night, as fires could be seen illuminating groups of travellers preparing an evening meal.

The children had drifted off to sleep. Jesse had snuggled up against Dan's broad shoulder; Eliza had my shoulder for support; but Mary, who was now seated next to her little brother, found room to curl up on the seat. I had passed a folded shawl to Mary to serve as a pillow.

The conversation on the coach gradually increased to an excited chattering in anticipation of arrival at our destination. The sleepers were either jolted awake by a sudden movement or a raised voice.

Weary from the marathon journey, we observed the evening activities of the mining community. Fires burned brightly, their scorched-wood aroma melding with the smell of beef and lamb cooking for the last meal of the day, whetting our appetites. A baby's cry was almost drowned by the sound of the pounding hooves of the horses, eager, no doubt, to reach their resting place for the night. The clusters of tents became larger and more numerous as the team of horses found pathways more defined.

After a few stops, where some travellers left the coach, Dan swivelled on his seat. 'Main Street coming up. Your stop here. I'm getting off further on.'

I viewed the street, amused at the sight. Most of the establishments were tents whether they were shops or dwellings, with a few more permanent buildings made from wood. 'I hope the hotel is not a tent,' I thought as our bags were handed down to us.

'Your hotel is just across there,' said Dan, pointing across the road.

We stood by the roadside and waved to our American friend. 'Goodbye, and thank you for your help,' I called.

'That can't be the hotel.' I tried to focus my eyes on the building across the dimly lit road. But as we approached, I was able to read the lamplit sign with the name clearly printed in faded black capital letters on a white painted board: 'BALLARAT TEMPERANCE HOTEL'.

'Well, it should be safe – no drunks here, I murmured as I led the children up the steps and through the roughly hewn doorway. The first thing that caught our attention was a glowing log fire blazing in the huge mud-brick fireplace. The fire radiated, filling the room with a cheery glow, greeting our jaded family with its friendly warmth and winning the contest against the cold night air.

A man with popping eyes like marbles and a big red nose, sleeves rolled up to his elbows, greeted us in a casual manner. I decided to book for two nights, after enquiring about the cost of a room, which was a little more than the Geelong hotel. 'Surely I'll find William by then,' I thought. Although I was reluctant to rely on William's generosity, my funds were quickly diminishing. After all, I didn't know what his circumstances were either. 'Perhaps he's struggling to support his family and living in one of the tents we've seen. On the other hand, maybe he's found a huge nugget of gold and become suddenly rich,' I pondered more optimistically.

Anxious to find the answers to the whereabouts of my brother, I questioned the man. 'Do you know a man by the name of William Dimsey?'

'No, sorry, I don't,' he replied, shaking his head. 'But you could ask my employer in the morning, 'e knows a lot of people round 'ere.'

Facing another night without an answer to my interminable predicament, I tried to focus on the children's needs.

'Have you had supper?' asked the pop-eyed man. 'They'll get you somethin' in the dining room if you 'aven't eaten.'

It had been hours since we'd finished off the remainder of the bread in the late afternoon.

'Yes, supper would be lovely. We're certainly hungry, aren't we?' I said to the children.

The small dining room, where another generous fire burned brightly, was accommodated by a huddle of people engaged in conversation. I found a table for four close to the fireplace and we were brought generous helpings of chunky vegetable soup of potato, carrot, peas and barley with bread and butter. The comforting food helped to calm my anxious mind.

Our meal consumed, I approached two men who had been deep in conversation, asking the question that I felt I'd asked a hundred times. 'Do you know a man by the name of William Dimsey?'

The men both shook their heads, obviously not pleased with the interruption, but, determined not to be dismissed, I continued to stand resolutely alongside their table.

'We're new round here – only arrived two days ago,' one said as an aside, before the pair resumed their conversation.

Once again disappointed, I retired with the children to our room to find it sparsely furnished, with calico sheets that I hoped were clean, on beds that proved to be quite comfortable. After reading to the children from Mary's book, I blew out the flame of the lamp and tried to sleep. I found myself tossing and turning until at last dim light infused the room declaring that the day had arrived.

I scrambled out of bed clad in my long winter nightgown, grasped my woollen shawl and drew it around my shoulders to counter the nip of the winter cold. I padded barefoot to the window and parted the curtains, wiping the vapour that had accumulated on the glass during the night. All I could see was the wall of a large windowless canvas tent.

The children were still sleeping soundly, all exhausted from the endless travel, I imagined they would probably need a few hours more. Pouring water from the china jug into the matching wash bowl with a fluted pale pink rim, I splashed water on my face, smarting at the icy coldness, and then dressed in my best winter gown in the hope that today I would see William. I tiptoed across to the bedroom door, closing it soundlessly behind me so as not to disturb the sleeping children.

I found a young woman in the dining room preparing to light the fire, obviously so the room would be warm by the time guests turned up for their morning meal. I resisted the urge to repeat my worn-out question and instead asked, 'How long will it be before breakfast is served?'

'Another hour at least,' replied the girl as she glanced up at the mantel clock above the fireplace that read five minutes to six. 'But I can get you a cup of tea when I've finished this, if you like.'

'Thank you. That would be lovely,' I said, grateful for a hot drink to comfort my insides.

The girl returned carrying a tray with a white china teapot, milk jug, sugar bowl and cup and saucer, all decorated with an English scene that reminded me of home.

'Thank you, I do appreciate your effort,' I said. 'What time do you expect your employer to arrive? I need to speak to him.'

'He's usually here at about eight o'clock. You should be able to see him then. His name's Mr Dodds.'

Feeling edgy, I glanced up at the hands of the clock. 'That's almost two hours from now,' I thought, agitated.

Sipping my tea, I noticed some newspapers piled untidily on a shelf. I picked through them and carried a few to the table where I'd been sitting close to the fireplace. Warmed by the hot tea and the increasing warmth of the sparking fire, I began to read news of the growing town from the local newspaper, the *Ballarat Times and Southern Cross*. The pages were full of stories of happenings on the goldfields, but unfortunately there was no mention of anyone by the name of Dimsey.

Checking that the children were still asleep, I returned to the dining room, where the inviting aroma informed me breakfast would soon be served. The young woman who had made me a pot of tea earlier breezed in, now wearing a spotless white pinafore over her drab grey dress. She brought me a large plate of crispy bacon and two plump soft-centred poached eggs on thick white crusty toasted bread that I had opted for instead of porridge.

After breakfast, I decided to explore the hotel's surrounds, conscious not to venture too far lest the children wake and find me missing. The caked hard earth of the Main Road was already bustling with people making an early start to the day. Stepping out onto the road, I surveyed the commercial establishments advertising their wares, beginning to prepare for the day's custom. Most vendors sold their merchandise from tents. Hammering and banging could be heard as builders worked replacing tents with more substantial buildings, once the traders had made enough profit to provide permanent constructions.

A frosty breeze was funnelling its way through the jumble of tents and buildings lining the road, driving me back into the warmth of the hotel's dining room, where I tried to wait patiently for the publican.

A middle-aged man entered the room, dressed in a white shirt with navy stripes and complementary waistcoat patterned in shades of blue, his stomach protruding slightly above his leather-belted waist. When the waitress reappeared a few moments later, she nodded towards the man and mouthed the words to me, 'That's him.'

I approached. 'Excuse me sir, you're Mr Dodds, aren't you?' I asked politely. Receiving a nod in reply, I continued, 'Do you know a man by the name of William Dimsey?'

He looked up and replied without hesitation. 'Yes, I certainly do. He's our secretary. Do you know him?'

'He's my brother,' I said, consumed with overwhelming relief, the words tumbling from my mouth with much enthusiasm and the feeling that such a huge weight had been lifted from my spare shoulders. 'I've come all the way from England, and I've been searching for him all over the colony for weeks. It seems I've found him at last!'

'Have you breakfasted yet?' he asked in a friendly manner that made me feel instantly at ease with this man I'd only just met. Learning that I had already eaten, he responded generously, 'Then join me for a cup of coffee while I eat mine. We make an excellent brew here.'

'Thank you, Mr Dodds.' I said, accepting his warm invitation, and feeling overwhelmed with gratitude, not so much for the offer of the coffee and conversation, but for what I anticipated as the end of my journey.

'By the way, my name is James – no need to call me Mister – and yours is…?'

'Lizzie, Lizzie Merritt.'

'Well, tell me about yourself, Lizzie Merritt,' said James in a kindly voice.

While James ate his meal, relishing the generously laden plate set before him, I recounted the story of my journey thus far.

James ordered himself a cup of coffee and a second cup for me, and proceeded to explain his plans to build a new hotel to replace this one. 'The temperance movement is growing from strength to strength here in Ballarat, but not as fast as the liquor problem. Be careful when you go out, for you'll see many people – not only men either – afflicted with drunkenness. The alcoholic beverages flow more abundantly than water here, I often feel,' he said.

'So you said my brother is involved – secretary, you said.'

'Yes, we've established a Temperance Association here to do what we can to discourage the abuse of alcohol. William is the secretary of the society, so he takes the minutes at the meetings, and writes letters when needed. He's very competent, and passionate about the movement and getting others on board to spread the message.'

'Do you know where he's living?' I enquired, full of hope.

'No, I don't really,' he said, returning his coffee cup to its saucer. 'I hear they moved recently,' and before my mood could sink to an irretrievable despair, he added, 'but there's a meeting tomorrow evening at the Temperance Hall. You'll find him there. You can come along with me if you like,' he added.

'Yes, thank you, James. I would like that,' I said as I fought the urge to jump up from my seat at the table and run around the room shouting my elation to all present. Perhaps it was fortunate I spotted a familiar tousled light brown head of hair pop up in the doorway of the dining room.

I sprang to my feet, almost knocking over the chair. 'Thank you so much, James. I'd quite forgotten my children. I must go to them now.'

'You're very welcome,' he said. 'I'll meet you here at half past four tomorrow then, and we'll make our way to the Temperance Hall.'

Grasping Jesse's hand, I returned with him to our room, where my excitement was unleashed as I shrieked the words, 'We've found him at last!'

'Who?' chorused the startled girls in unison.

'Your Uncle William, of course. He's here in Ballarat. We'll see him tomorrow.'

Monday breezed in with fresh anticipation, for I was certain that today my hopes would be fulfilled. Clad in our warmest clothes, we began to explore the area; the sights and sounds revealing that the town was in transition from an embryo to a place of permanent prominence. The wide road was lined with shops and establishments of all sorts, most in tents but some built from timber. The roughly hewn timber had been cut from the surrounding bush, the prolific stringybark trees providing useful slabs of bark used to roof the structures. Some buildings were a combination of wood and canvas.

Enterprising shop keepers were selling food, clothing, household goods, mining tools, canvas and supplies for horses; there were banks, lawyers, hairdressers, dancing salons, sly grog shops, brothels, gambling dens and churches.

The main street was vibrating with a countless variety of British dialects and accents, mingling with foreign languages of people socialising on this late winter morning. The Chinese were easily identified, their flowing shirts and pants loosely cladding their slight figures. Upon their heads balanced distinctive wide circular cone-shaped straw hats, unlike any we'd made back at Luton.

There were sailors here too, recognisable not only by the clothing they wore, but the familiar oaths heard on our voyage. 'Shake a leg, mate,' we heard an older sailor call to a young lad who appeared to be drunk. 'I suggest you give 'im a wide berth, ma'am,' he called when he noticed me. I had to restrain Jesse from approaching the sailors, so eager was he to learn of their adventures at sea.

A brightly coloured flag that lifted featherlike in the gentle breeze caught my attention; three women of about my age sat upon upturned wooden crates, absorbed in conversation, probably sharing the latest gossip, I imagined. I approached the women, seizing the opportunity to have some of my questions answered about life in this unconventional town. Greeting them with a cheerful 'Good morning', in the hope that they might engage in conversation with me, my smile was met by a cheery grin in return from the woman draped in a shawl of orange and yellow shades. The skirt of her cotton dress, in chocolate hues, billowed as she swung herself around in a casual manner. Her golden curls fell from a bonnet lined with the same fabric as her dress, completing the picture of warmth and friendliness.

'Hello. Are you new to Ballarat?'

'Yes, we just arrived on the coach last night.'

'Well, one of the first things you'll learn here is that the cost of everything is outrageously expensive. You may not believe it, but a pound of potatoes costs a shilling in there,' she said pointing to the shop flying the flag that had caught my eye. 'In Melbourne, they're only fourpence.'

'My goodness,' I responded. 'Why is that so?'

'Everything has to be brought in from Geelong or Melbourne. Hardly anything's grown or made here. They're all too busy looking for gold. So if we want to eat, we don't have a choice.'

'I suppose clothing is expensive too.' I realised we had no summer clothing with us.

'Yes, my goodness,' said the woman. 'Even if you can make your own, the material is so expensive – the threads and trimmings as well.'

'We've left most of our belongings in storage at Melbourne, so we'll need to have them delivered here – if we stay until the summer, that is,' I added.

'Oh my,' said the woman slowly shaking her head. 'That'll cost you a fortune too. Cartage costs are extraordinarily high. I don't think you'll do much better than one hundred pounds per ton.'

'Gosh, it's just as well our boxes don't weigh a ton then,' I laughed.

'You need to take care around here. I'd keep the children with you, so people know you're a married woman.' She glanced at the children and turned her head so that the children couldn't see her wink at me. 'Most single women are here to satisfy the needs of the single men. There aren't many women here. Most of the wives have stayed back in Melbourne or Geelong. I don't blame them,' she said, as she turned to her companion. 'It's hard going, isn't it?'

The children were becoming fidgety, and I realised it was time to look for something to eat. Further down the road, I observed a tent advertising 'Soups Meals Coffee and Other Drinks'. Pea and ham soup was offered, but we'd eaten enough of that on the ship to put us off it forever. The mutton and vegetable soup sounded good, so we sat outside the tent on a bench and ate large steaming bowls of the hearty concoction served with generous chunks of damper. The damper was dry and crusty so the children followed my lead, dipping it in the broth to soften it. I finished off with a cup of tea; lemonade was served to the children. Fortunately, the price wasn't as exorbitant as the woman I had spoken with in the street had led me to believe.

Well before the appointed time, the children and I were waiting expectantly by the fireplace in the hotel dining room ready to be taken to the Temperance Hall. Just before the hands on the mantel clock reached half past four, James appeared.

'I'm glad to see you've warm cloaks. It's cold outside, and that dratted misty rain has returned. It's only a short walk, though, and they'll have a fire going in the hall. It's not far – just along here at Bakery Hill,' he said as we followed him into the street.

On entering the hall, I felt an overwhelming sense of relief, immediately recognising my brother. He was absorbed in conversation with another man.

He looked up to see me smiling at him. He scrunched up his forehead and nose with a look of confusion, followed moments later by a courteous smile. 'Lizzie, my dear sister,' he said, his hands extended to welcome me and the children. He took my hands in his own. 'What a surprise! I didn't know you actually made the journey.' He turned to greet his nieces and nephew, grasping each child's hand firmly as his eyes met theirs.

'He may not be wearing a uniform, but he still presents a figure of authority,' I thought as I observed my brother. It wasn't just his height and upright stance, either. He was dressed neatly in clothing fit for a gentleman, neat and tidy as ever. His ginger beard was carefully trimmed and his hair had obviously been attended by a barber in recent days. His face was wearing its friendly expression, but I knew it could harden in an instant.

'Why aren't you wearing your constable's uniform?' asked Jesse.

'I'm not a constable any more, Jesse,' said William. 'They don't really have constables here like those we had in England. They do carry a baton like the one I used to have, but they carry muskets as well, and they fire them too. You've probably seen some of them about in the streets. Most of them are ex-convicts. Many of them are drunk on the job, so do be careful to avoid them,' he said as he turned his attention to me.

'Look,' said William. 'I'll have to attend to my duties here. It will soon be dark, so you'd best get back to the safety of the hotel. I'll come and see you there tomorrow,' and he turned and strode to the front of the gathering.

Retracing our steps back through the misty rain, I felt dissatisfied. I sensed William's disappointment at my presence here in Ballarat; I was probably an unwelcome interruption to his life. I couldn't help but feel hurt that he wasn't more pleased to see us. On the other hand, I felt certain I could depend upon William for support. He will do what is right, no matter how inconvenient it is for him, I concluded.

The sudden sound of gunfire roused me from a deep sleep. I'd not yet become used to the disorderliness of the goldfields. I wondered what the time was; surely it must be close to dawn, and yet there was no signal through the thin muslin curtains that the day was about to begin. I lay awake, my thoughts drifting to the day's potential. With a feeling of concern that William might try to determine my future fate, I almost wished I hadn't come to Ballarat. Would it mean the end of the freedom and independence I'd come to treasure? My ruminations continued until a faint pre-dawn light began to filter through the curtained window.

Not knowing when my brother would arrive, I rose, dressed and proceeded to enquire about baths for the children and me; it was more than a week since we'd bathed. Hoping this day would spell the end of our journey, I wanted my little family to be looking spick and span for the momentous day. Knowing that William would not abandon us, I felt I had no other option than to rely on him for support. Some stability for the children was needed: school for Jesse and Mary, if not Eliza who was already accomplished at reading, writing and numbers.

By nine o'clock, satisfied with the children's appearance, I was anxiously waiting for my brother to turn up. At ten o'clock on the dot, I heard a firm knock on our door. William led us out into the street, explaining that his home was within easy walking distance. The sun was a silver orb glowing in the sky, seeking to find a way through the film of cloud.

'Mary is expecting you to come for dinner,' he said, as we traipsed along the gravel road, dodging puddles. 'Eliza and Ralph are at school today. Will helps out at the school at times. He hopes to follow in Father's footsteps and become a schoolmaster one day.'

'Where is the school?' I asked.

'You'll see it shortly. It's in the Methodist church.' Moving further along the road, he continued, 'You can see it from here actually,' as he pointed to a grey stone building on a slight rise. 'The Methodists are the only ones with a proper building at this stage. The other churches all hold their services in tents. We've been attending here because it has a school, and being close to where we're living is a big advantage. Most of the schools here are run by the churches. There are quite a number of them. That's our place over there,' said William waving his arm toward a small humble dwelling. 'Many people are living in tents here. We were lucky to acquire this cottage. There are only two rooms, so the girls have to share the bedroom with us, and the boys sleep where we eat. It certainly is cramped, but we're warm and dry, and managing well enough under the circumstances.'

'Really, William?' I asked, recalling the substantial home they'd left in Ashwell.

'Well, you've seen how it is here by now, I imagine,' said William as we approached the roughly built cottage made from hand-hewn local gum trees. 'We've decided to stay in Ballarat, so we'll apply for a plot around here and build our own house as soon as we can afford it.'

William's wife Mary, and his eldest daughter, Mary Ann, came down the path to meet us. My sister-in-law gave me a warm hug. 'Let's go inside. It's warm in there.'

I was shocked to see how small their home was.

'It's so good to see you, Lizzie. I was really excited to hear you were here. There's so much for us to catch up on,' said Mary.

'I'm so sorry,' I said. 'Little Anna Maria. How sad for you all that must have been. I learnt about her death from the vicar at Geelong.'

'Yes,' said Mary, her voice catching at the remembrance of her baby girl. 'She'd just begun to say a few words and was quite steady on her feet, toddling around happily before we set sail, but then she became ill. As the voyage progressed, she became increasingly weak and died soon after we arrived in the colony.' Mary took a handkerchief from her apron pocket and wiped away the tears that had begun to slip down her plump cheeks. Returning the handkerchief to her pocket, she continued, a tremor of emotion in her voice. 'But those are the hardships of this new life. How did you manage the journey, Lizzie? It must have been difficult on your own with the children.'

'Oh, we've managed all right,' I said.

Eliza was already engaged in lively conversation with her cousin Mary Ann as they shared their experiences of the ocean voyage. Eliza had always admired her older cousin; the difference in age posed no barrier to their friendship.

'When will we see Ralph and Eliza?' piped Jesse, anxious to see his cousins.

'They'll be home for dinner any moment,' said William.

A few minutes later, the two youngest members of the Dimsey family burst through the doorway. Jesse ran up to greet Ralph; Mary stayed close to my side until her cousin Eliza approached and invited her to look at some embroidery she was working on — a doily with soft pink gum blossoms and grey-green gum leaves.

William's wife went to check the huge pot hanging over the fire in the crudely formed mud-brick fireplace. As she lifted the lid, the savoury aroma from the bubbling concoction confirmed my guess that it was a stew of some sort. I wondered how the large family group would manage to eat dinner. There were not enough chairs and the roughly hewn wooden table would barely seat William's family of seven.

'The children can eat first,' said my sister-in-law as though she'd read my mind.

Four of the cousins sat to eat, each confirming that they still identified as a child. Eliza must have felt quite grown-up to be included with the adults, as she continued to converse with her older cousin.

'And Davey – what's he up to? He must be sixteen, or is he seventeen now?' I asked.

'Almost seventeen,' said Mary. 'He'll be home for dinner too. He's working at the diggings.'

'Come, Lizzie,' commanded William as he held out his bent right arm for me.

I took hold of it obediently as he led me outside.

'I'll show you what I've been doing.'

Not far from their humble home, I spotted my nephew Will, bent over, cultivating rich dark soil. There were rows of grey-green cabbages beyond him.

'We're growing vegetables, not just for ourselves, but with the plan to sell them to the public. The only ones who grow their own vegetables here seem to be the Chinese. All the fresh produce has to be brought from Melbourne or Geelong, so without the cartage costs added on, we'll be able to sell ours at a lower price. They'll be much fresher too.'

'Hello, Will,' I said, greeting my nephew.

'Hello, Aunt Lizzie,' he responded, straightening his back and displaying his soiled hands helplessly, signifying that a polite handshake was not possible.

'What are you planting, Will?' I asked.

'Potatoes here – and onions along there. The frosts should be gone before the potatoes begin to shoot.'

William interrupted before his son could explain further. 'You'd better finish off and come for dinner, son.'

Turning to me, again extending his arm – as if I need his support, I thought – William continued to explain as we strolled back to the cottage. 'We've got this small plot for a start, but I intend to lease a larger piece of land if this venture works. I can't see why it won't. Will does much of the physical work. Do you remember how we used to help Father in the garden behind the school in Hitchin?'

'I don't remember having to do any of the work,' I said with a chuckle, 'but I do remember picking the apples that grew there.' My mind retreated. I was back in the orchard behind the school, my teeth crunching through the rosy apple skin, the juicy tartness dripping from my chin.

'Will spends a couple of days at the school, so he has plenty of time to help me in the garden.'

'What does he do at the school?'

'As I mentioned, he wants to be a teacher and there are no teacher training schools here, so the best way is for him to get some practical experience. I suppose it's a bit like the monitors we had back in Father's school at Hitchin.'

'Mother's school too,' I added, feeling disappointed that William hadn't acknowledged that our mother had also been a teacher. 'You know it's not the usual case that a married woman with children would be teaching,' I added, indignantly.

We reached the Dimsey home again, to find the children had finished eating and David had returned from his mining work.

Jesse, eager to learn about gold mining, approached David. 'So are you working down one of those holes we've seen?'

'Yes, I'm working with a couple of older men,' said his cousin. 'It's not far from here. You've seen the diggings. There are hundreds of mines. My word, it's hard work, Jesse!'

Mary had prepared a bowl of water and soap for her sons to remove the grime from their hands that had accumulated from their respective working endeavours. Soon we were all enjoying the hearty stew with damper that Mary had made earlier in the morning.

'So, tell me. Have you found any of the gold everyone is talking about?' I enquired.

'No, nothing much,' said William. 'Davey was working with another fellow, but they didn't seem to have much luck and so the claim was abandoned. He's working on another now. Doing okay, would you say, Dave?'

David responded with a nod. 'The unwritten rule here is to keep quiet about what you've found. Otherwise, you might get it stolen from you – quick as a flash.'

'I'd love to have a look round the diggings,' I said. 'Could you show us around, William?'

'Certainly not. It's no place for a lady, Lizzie. You'd be wise to stay indoors. It's not safe to be out and about. Besides, I've a meeting of the Benevolent Society this afternoon. What's the time, I wonder?' he said, retrieving his watch from his waistcoat pocket. 'I must be off shortly. I need to have a talk with you, Lizzie. I'll come to the hotel tomorrow morning,' he said rising to his feet, stamping them on the beaten earth floor, eager to be on his way.

'Gosh, Mary, William becomes more like Father every day – always busy with some cause or other.' I glanced around the primitive dwelling with its rough walls, low bark ceiling and improvised furnishings. 'It must be difficult for you living like this.'

'Well, it's not too bad, really. It's far better than the tent we lived in when we arrived. We do have a fireplace now. When we were in the tent we had to cook on a fire outside, which was very difficult when it rained. Someone came up with the idea of holding an umbrella over the fire to keep it from going out until the meal was cooked. The fire makes it nice and cosy in here and the bark roof helps to keep out the rain and keep the warmth in.'

'I notice you've given up wearing crinoline skirts, too,' I said.

'Well, yes, just at home,' replied Mary. 'After we saw a woman's skirt catch fire, William decided that petticoats should be abandoned at home. It was dreadful. The poor woman screamed in agony. We heard that she later died.'

'How dreadful. I haven't worn a hoop under my skirts since we reached the equator on the journey here,' I said. 'It was so oppressively hot, I stowed my hooped petticoat away in our luggage. I doubt that I'll ever wear it again.'

Mary's face wore a surprised expression. 'William still wishes me to wear mine whenever I go out. He's just afraid that if I wear it at home my skirts may catch fire as I attend the cooking.'

'Where do you go?' I asked, imagining a variety of interesting excursions.

'Just church on Sunday and William takes me to the store every Wednesday. He won't allow me to go out alone.'

'Hells bells! That's absurd! What a fusspot my brother is!'

Mary didn't respond, obviously feeling uncomfortable at this remark, so after a pause I decided to change the topic.

'So, tell me what happened to Anna Maria – that is, if it's not too distressing,' I added.

'I do find it painful still, although William says I should be over it by now. You understand, because you've been through it too, Lizzie. It was dreadful on the voyage. My poor baby was so sick, I felt so helpless. I was relieved when we reached Geelong, where we could get her to a proper hospital, but it seemed it was too late. I tried to hide my tears from William and the children, having a good cry when no one was about.'

'Yes, I can well imagine,' I said, knowing William would expect stoicism to prevail. My brother would keep a stiff upper lip, and expect the same of his wife.

'We're fortunate our children are older,' said Mary. 'The deaths of children here are even greater than on the ships. I've heard about half the children here die before they reach five. It's the poor hygiene. We've very limited water for washing. Water is piped from the swamp and we have to pay a carter to bring it to us from the central pump.'

'Where do you go to do...' I paused, searching for an appropriate word and continued, 'you know what.'

'We're lucky to have our own privy round the back, but it's a big problem on the diggings. Dysentery is the cause of many of those young deaths.'

'I remember as a child in Dead Street. Admittedly it was named after the plague, when almost everyone in the street died, but there were still countless deaths there when I was growing up. We had a water closet, of course, but along the street people in the yards had to share. In one yard, there were twenty-six houses sharing just three privies between them. Can you imagine that! I even saw some children unable to wait squat in the street,' I said, recalling the appalling conditions that many had to endure in my village.

Time hurried by as we talked of the old country, when suddenly William returned.

'Time for us to get moving,' I said, rising from my chair by the fire. 'I'll see you in the morning, William. Thank you for the wonderful meal, Mary. I've so enjoyed spending the afternoon with you.'

My spirits rose as I wandered back to the hotel with the children. It was a great relief to be in touch with Mary and William. I began to imagine settling here, knowing my brother and sister-in-law would be close by to provide support for me and the children. I'd just have to learn to stand up to William's assumption that I needed a guardian.

Shortly after returning to our hotel room following breakfast, there was a sharp knock on the door. 'Surely not William already,' I thought. But there he was, looking as self-assured as ever.

'We can talk in the dining room,' he said, his tone officious.

I turned in the doorway and spoke to the children. 'Get out your books and do some reading. I'll be in the dining room talking with your uncle.'

'Right, now,' said William, once we were settled in chairs by the fire, 'what are your plans? You do realise it's not possible for you to stay in Ballarat.'

'Why not, William?' I asked, alarmed.

'Well, you can see what it's like. Where would you live? You've seen the cramped conditions we live in. It's not safe for you either, without a man to protect you. There's so much depravity here – drunkenness and debauchery. It's the criminal element too. Many of the men carry guns and fire them recklessly when there's a dispute – and disputes are frequent.'

'Oh, William, I'm quite capable. Surely you're exaggerating! I made the journey all the way from Luton without any mishaps. I'm sure I'll manage here. I could find somewhere for us to live. And the children could go to school.'

'No, Lizzie. It won't be possible,' insisted William. 'There are no houses available. I thought you understood that. Don't you think we'd have found a better home if one was available?'

I felt anger rising within me, but remained mute, having no argument to support my position. Of course I realised my brother's circumstances had altered dramatically.

'Have you seen Jasey yet?' asked William.

'No, I don't even know where he's living. Is he here in Ballarat too?' A sliver of hope surfaced. I was afraid William might see my chest heaving with emotion, but of course not.

His eyes were piercing intently into mine. 'He's living in Melbourne. He has a house in Kew and he's working as a stone-carver on some of the new buildings. Surely Jasey would want to see you, and he probably could afford to help you out with accommodation. He's doing well, I hear. I imagine there's great demand for his skill with all the new building constructions. Perhaps you and the children could stay with him until you decide whether to remain here or return to England.'

'Mmm, I know the girls want to see him and I guess Tom is with him. I really do want to see Tom. The children have been looking forward to seeing their father and brother too.'

'I've got Jasey's address, so I suggest you write to him, letting him know you're here,' he said, handing me a piece of paper with the address written on it.

'Typical William,' I surmised. 'He has come here well prepared with a plan for my future.'

'James can provide you with paper, pen and ink, I imagine,' he said, as he proceeded to the front desk, returning shortly after with the letter-writing equipment. 'There, that's settled then,' he said.

I hesitated, unwilling to give in to William's commands. 'I'll think about your suggestion, but in the meantime could Mary and Jesse attend the school where your Eliza and Ralph are going? While we're here, that is. There was no schoolmaster on our ship, so they haven't attended school since we left Luton.'

'That should be possible. Just bring them round before nine in the morning and I'll take them over.' William retreated, his business complete.

I returned to the children to find them quarrelling about something trivial. My patience at a low ebb, I shouted at the children. 'That's enough!' and addressing Mary and Jesse, I continued, 'It's off to school for you two tomorrow!'

I felt the need for some space or I'd go mad. Thoughts flew around in a confused arrangement in my mind, my dreams of a reunion with Jasey nudging me. I needed to consider William's advice. It seemed this was a never-ending journey I was on; always another decision to be made. Tomorrow, the two younger children would be at school, and Eliza seemed to enjoy Mary Anne's company, so perhaps she could spend the day with her cousin, affording me an escape from the children for a few hours.

I delivered the children to the home of William and Mary, being assured by my sister-in-law that Eliza could spend the day there and it would be quite convenient for me to return to collect the children later in the day.

Setting out along the route that led to Creswick, I reached the top a hill where I could see trees in the distance, and set my path in that direction. I needed to escape the madness of the congested embryonic town. Up hills and down slopes I strode, kicking at the loose gravel with the toe of my boot, lost in thought, the sounds of the thumping machines and the multitude of voices fading, drowned out by the screeching of a flock of white birds that fluttered to rest among the leaves of a seeding gum. I eventually reached a clearing and, tired from my exertion, found the smooth surface of a fallen tree to sit for a rest. The stillness was only broken now by the carolling of the numerous black and white songbirds I'd seen on the outskirts of the towns. Their warbling songs were a comfort, and masked the odd distant sound of musket fire.

My mind mulled over the events of the past weeks. I needed to revisit the vision I'd had when I set out on this quest. My fanciful notion that Jasey would be there to meet us in Melbourne with the possibility of a fresh start was a delusion. I knew I had to face the truth that his affection for me didn't match mine for him. The hurt of that knowing welled up in me as I fought the loneliness I'd been feeling since leaving my homeland.

I'd pictured my brother's lifestyle being much as it had been in England, and was shocked to discover that life in the colony was unpredictable, and so unlike the one I'd known. I'd heard there was plenty of work in Victoria due to the gold rush, and I'd imagined supporting myself and the children, if not through becoming a milliner with my own business, at least working in the hat-making industry.

However, as on many previous occasions, my grand scheme had not been thought through and, it seemed, would fail to reach its desired outcome. How foolish of me. I had no idea what it would be like on my own with the children. As usual, yet another decision I'd made on a whim – straw bonnet designer indeed!

I couldn't blame William for believing me to be an irresponsible mother. Although he'd not said so, I sensed that was how he felt. It seemed that living in Ballarat would not be possible.

Yes, it seemed Jasey was my only option right now. I was looking forward to seeing him again, but knew making contact with him would be awkward. Then there was Tom – I longed to see my firstborn. He would be almost a man now, so he might prove to be a helpful support for me.

'What other choice do I have but to follow William's directive?' I conceded.

Realising it must be close to dinner time, I began the descent to the town below. Casting aside William's words of caution, I headed straight for the diggings instead of following the main road.

The recent rain carried the muddy contents of the discarded piles of earth, creating brown rivulets that trickled toward the gullies. There were mud-spattered faces and mud-spattered tents; the clothing the miners wore was caked with the clay that had dried where it landed; hats and hairy beards carried flakes of it.

Holes in the ground abounded: round ones, square ones, wide and narrow, some with poled structures that carried winches with handles and a hook at the end of a rope to draw out the baskets of soil. The miners worked in silence, their backs bent to the task. The only sounds were the thuds of shovels as they dug into the rock-hard earth and the pick, pick, pick of the iron picks to loosen the hard surface as they chipped away in the hope of finding some of the precious metal each man dreamed of. Muffled echoes of male voices swam to the surface from the shafts below.

Reaching the creek, different sounds reached my ears; a wheelbarrow being trundled toward a wooden device that was being rocked like a baby's cradle. I watched as the contents of the wheelbarrow were shovelled into the top of the machine. The operator rocked the cradle with one hand, and held a stick in the other to break up the clods of dirt. Water ran through the device, washing the gravelly soil away, with the hope that a glittering prize would reveal itself.

Beside the creek, a few women worked with tin dishes, picking up the crumbly rejects from the cradles, swilling them around with water from the creek in the hope of finding some tiny pieces of gold that had been missed. These were the only women gold-seekers I'd seen, hoping to find in their pans a few sparkling specks that had been overlooked by the men. 'No nuggets for them,' I thought.

William's prudent words were proving to be groundless, when suddenly I heard the crack of a musket and a trooper came galloping up on his horse to sort out a violent dispute between two enraged miners.

'Out of the way, lady!' he cried, waving his musket; which sent me scurrying off toward the town, passing some barking and yelping dogs on my ascent up the hill.

Slipping on the muddy surface, I ignored the bawdy comments of a couple of miners as I hurried on.

My breath ragged from my hasty retreat, I noticed a tent advertising lemonade, so I stumbled inside and purchased a glass of the thirst-quenching brew.

Reaching the main street, a woman could be heard, obviously in a drunken state singing a familiar song.

> She wheels a wheelbarrow,
> Through streets wide and narrow,
> Crying cockles and mussels,
> Alive, alive oh!

'Plenty of wheelbarrows here, but there are certainly no cockles and mussels to be found in this place,' I mused.

Most of the afternoon was taken up with writing to Jasey. It took great effort to get the wording right, and I needed to return for another piece of paper on two occasions. No blotting paper was provided, so one of my attempts was discarded due to the smudges on the page. Finally satisfied, I returned the ink pot and pen to the receptionist and carried the letter to the post office, where I bought a stamp. I addressed the envelope to 'Mr William Merritt, Cotham Road, Kew, Melbourne'. I knew he still used his formal name for business purposes, but he'd always been Jasey to me. I'd not known his birth name was William until our marriage, when it was recorded on the certificate.

I felt that 'Jasey' was much more appropriate for this warm, soft-hearted man. 'William' was much too formal for the casual Jasey. Anyway, my brother bore the name 'William'; it suited him perfectly.

The days passed slowly as I waited for a reply to my letter. Mary and Jesse were now occupied during the day, and were happy to set out each morning for school, where they had begun to make some new friends in addition to their cousins. They enjoyed their older cousin Will being there on some days too. Eliza passed the time with me or her cousin Mary Ann.

Two days after I posted my letter to Jasey, I began to visit the post office each morning in the hope that a letter would be waiting for me.

Several days had passed when the postmistress said, 'Yes, there is a letter for you, Mrs Merritt.'

I recognised Jasey's familiar hand as I took the letter, clutching it firmly in my hand as I retraced my steps to the hotel. I unfolded the letter, appreciating the fine quality of the cream parchment, and pleased to discover Jasey had taken the effort to provide three pages of news.

'Dear Lizzie,' he began. Before long, I was lost in his words, as I remembered the kind, sensitive person I'd known before everything began to unravel. His warmth flowed through the words he had written with obvious thoughtfulness. It was a great relief to discover that he was still the same Jasey.

'Yes,' he said, he would be happy to have the children – and me too, of course. I was disappointed, but unsurprised, that he'd not said how glad he was that I was here and that he was looking forward to seeing me. He'd made no mention of Tom, however, and I wondered at the omission.

Excited now, I hurried around to share my news with Eliza, who was spending the day with her cousin at the home of William and Mary. Finding them all at home, I proceeded to tell them the news. Eliza, who had been enjoying rebuilding her relationship with her cousin, was not able to share my enthusiasm.

'Oh, Mother!' she exclaimed, exasperated. 'Surely, we're not moving again. We've only just got here.'

'I'm sorry, Eliza, but we can't afford to continue to stay at the hotel, and you can see there's no room for us here. You know you can trust your father to take care of us, and his house in Kew sounds very comfortable. He says it's a friendly neighbourhood and your Uncle Thomas is living nearby.'

When Mary and Jesse returned from school, Mary's reaction was similar to her older sister's.

'We're just beginning to make new friends at the school,' she said, with a worried expression.

'When are we going?' asked Jesse excitedly.

'Right,' intervened William. 'So when do you plan to go to Melbourne, Lizzie? I'll organise a coach. They leave every morning at six o'clock.'

'Jasey said he needs a week or two to organise the house to accommodate us, so I plan to write and suggest early September.'

'Good,' said William. 'Once you've set a date, I'll book the coach for you.'

Next day I wrote,

Dear Jasey,
    It was pleasing to receive your letter, especially with your gen-

erous offer to have us stay with you. I can imagine my letter coming as a shock and I'd not have been surprised at your disappointment that I'm here in Australia. Once William and his family set sail for the new land, I felt completely alone, with all of you over here, so I decided the only thing to do was to take the voyage myself. I had planned to settle close to William, but I've found it's not possible for us to live at Ballarat – for the time being anyway. I had no idea what it would be like on the goldfields. I had no intention of being a nuisance for you. You needn't worry about me. I'll soon find somewhere for the children and I to live where I'll be out of your way. I certainly don't intend to create further problems for you, as I did in the past. I've put you through more than anyone could be expected to endure, and you were so patient with me over those early years of our marriage, so I'm not surprised you're prepared to take us in. I'll try my hardest not to disrupt the life you sound to be succeeding with in Melbourne.

Mary and Jesse are attending the Methodist School here in Ballarat, and I'm hoping there's a school close to where you live that they'll be able to attend. Can you check that out for me, please? You may remember Eliza was always mature for her age, so she needs no further schooling. She's competent in so many ways. In fact, I don't know how I'd have managed without her on the voyage out.

I realise I didn't mention much about Jesse in my first letter. I realise you and he hardly know each other, but I believe you'll enjoy his enthusiasm and interest in the world around him. You might need to brush up on a few topics, because he's full of curiosity so he'll have lots of questions about what's happening in Melbourne town. I hope it won't be an irritation for you.

I noticed you did not mention Tom in your letter. I expect he's with you, but could you confirm that when you write back, please.

Would you do something else for me, please, Jasey? When we disembarked at Williamstown Dock, I placed our baggage in storage. There are three trunks and three boxes being stored there. Would you arrange for them to be delivered to your home, so they are there when we arrive, please? That is, if it's not too much trouble. The warmer weather will be arriving soon, I imagine, so we'll need our summer clothes. We've heard so much about the heat of a Melbourne summer.

Now, as you said, you'll need a week or two to be ready to receive us, so I'm wondering if it would suit you for us to come in
early September. Please let me know if that will be all right.

Yours ever,

Lizzie.

As expected, Jasey wrote a brief note back without much delay,
agreeing to my requests, but with still no mention of Tom. In the days
waiting for our departure, I became concerned about my son, wondering why Jasey had been silent on the topic.

On 9 September, the children and I farewelled the Dimsey family
at Ballarat and were on our way back to Melbourne, where we had
landed in the Victorian colony several weeks earlier.

Arriving in Melbourne, I observed the after-dark activities as people moved about the town at a sedate tempo, the glow of oil lamps softening the scene. As the coach drew to a halt at the depot in Bourke Street, I cast my eyes back and forth scanning the street for a sign of Jasey. Yes, there he was, easily recognisable even though it was more than two years since I'd last seen him.

There he stood, hands in his pockets, smiling warmly as the coach approached. My mind returned me to another place – a place where I felt loved, wanted, needed, accepted. I'm back in Chelsea. It's just months since Jasey and I married.

The overwhelming feelings that welled up inside me were a reminder of how I'd always felt I was a worthwhile person when I was with Jasey. He made me feel as though I had some value. My apprehension at the thought of meeting him faded with the realisation that I would be able to communicate with him despite the years of living apart.

The comfort I felt at seeing Jasey was tempered by the fact that Tom wasn't standing there beside him. Realising the reunion between the three younger children and their father was the priority right now, my questions about Tom would have to wait.

While the children were being greeted by their father, I retrieved our bags that were being unloaded from the coach. I stood apart, waiting expectantly for Jasey's eyes to meet mine; when at last they did, my hesitant smile was met by one of generous proportions and a meaning-filled moment was shared. Jasey clasped my hands in his warmly, as we murmured our greetings. Remembrance was all that remained of the early bonds, it seemed; the past could not be revisited.

'Where's Tom?' I asked.

'I'll tell you all about Tom later,' said Jasey evasively, as he glanced at our other children. 'Yes, yes, he's fine, Lizzie – nothing to worry about.'

Jasey, as always, was dressed in his own individual style with a flair that was unpretentious. He'd removed his felt-brimmed hat to reveal the thick golden waves of his obviously barberised hair, swept back from a brow that was beginning to show the creases of age. His clean-shaven face that had filled out since I last saw him was framed by side whiskers giving him a distinguished look.

Jesse warmed quickly to his father, such a friendly outgoing lad that he was. I had expected establishing a relationship with his father would come naturally for the boy.

Jasey explained that his own vehicle – a jinker – could only carry one passenger, so he'd hired a larger carriage to take us to his home. 'Kew is a short distance from town,' he explained, 'just a couple of miles.'

The carriage slowed as it reached yet another hill; now when we turned in our seats we could see the lamplit town of Melbourne below.

'This is Cotham Road – not far now,' said Jasey, as the horses slowed in their effort to approach another steep incline.

The horses were drawn to a halt in front of a neat cottage placed unpretentiously in a row of similar wooden dwellings, each with white picket fences and verandas in front.

Jasey assisted with the bags as he led us through the wooden gate, up the steps onto the veranda and through the front door, down a short passage and into the parlour. A fire had been lit earlier, sending a warm glow to every corner of the room as Jasey moved to the hearth, picked up the poker and stoked the glowing embers, stirring the fire to life. Lamps were lit, revealing the contents of the room. The piano with its polished surface glowed mellow in the lamplight and against another wall stood a tall bookcase guarding many of Jasey's cherished volumes. Comfy sofas and chairs were positioned in a friendly arrangement on the familiar patterned floor rug, giving the room a feeling of domesticity that spoke of a permanence that was reassuring for me. This felt like home and surely the children would feel secure here.

'You must be hungry,' said Jasey as each of us confirmed with a word or a gesture that we certainly were. 'We'll get some supper then,' he said as Eliza and I followed him to the kitchen, where a wood stove created a cosy feeling. Jasey passed a loaf of bread to Eliza. 'Would you slice the bread, please?' He retrieved a bread knife from the drawer of the dresser, handing it to Eliza.

Jasey produced a piece of cold roast beef from the water cooler, and a block of cheese, butter and pickles from the cupboard, placing them on the polished surface of the table in the centre of the room. 'Dishes and cutlery are in the dresser, Lizzie – and a tablecloth too if you like.'

Together we prepared the simple meal, with a comfortable ease that brought back happy memories of domesticity for me.

'Would you go and tell the others supper is ready,' said Jasey to Eliza.

It was easy to see she was very much at ease in her father's presence.

Once we'd had our fill, Jasey placed a bowl of oranges on the table, fresh from a little orchard nearby, he said. We all found room for the delectable fruit. When the sweet juice trickled down Jesse's chin, Jasey handed him a napkin.

'How are Thomas and Sarah? I noticed you didn't mention Sarah in your letter,' I queried.

'Oh, I hadn't realised you didn't know,' said Jasey as his hand flew to his mouth. 'Sarah died last year – and the baby too. Poor Thomas, though. It was really tough for him losing both his wife and child.'

'Oh, that's so sad.'

'Yes, such a sweet young woman she was too. She and Thomas were so looking forward to the arrival of their baby. They'd only been in Melbourne just about a year, and were beginning to settle in nicely. Thomas has a well-paid job working for a man by the name of Miller near his home in Richmond.'

'So many mothers lose their lives in childbirth. It's just not fair!' I lamented. 'And the babies too!'

'I know,' said Jasey.

'It's all right for you,' I retorted, 'being a man.'

Eliza grasped my hand firmly beneath the table, in unspoken warning.

'How about a cup of tea?' asked Jasey as he rose from the table and crossed to the stove, where the kettle was boiling merrily. 'Would you get cups from the dresser, please, Eliza,' he said, as he moved the kettle to reduce the flow of steam from its spout.

The table was cleared, the dishes washed and the kitchen restored to its former state.

'I'll show you to your rooms. I've organised a room for you three girls, and Jesse can share with me,' said Jasey.

'That sounds perfect,' I said with genuine gratitude.

The children snuggled beneath the generous quilts blanketing their bed and were soon asleep, tired from the long journey. The girls had been eager to open the trunks, but I persuaded them to wait until the morning to be reunited with their belongings.

I sank suddenly into the armchair, surprised by its softness. Jasey noticed it was far too deep for me and passed me a velvet cushion to support my back, before carefully positioning another log on the fire. A few sparks spluttered onto the rug. He jumped to his feet, stamping out the tiny embers.

'Now tell me about Tom. Where is he?'

'It's a long story,' Jasey shifted in his chair. I could see the unease in his pose. 'I really don't know where to start – the beginning, I suppose.'

Becoming impatient, I repeated my question, growing more agitated.

'Shhh,' he cautioned, 'let's not disturb the children. It's best that I start at the beginning. Please try to be patient with me.'

Bracing myself, I clasped the brocade of the chair arms, as if trying to hold myself together, waiting for Jasey's news of our eldest child.

'Tom settled in at Eton – was doing quite well with his schooling

– I know I told you that. When he came home for the holidays, naturally he was out and about while I was at work, and I suppose I was a bit distracted and unaware of his daytime activities. I thought everything was fine, but you know how it is with young men, they don't tell you much. At the same time, I began to consider coming to Australia. As you know, Thomas and his new wife had come out here, and he'd been encouraging me to join him. I was reluctant because I wanted Tom to continue his studies, but then I discovered he'd been spending time with a girl. It seemed to me he was becoming too involved and I was afraid he might get her in the family way, so I tried to get him to end the relationship. As you know, our Tom is quite headstrong and he rebelled. That's when I decided it would be best to make the journey here.'

'But why didn't you tell me this at the time?' I demanded.

'For goodness sake, Lizzie!' Jasey was becoming impatient. 'For one thing, I didn't want to trouble you – didn't know what mood I'd catch you in, so I felt it best not to give you the full story.'

'But you still haven't answered my question.'

'What was that?' he asked.

'Where is he?'

'Back home again,' said Jasey, his voice flat.

I sprang from my chair. 'Not here then?'

'No, let me explain,' he said as he raised his hands in a gesture that implied restraint.

I struggled to reign in my emotions, retreating to the chair and stiffening myself into an obedient pose.

We sat in silence and the seconds ticked by before Jasey continued to recount the events concerning our son.

'Soon after we reached Melbourne, a letter came for Tom. It was written by a woman at the Renfrew Road Workhouse in Lambeth. The woman said she was writing on behalf of a girl by the name of Ellen Evans, who was in residence there. The girl was expecting a child and said the father was our Tom.'

My hands flew to my head. 'Oh no, surely not! Tom would have been barely sixteen then. How old is the girl?'

'A little older than Tom, apparently.'

'What was Tom's reaction to the letter?'

'After reading it, at first he was reluctant to speak at all – afraid of my reaction, I imagine – but then he admitted it must be true.'

'So he decided he must go back. Did he want to go, do you think?' I asked, trying to guess what my son would do in a situation such as this.

'He said he wanted to go. I believe he'd been pining for her, especially in the first weeks of the voyage. But he seemed to be getting over it as the journey progressed.'

'So he was only here for what – a few months?'

'Yes, I thought once the decision was made it best he get back in time for the birth.'

'Yes, the poor girl – in the workhouse, all alone. I'm glad he went to her. So the baby – did you hear of the birth?'

'Yes, a baby girl – Martha, they named her. Of course they're unable to marry, although Ellen has now turned eighteen. Tom said when he turns eighteen in a few months, they intend to marry.'

'I can't believe you've kept all this from me, Jasey!'

'Well, I sat down and began to write to you on two occasions, but put it off, and as things proceeded, I decided it best to wait until things had settled down and everything was sorted. What could you have done – and it would have caused you a lot of unnecessary anxiety,' he added, defending his position.

Concurring, I shook my head reluctantly. 'I really don't know. I'd just like to have known, that's all.'

'I'm sorry, but I did what I thought best,' he said.

'I know, I accept that,' I said with resignation. 'Where are they living – surely not in the workhouse, I hope.'

'No, of course not,' said Jasey indignantly. 'I wouldn't wish anyone I know to have to live in one of those dreadful places – working every day under deplorable conditions for little or no pay. Punishment for being poor, really. I gave the lad enough to get them settled. He found a position in the building trade with a reference from me – a labourer's job, laying bricks. Ellen is taking in washing too. So they're doing all right by the sound of it – at least, Tom says so in his letters.'

'You've kept his letters, I hope,' I said expectantly.

'Yes. I'll get them for you shortly.'

'So when were you going to tell me all this?'

'Well,' he seemed to be searching for an answer. 'Well, once they had married, I guess.'

I suddenly had another thought. 'That means we're grandparents, Jasey. Fancy that!'

'Yes,' he smiled, nodding.

'What will we tell the children?'

'We could tell them Tom's gone back home – has a building job over there. That would be true. Then down the track we could tell them he's married with a child. How does that sound?'

'Mmm, I suppose so. Yes, you're right – let's tell them that. They're bound to be asking in the morning, as we've all been eager to see Tom. I think they'll accept it, though. Besides, they'll have plenty of other things to occupy their thoughts tomorrow.'

I heard Jasey in the kitchen when I awoke, so took the opportunity to spend some time with him before the children arose. I was feeling sorry I'd been somewhat fractious during our conversation about Tom, and wanted desperately to be on good terms with him.

I sat at the table and sipped the coffee he had just prepared. 'It's nice and quiet here. I could hear a little bird in the early hours. What would that have been?' I asked.

'Well, it might have been a willy wagtail, I expect. It's nesting time now, and their song sounds a bit like "sweet pretty creature". Did it sound like that?'

'Yes, that would be it. Are you noticing a lot of different birds to those we have back home?' I asked, continuing on a topic I knew was of great interest to him.

'Yes, most definitely. We're out in the country here – the bush, they call it. Yes, I often go for walks observing the variety of plants and wildlife they have here – very different to home. I've bought some new books on Australia's natural history recently. I wonder if Jesse will be interested.'

'I'm sure he will,' I assured him, as I moved to peruse the books in Jasey's bookcase. 'I see you've got a copy of *Uncle Tom's Cabin*. I'm reading it now,' I said. 'It was all the talk of town in Ballarat.'

I picked up Jasey's silver-keyed flute that was sitting on a shelf next to some books. 'I see you've still got your flute. Do you play it much these days?'

'Not much.'

'I hope you'll play for the children and me. I'm sure you remember my favourite piece,' I said with a smile.

When Jasey simply smiled in return, I decided to change the subject. 'Perhaps he doesn't remember,' I thought, disappointed. 'Have you been able to find out anything about local schools?'

'Yes. We've a couple of choices. Most of the schools are run by the churches, but there are a few national schools now too. They'll have a bit of a walk, but I suppose that won't bother them much. Perhaps I could take you to check them out this afternoon.'

'Yes, thank you. Let's do that.'

'There's a school at Collingwood run on the British and Foreign Society system. That organisation took over your parents' schools, didn't it? I hear the one at Collingwood is very good. Perhaps we could try that one first. See how you feel about it, anyway.'

'That sounds perfect,' I said, feeling completely satisfied with Jasey's suggestion.

'There's also a national school at Heidelberg, so we could consider that as well. I've been wondering about Eliza, too. You said she is well advanced. They're really short of decent teachers here. I hear some of the teachers can barely write and only know basic arithmetic. Very few are trained. Eliza shouldn't have much difficulty finding a position in a school as a pupil teacher, I should think.'

The children joined us in the kitchen, still in their nightclothes.

'Good morning,' said Jasey cheerily. 'I'll get you some warm water to wash in, then you can get dressed and we'll have breakfast. I've got a pot of porridge on the go, and even some fresh cream I bought from the farm down the road.'

I went outside to see the sunlight filtering through the trees I now recognised as gums. Birds were singing and chattering, busily engaged, no doubt, in finding food for their newly hatched young. The only bird songs I recognised were the magpies, and now I could add the willy wagtail to my list. Surely my knowledge about the local birds would grow now I was in the presence of Jasey.

'What a lovely spot you have here,' I told Jasey when I returned to the house.

'Yes, they say it's the prettiest part of Melbourne. Did you go as far as the river? It's called the Yarra after the Yarra Yarra native tribe.'

'Are any still living round here?'

'You do see them occasionally.' He paused, and then continued, 'They are treated abominably – don't seem to have any rights. John Batman, a huge landholder, made a treaty with the chief of the Yarra Yarra people – and the rent was supposed to be paid to them for the use of their land. There was a Quaker settler, though, I hear, who paid a yearly rent to the Aboriginal owners. It was very generous too – one-fifth of the value of the land.'

'He must be a good man. My grandmother used to go to Quaker meetings in Hitchin. She agreed with their views,' I said. 'You'd remember her, wouldn't you?'

'I do indeed – I know you were close to her.'

After a hearty bowl of porridge sprinkled with sugar and smothered in thick cream followed by a cup of milky, sugared tea, the girls returned to the bedroom. I entered the room to find them absorbed in eagerly searching for particular items in the trunks and boxes that had been waiting for their arrival. Some of their clothing would need a good airing, or better still a wash, as it had been worn on the ship, the fusty odour arising from worn garments no doubt reminding them of the ocean journey.

'I think we'd better wash everything in that trunk,' I told them. 'It's just as well we only put clothing from the voyage in that one. The other trunk and box will be unaffected, as they weren't opened on the voyage out – they'll just need an airing. I'm going to toss this out,' I said, throwing my hoop petticoat across the room in disgust.

Following dinner, the children and I were taken by Jasey in a hired carriage to investigate the schools he had mentioned. I took Jasey's advice and agreed the school at Collingwood would be suitable; an added advantage was that the headmaster was happy to offer Eliza a position as a pupil teacher. Eliza seemed to be feeling quite positive at the thought.

Within a few days of the children starting school, I became restless. Jasey was away at his work during the long hours of the day and after a few excursions around the hamlet and the surrounding area, I soon became bored. I had discovered a spot I'd claimed as my own. It was a comfortable walk downhill to the Yarra River, where it became one with the Merri Creek. It was now mid-spring and the wattles were blooming, their yellows complementing the grey-green foliage of the gums and other trees and shrubs that grew along the banks of the stream. I would sit on the riverbank, viewing the native splendour reflected off the glassy surface of the clear, still water.

I began to crave more excitement in my life. The children were happily filling their days at their new school; they hadn't complained even though Collingwood was a long walk there and back. They'd been through so much upheaval in the last few months; perhaps in this new phase, they could appreciate the new life of stability Jasey provided. I was pleased to observe a relationship developing between the children and their father.

Jasey had arranged for a neighbour, Mrs Jones, to come in every day to help run the household and each of the children had been given regular chores by their father, leaving me feeling useless and superfluous. All my dreams of life in the new land seemed to be unachievable. It was hard to imagine reaching a point where I could set up house for myself and the children, let alone establishing myself as a straw bonnet designer. I would need a highly paid job if I was to afford a housekeeper and that seemed unreachable.

As I retraced my steps through the bush, dry twigs crackled as they snapped beneath my boots. Suddenly I was startled by a whooshing and a click above my head. Looking up, I recognised a magpie, turning back as though to swoop at me again. I ran ahead, laughing, glad I was wearing my straw bonnet. Of course, I realised, it was nesting time. The bird was just protecting its young. 'I've done my bit,' I thought. 'My young are almost ready to leave the nest – Tom has flown, and Eliza is almost ready to spread her wings too. Jasey can take more responsibility now. It's his turn.' And with that, my mind was made up. It was time to move on to something more stimulating. Kew is too quiet for me,' I decided. 'I need action. I'll move to the town.'

Returning to Jasey's home, I began to pack my belongings in one of the trunks. When Jasey and the children returned from school and work, I surprised them with my decision: 'I'm going to move into town. You'll all be okay with that, I hope.'

Not one of the four family members spoke a word at first. The girls were used to my sudden impulses.

Jasey answered on behalf of the children. 'That will be all right, won't it? We'll manage quite well, I believe,' he said as he turned to the children. 'We've got Mrs Jones too. She's a good soul and an excellent cook, isn't she?'

'You will come and visit us, though, won't you, Mother?' asked Mary anxiously.

'Of course I will. Goodness, I might even find somewhere close enough to walk up here. You'll probably see me almost every day.'

Now that I'd made up my mind, I was eager to set out on this new venture. In *The Argus*, I'd seen an advertisement listing a vacancy in a lodging house in Bourke Street. This sounded like just the thing; right in the centre of the town. I would make enquiries.

I mentioned what I was planning to Jasey, who cautioned me. 'Some lodging houses in town are pretty wild, I hear. Many of them are grossly overcrowded and sell sly grog. I've read about some of the goings on at a few places, so be careful not to commit yourself, won't you, Lizzie.'

I let Jasey's warning words fly over the top of my head.

Next day, once Jasey and the children had set out in the morning, I walked down to the stables and hired a horse. The stable hand apologised for not having a special saddle available for me to ride side saddle, but I dismissed him. I'd much prefer to ride the horse the way men did. I hoisted myself up onto the saddle and set out for Melbourne town astride a chestnut mare, conscious that I was the only female on horseback among the traffic on Cotham Road.

The heat had already grasped hold of the day when I arrived at Bourke Street. I rode through the myriad of foot traffic, guiding my steed among the other horses and horse-drawn vehicles as I searched for the lodging house named in the newspaper advertisement. I relished the fact that it was right in the lively centre of the growing town. It was just what my rising spirits were craving. I soon found what I believed to be the establishment.

'Is this the lodging house that was advertised in *The Argus* as having a vacancy?' I asked the buxom woman who answered the door.

'Yes, so it is, lovey, but I'm not sure it's the place for the likes o' you,' she said, her hands settled on her ample hips as she looked me up and down from the peak of my bonnet to the toes of my smart boots. 'They're a pretty wild lot 'ere. I doubt that you'd fit in. Anyways, they're crammed in 'ere close to bursting point. There's 'eaps of other places to stay. I s'gest you find something more to your suiting a bit further out of town.' Stamping the end of the conversation with a nod, she turned abruptly and slammed the door in my face, leaving me in stunned silence.

Upset and deeply disappointed that my excited expectations had been squashed, I returned to the street and untied the horse that was waiting patiently. Once mounted, I turned the mare in the direction of Kew.

As I rode down the busy street, I caught sight of a familiar face. 'Monica!' I called. I observed the look of horror on her face as she quickly hurried on. It was difficult turning my steed in the busy street, but once she was turned, I followed until I spied Monica disappearing into the lodging house I'd just left. I gave the knocker a few sharp raps.

The buxom woman opened the door. 'What do you want now?'

'I want to see Monica – she came in just then.'

'No Monicas here,' she said. The door was slammed in my face a second time.

I wondered if I should try again. No, best not risk a third.

Jasey arrived home before the children and enquired how my excursion to the city had gone.

'No good – not suitable,' I said, feeling irritated.

'You probably need a boarding house – not a lodging house. Lodging houses here are not like the one you ran in Luton. You need something called a boarding house – just a small place run by a decent woman. It would be much friendlier. The only thing is, they're more likely to be out of town a bit. There are a couple in Kew, I hear.'

'But I need to be in town. It's so dull out here. There's nothing to do.'

'Would you like me to make some enquiries – find out what's available – something closer to town?'

'All right, Jasey, I'd appreciate that,' I replied reluctantly.

When he returned from work the following day, he told me someone had recommended a place to him that might suit my needs.

'It's in Gertrude Street, not too far from the children's school and not too far from Melbourne town either. In fact, you could walk to visit us here as well. The person who told me about it thought there might be a vacancy. Would you like to check it out?'

I was relieved Jasey was asking me, rather than telling me to check it out. Otherwise, I might have reacted with a negative response, but as Jasey was asking, my response was amiable. 'Yes, I might make enquiries. Can you give me the address and I'll go tomorrow.'

I set out with the children on their way to school the following morning and, finding the address without much difficulty, I approached the solid timber dwelling, which had a friendly look about it. 'It must be quite new,' I thought, noticing the garden that was in its early stages of growth.

A woman of about my own age, wearing a floral apron and with rosy cheeks and a winsome smile, answered the harsh sound of the door knocker.

'Do you have a room available?' I asked tentatively, half expecting the answer would be 'no'.

'Well, now, let me see,' said the woman pausing. And then with a chuckle, she said, 'Yes, I think we do. Would you like to come in and have a look?'

'Yes, thank you.'

'My name's Bertha. What's yours?'

'It's actually Eliza, but I'm known as Lizzie.'

'Well, Lizzie, this is the room here. We've got a bathroom too and a water closet as well. I think you'd find it quite comfy.'

The room was small with minimal furniture, but I had taken an immediate liking to Bertha, so decided I would take it.

'How much is it?' I asked.

'It's one pound per week, and that includes all meals,' replied Bertha, 'and I'd need you to pay weekly in advance.'

I had not done my calculations, simply acting on impulse, and suddenly I realised the pounds I had left would soon run out, unless further payments from uncle's will were forthcoming. But I pushed away the thought and produced a sovereign. 'Thank you,' I said, without hesitating. 'I'll take it.'

With the satisfaction that my plans were delivering their desired outcome, I felt the familiar elation rising within me, and so I set off striding along toward Melbourne town at a vigorous pace, eager to find out how close I was to the action. I had to admit, the place would be much more suitable, so it was a sensible choice.

I was surprised to discover that before long I was in Spring Street. I walked on, soaking up the atmosphere as I turned into Bourke Street. I needed to look for Monica. I was convinced it was her I'd seen in the street. Should I try the lodging house again? I knew I'd probably find the door slammed in my face for the third time, so I decided not. No, best to look out for my dear friend in the hope that I could talk to her. I wandered up and down past the lodging house, looking in shop windows, trying not to look too conspicuous.

Finally, I gave up. I'd just have to keep a lookout for Monica whenever I was in town. It would give me a good reason to come in here more often.

Back at Kew with energy to spare, I finished packing my trunk, having made arrangements for it to be transferred to the boarding house the following day.

Jasey seemed pleased I'd found the place to my liking, but still felt the need to warn me. 'Now, Lizzie, please do be careful. Melbourne town is not a safe place for a woman, especially after dark. It's different to Luton or Hitchin. And the police clamp down on any deviant behaviour, so don't go getting up to your usual antics, or you might find yourself in trouble,' he said.

'Oh, Jasey, you're sounding like William. All I want is a little fun. I won't do anything to break the law. You know that!'

Jasey gave up with a shrug of his wide shoulders and a sigh. 'I know. It's not what I meant.' Tentative, he asked, 'Can I help with payment for the accommodation?'

'Certainly not!' I snapped in return. He would know I'd want to be independent if I possibly could. He might have guessed my funds were low, but my response to his question would have warned him not to delve further into the matter. We'd had so many heated arguments about money in the past; he'd surely learned not to press on with the matter.

'I haven't told you about Uncle Ralph's will, have I?'

'No.'

'William and I were both beneficiaries. It was quite a substantial amount. I received my first lump sum a few weeks before we set sail. Otherwise, I wouldn't have considered making the trip out here with the children. So, thank you, I can well manage to pay my way,' I said with satisfaction.

'I'm glad to hear that,' said Jasey. 'Your Uncle Ralph did very well – captain in the army and all that, but I'm guessing his prosperity came from his first marriage to the Lewin woman – all that status and wealth!'

I didn't respond to this comment, although Jasey probably expected I would. I continued to gather my few remaining belongings. I embraced each of the children before they set out next morning, reassuring them that I'd be back to see them once I got settled.

The room was modest and sparsely furnished. A single bed with a simple covering, neutral in colour, was positioned beneath a small open window. Alongside the bed, a large chest of drawers stood on clean bare polished floorboards. Although unappealing, I realised I could make the room my own by adding some colour. I was still excited at the thought of living independently; being close to town and free from the responsibility of the children. As I sat on the bed, I convinced myself that this was just the beginning of my new life here in the bustling town.

The trunk containing my belongings was wedged between the end of the bed and the wall. I climbed onto the bed and leant over the wooden bed end to open it and unpack my things. Sorting through the contents, I found my books, hairbrush and other necessities and placed them on the top of the drawers.

Now what else could I find to make this room my own? I wondered. Delving into the trunk, I retrieved a wooden box from among a jumble of clothing. The rosewood box was inlaid with mother-of-pearl and lined in a soft shade of green silky material. It had been an anniversary gift from Jasey early in our marriage.

I retrieved an item I cherished above all others. It had belonged to my grandmother. I remember her pressing the pretty little silver fob watch into my hand – its fob no longer attached – saying, 'I want you to have this, Lizzie. It belonged to my mother. I've carried it with me since my parents died, and now I want you to carry it together with memories of the grandparents you never knew. I'm well past my three score years and ten, so my time must be coming soon,' she had said, as the words were formed in her precise Scottish brogue. It was her eightieth birthday. That was typical of Grandma, her giving me a gift instead of the other way round.

I was so grateful to have this small memento I could hold in the palm of my hand. I snapped the watch case open. Giving it a good wind, it began ticking again, so I set it at ten o'clock. I'd find out the correct time from Bertha later. The little piece of memorabilia reminded me of my childhood. It also had the practical benefit of keeping me informed of the time. Time had been so important in my home as a child. I recalled one of the rules at my parents' schools: 'BE EARLY ALWAYS'.

I drifted across the oceans to a place where I felt loved, accepted. Grandma is sitting on my bed trying to console me. I've just had another fight with Mother. Thoughts of my grandmother led to a lump of emotion gathering in the back of my throat. I reached for my handkerchief. Grandma was the only one who really understood how I felt; if only I could go back to those days when my grandmother and parents were still alive. If only my sister had lived instead of dying as a toddler, I would have had a sister five years older than myself, instead of only having brothers who didn't understand what it was like to be born into the world as a female, let alone a female such as my problematical self.

I laid the watch in a pride-of-place position on the drawers.

I found in the box a small picture that Jasey had painted of Wain Wood near his home at Preston Hamlet. It depicted a favourite place in the woods where the bluebells grew in abundance each spring. The place was named Bunyan's Dell after the famous non-conformist preacher who held meetings there in bygone years. Jasey's family were non-conformists and no doubt his ancestors would have been there to listen to the popular controversial preacher. Jasey descended from a line of woodmen, hard-working honest men, who had charge of the wood that supplied fuel to cook food and warm the homes of those who lived in the hamlet.

While expecting my second baby, it became impossible for Jasey and me to continue in the same household. After a bout of conflict over something trivial, probably about Tommy – we never seemed to agree on how the children should be raised – Jasey suggested I go down to Preston to stay at his family home until the birth. It seemed to be the best solution. With Jasey gone all day at his work, I was alone with our son Tommy and, I had to admit, not coping at all well. I suppose Jasey realised I needed female company, and he knew I enjoyed the company of his younger sisters Miriam and Mary Ann.

I stayed with the girls, their father and younger brother until the birth of the baby. Jasey came down for the christening. We named him John. He only lived for five short weeks. I would spend hours in the Dell when overcome with grief. In this naturely place, I would find solace as I yearned for my lost baby. One day as I sat on the ground watching Tommy chase a squirrel up a tree, my heart almost at breaking point, the tears began to trickle down my cheeks. John would have been running about here with his brother in a few years. Tommy came back and noticed my tear-stained cheeks and said, 'Mama cwy,' in a sad little voice as I tried to wipe away the tears with my shawl. Then the three-year-old ran off and returned with some bluebells clutched tightly in his little hands, as he said, 'Sowee, Mama,' and the tears welled again at the kind gesture of my little boy.

I sat the framed watercolour upon the drawers, leaning it against the wall where I could see it easily, rather than hanging it from the picture rail that was much too high for such a small picture. I sank again into thoughts of home. No, I'd decided this was a new beginning. No use dwelling on what could never be undone.

Colour was needed, so I removed the items from the drawers and draped a light fringed shawl in my favourite shades of purple and red tones, over the drawers before reinstating my few treasures. With the room organised to my satisfaction, I set out to browse the shops to see what I could find to stamp this tiny room with my own personality.

Over the following weeks, I purchased some items to decorate my room in the Gertrude Street house. I'd found a pillow embroidered in vibrant oranges and purples that added cheer to the otherwise plain room, and I'd managed to buy an oil lamp from a man down by the wharf. He was obviously destitute, and had resorted to selling his family's treasured possessions for money to buy necessities. The oil lamp replaced the candles that were provided at the boarding house. It cast a stronger light for reading, and besides was much safer.

Whenever I went into town, I was always on the lookout for Monica, particularly around the Bourke Street area. Finally, one day, I was sure I spotted her walking ahead of me in the crowded street. I hurried along, catching up with her, turning to be sure it was Monica. It was.

'Oh, Monica, I'm so glad to see you.'

Monica didn't seem pleased to see me at all.

'What's wrong?' I demanded. 'Don't you know me? It's your friend Lizzie.'

'Leave me be,' she said, her head down.

'What's wrong? Please stop. I need to talk to you.'

'Leave me be.'

'Why? What's wrong?' I clutched the sleeve of her gown. 'Please stop.'

She stopped.

'Let's go over here and have a drink of ginger beer,' I said.

Once settled, cool drinks ordered, I pleaded with Monica to tell me what had happened since we'd parted in Melbourne some months earlier.

She was reluctant to speak, but once she had started, her story poured forth. She'd managed to obtain a position with a well-to-do family, but when the lady of the house noticed her husband becoming rather fond of their housemaid, she was dismissed. Monica said that it was a relief to some degree, because she had been most uncomfortable with her employer's inappropriate advances. So she'd returned to live at the Houseless Immigrants' Home once more. She had tried unsuccessfully to obtain another position. Once her savings expired, she felt she had no other choice than to join another young woman she met, who assured her there was a good living to be made in the streetwalking trade.

'I feel so ashamed,' lamented Monica.

'It's all right, you're still my friend.' I said.

'I'm not worthy of your friendship.'

'You'll always be my friend, Monica,' I said with genuine warmth.

'I'm not Monica any more.'

'What do you mean?'

'I changed my name to Tilly. I'm Tilly now.'

'You'll always be Monica to me.'

'I need to go now. Please forget about me, Lizzie. Promise me you won't try to see me again.'

'Oh, Monica, I do wish I could help,' I said, and I really did mean it.

She hurried off, leaving me standing alone, feeling desolate. What could I do? I wanted to follow her, gather her in my arms and take her home with me.

Spring frolicked into summer. The hot weather descended with a fiery vengeance. Christmas Day was oppressively hot and dry with a northerly wind puffing dragon-breath dust across the town. The sticky flies were an unrelenting annoyance. It was almost impossible to imagine Christmases in the old country, where some years snow arrived and the family gatherings around a roaring fire and a hot roast dinner were appropriate.

Returning to Jasey's home after attending the Christmas service at the Methodist Church in the morning with Jasey and the children, we found a roast dinner in the oven, prepared earlier by the housekeeper.

The day was really too hot for the meal, but it was good to be eating together as a family. Jasey's brother Thomas and his new friend Lucy joined us.

'It's so hot,' I complained. I had no appetite for the heavy meal on offer.

'I know, but Mrs Jones has provided a wonderful spread, just like we have at home,' said Jasey. 'However, you'll be sorry to hear that she will be leaving us about the end of January. Her daughter, who lives in Geelong, is expecting her fourth child about that time, and she needs to go down to look after the children. She may be gone for some months, she says. We'll need to find someone else to come and help us,' said Jasey.

Monica was never far from my thoughts, and a few days later, I suddenly came upon a wonderful idea. I set out for Jasey's immediately, eager for his approval. The children had arrived home from school, so I took Jasey aside to tell him of my solution to the problem of replacing Mrs Jones.

'Jasey, I think I know someone who could be suitable. A young woman we met on the ship. The children loved her, so she'd fit in very well. I've been talking to her recently and, although she had a job as a housemaid, she's no longer needed there, so she could be available. Would you like me to check – see if she wants to come? She'd need to live in, but that would be even better than the arrangement with Mrs Jones.'

'Mm, let me think on it, Lizzie. Are you sure she'd be suitable?'

'Oh, yes, yes, please say yes.'

'What's her name? How old is she?'

'Her name is Monica. She's Irish. She'd be about twenty, I imagine.'

'Perhaps you could bring her to meet me. I don't want to commit without having met her.'

'I will, thank you, Jasey. It would make me so happy, and the children too, I'm sure.'

I set out immediately for the lodging house in Bourke Street. Rapping on the door knocker, I was met by the same woman and asked to see Tilly.

'Who shall I say wants to see her?'

'Oh, just say a friend.'

'Wait there then.' The door slammed in my face once again.

I waited for several minutes, until eventually the door opened, and there stood my friend Monica.

Monica was reluctant at first. 'How can you want me to be around your children, knowing what I've done?'

'They'll never know. You're Monica. Not Tilly. The children and I only know Monica – to me, Tilly never existed.'

Finally, my friend was persuaded. I left, giving my word that I'd be back to arrange for her to visit Jasey's before the end of the week.

The children were delighted when they saw Monica walk in. Jasey and I had kept it a secret from them, so as not to raise their expectations. Jasey warmed to Monica, just as I expected, and it wasn't long before she was settled into the household.

Unused to the heat, I was finding it hard to cope. I would lie awake, tossing and turning at night. Sometimes I felt trapped by the heat – a claustrophobic feeling from which there was no escape. The little window of my bedroom facing in a northerly direction drew no cooling breezes and absorbed the heat from the scorching sun during the day. The constant droning of the odd mosquito that found its way into my room drove me to distraction. There seemed to be no relief from the relentless hotness of the long days and nights.

I lay awake becoming distressed about my future. My money would soon run out, a threat to my desired independence. My visits to the post office had been unproductive, with no further payments from Uncle Ralph's legacy. I really didn't want to rely on Jasey and it seemed unfair to expect anything from William.

I thought again about the advertisement I'd seen in the paper some weeks earlier that read, 'WANTED Straw Bonnet Makers, good hands only need apply'. That was something I knew I could do. I knew I had the good hands they were looking for in the straw bonnet industry. I'd certainly had plenty of experience from my straw plaiting days as a child and, more importantly, making up the bonnets themselves.

I made up my mind to watch the daily papers for further opportunities, and within a week there was another advertisement. This one didn't even ask for good hands, so perhaps they were getting desperate. I wrote down the details: 'WANTED Straw Bonnet Makers, 78 George St near Royal Exchange Hotel, Gertrude St, Collingwood'. So it was in my street and, knowing the hotel mentioned, I immediately approached the establishment.

My application was snapped up when they learnt of my experience at Luton. 'That's the home of straw bonnet making!' exclaimed the man I approached about the job. 'When can you start?' he asked without further questioning.

I was happy to be occupied once more. I enjoyed the companionship that working alongside the other women provided, and it wasn't long before I had a new group of friends. Talking while we worked was frowned upon by our boss, but once he was out of sight and earshot, we women engaged in muted friendly banter as we worked. My skills were much appreciated and some of the ideas I'd carried with me from Luton were adopted. Before long, I had a pay rise and found the financial security a relief, earning more than I had at Luton.

Spending time with my newfound friends at work, along with visits to my family, provided me with the full life I craved. I felt that at last my life seemed to be under control, relishing the unrestrained freedom my new circumstances delivered. Visits to see the children were no longer duty-driven. I'd been critical of Monica initially, a little irritated by the way she seemed to agree with almost everything I said, admiring my clothes, even wanting to dress like me. However, I noticed a change in the young woman. She had become more independent and I liked the way she sometimes ventured to give her own opinion. I found myself visiting more often, much to Mary's delight. It seemed to me that all three children were happier with Monica becoming a part of the family.

Eliza was blossoming into an independent young lady, enjoying her work at the school and sharing Jasey's interest in music. Her father had arranged for a music teacher to come to the house to give her piano lessons.

I was delighted to see Jasey and Jesse developing a father-son relationship. On my visits, I was met by an enthusiastic young boy, eager to tell me all that he was learning from his father. On one occasion, he brought out a cardboard box, lifting the lid to expose a nest of baby mice. I shrieked with fright. I was not amused. Jesse was! His little head was bursting with new knowledge and in the end I would say, 'That's enough for now, Jesse. I need to hear what the girls have been up to.'

It was now autumn and I was relieved the hot nights and long days of oppressive heat were over.

As the holiday to commemorate Queen Victoria's birthday approached, my friends at work discussed how they would spend the day.

'Last year, we all went to the celebrations in town,' said Jane. 'We had a wonderful time. Do you want to join us?'

'Oh yes,' I said, glad to be included.

'Shall I meet you all somewhere tomorrow?' I asked as we left work on the day before the holiday.

'Yes,' said Jane. 'We'll meet at twelve noon outside the Olympic Tavern. You know where that is, don't you?'

'Yes, it's next to the Olympic Theatre, isn't it?'

'That's it. See you then.'

I was excited at the thought of spending a day with my friends. I'd always been delighted to observe Her Majesty's birthday; in fact, I had great admiration for the Queen, bestowing the affectionate name 'Queen Vickie' on her, as though she was my personal friend. Being of a similar age to me, I felt sympathy for the young woman who must live a restrictive life in her role as Queen. Celebrating her birthday in the new colony of Victoria that had been named after her would be a great pleasure.

Paying more attention to my dress than usual, I chose a new costume I'd had made for the cooler weather that had recently crept in. I had considered making the new garment myself, but once I discovered that a needle alone would cost sixpence, let alone all the other tools I'd require, I decided to find a dressmaker. I was delighted to find a woman in Collins Street, who claimed to have served under a dressmaker of the Queen's. From the designs shown to me, I chose a style that required a striped fabric, choosing a heavy silk in stripes of varying width in a warm cream colour contrasting with navy blue. The design consisted of a bodice that used a clever arrangement of the stripes, and long pagoda sleeves finished off with a braided trimming in the colour of the darker stripes of the fabric. The full skirt would only require me to wear one petticoat beneath it. I asked that the skirt be a little above the ground so my new side-buttoned cream kid boots would peep beneath the hem. Besides, I thought, it would help to keep the dress from picking up grime from the road.

After seeing the bonnets on display in Mrs Dick's Collins Street establishment, I decided that rather than buy a new one, I could add fresh decorations to my tuscan straw bonnet to create a look that complemented my outfit. Mrs Dick had been kind enough to sell me some of the braid used on a bonnet displayed in her window that was a close match to the fabric of my new gown. In town, I'd purchased ribbons and a rose in a deep red to add a touch of colour. I thought Queen Vickie would approve. My outfit not only created an impression of ease and comfort, but actually felt comfortable, unlike many of the gowns I'd worn in the past with all their fuss of restricting undergarments.

Setting out, gaily swinging my new parasol in case the clouds should produce some rain, I hurried along to meet my friends in the centre of town. There well before noon, I stood watching the passers-by strolling along at a relaxed holiday pace; many women promenading in their hooped skirts. How glad I was to be free of my cumbersome petticoats. Men of new-found wealth were easily identified; cigar-smoking, cane-carrying men fresh from the goldfields. They portrayed a picture of affluence with their gold watches tucked into their decorative waistcoats. Their bushy beards and unkempt hair suggested a different story.

Once our party was complete, Katie led us into the popular tavern. 'Let's go in here for a drink,' she said.

I had never been inside a tavern before, and the thought caused my heart to thump in anticipation. William would certainly not approve. We entered the crowded tavern to a hub of celebration. Music was blaring, and many of the patrons were already showing signs of intoxication with their ribald behaviour. Not wanting to be the odd one out by refusing alcohol, I was relieved when Jane asked for a glass of lemonade.

I soon became engulfed in the exhilarating festivities. As the afternoon wore on the streets were crammed with people singing and dancing and rollicking. My spirits rose and I found my irrepressible mood rising past a point where I was able to rein it in.

I began singing a favourite of my beloved Queen.

Home! Home!
Sweet, sweet home!
There's no place like home!
There's no place like home!

I danced down Bourke Street weaving in and out of the traffic, stumbling over a dog that crossed my path, but scrambling to my feet, I continued, repeating the chorus of the familiar song. I thought I heard Jane calling out something, but the song and the dance had overtaken me.

Suddenly I was stopped in my tracks; I felt firm hands grasping my arms; I struggled to free myself. Panting from the exertion, I screamed between breaths, 'Let – me – go!'

Pulling at my arms were two men wearing dark blue jackets with red stripes on the cuffs. Although my mind was still in a state of confusion, I was able to recognise the familiar police uniform.

My breathlessness easing, I cried again, 'Let me go!' as I struggled in vain against the burly policemen.

By now, Jane had caught up. 'Please let her go,' she pleaded. 'She's done nothing wrong – just a little excited.

'She's drunk,' pronounced one of the policemen in a sharp voice as they continued to propel me onward toward William Street.

'No, no,' shouted Jane above the din of the crowded street. 'No, she's not had a drink at all.'

Eventually, we reached the police station, where I was restrained with handcuffs. I was seated on a bench.

Jane sat down beside me. 'Don't worry, Lizzie,' she said to me, concern in her voice. 'I'll explain and I'm sure they'll let you go.'

Jane concocted a convincing story, explaining persuasively and pointing out that it should be obvious to them that I was a respectable lady. She promised to return me to the safety of my home, assuring them there would be no further unruly behaviour. Having sat quietly for more than an hour, calmed by my friend and exhausted from the ordeal, finally the police agreed to release me into the care of my friend.

'But I'd be careful if I was you, lady. Do somethin' like that agin and y'll end up at Kew.'

I was greatly relieved as Jane took my arm, handing back my parasol and reticule; I must have dropped them in the street when the policemen took hold of me.

'You know what they mean – about Kew?' asked Jane.

'No. As you know, my family live there, but the police wouldn't know that.'

'They mean the lunatic asylum, Lizzie. It's a dreadful place where they send people who are charged with lunacy. You wouldn't want that, would you?' she said as we continued back toward Gertrude Street.

Following the arrest, I avoided the town for some time, resolving to try to manage my uncontrollable moods. When my mood was elevated, I felt as though I was like a wind-up toy, wound so tight there was a risk that if I broke it would be with a shocking snap.

I resolved not to be caught again; lying low like a hunted rabbit avoiding the hunter; trying not to be noticed; staying away from places where the police might be waiting to pounce upon anyone who dared to step out of line.

My spirits descended to a depressing depth, and the gloom of days with clouded skies and drizzling rain corresponded with my mood. I would go to my favourite place near Jasey's. Instead of visiting the children, I'd spent the day sitting watching the Yarra's progress as it threatened to overflow after the recent torrential rains. On these occasions, I would gain relief, imagining the fast-flowing waters carrying away my bundle of contentious thoughts, washing them out to sea.

Winter passed uneventfully, and spring burst forth, bringing fresh hope tainted by the thought of another summer to follow.

Early in October, I became concerned that another of my muddled mind episodes was approaching like the distant roll of thunder that signals either a storm approaching or receding. I longed for it to be the latter; I feared what might happen if the storm arrived. 'I've got to get my scrambled thoughts under control,' I agonised.

I hadn't told Jasey about the arrest, or Monica, as I wanted to shield the children from my shame. I wrote to William regularly, but didn't dare to mention it to him, being ever careful to tell him only the things I knew he'd be pleased to hear. I felt that my brother would be quick to pass judgement on me.

Eliza's birthday was approaching, and I had planned to buy her a pretty new parasol for the coming summer. I'd seen some suitable ones in the shops in town, but struggled with my dilemma. Should I risk going into town, breaking my resolve to avoid public places? The alternative would be Eliza's disappointment, as I had promised to buy her a new parasol for her fourteenth birthday. I was determined not to let her down, as I so often had in recent years.

'Yes,' I decided, 'it should be fine. I'll need to be careful, though. I can avoid the police station if I go to the Queen's Arcade and if I can't find a silk parasol there, I'll surely find one in the Victoria Arcade.'

I could hear the bells ringing, bong, bong, bong, bong, bong, as though in time to the throbbing of my head. Time for church, Father will be there already. He'll be cross if I'm late again. Bong, bong, bong, the bells continued as I gradually became half awake. My head was throbbing in time to the bonging of the bells, slowly, and then faster they bonged. I must get up, but when I tried to move all I was able to manage was to raise my granite head a few inches, but it quickly returned to meet the rough surface of the rock-hard pillow.

My whole body was shuddering; I struggled to still it. Was I cold, I wondered? What was this strange quivering of my body? I lifted my eyelids a fraction, trying to focus on any shapes or outlines in the almost dark that would help me to guess at where I was. I closed them again. The sound of the clanging church bells turned to a distant thud, thud, thud, and my body hammered in time to the distant sound. Or was it distant? The sound seemed to be within my head. No explanation came to my question, just the continual thud, thud, thud, as my body continued its involuntary shuddering.

I lay there, oblivious to time until I eventually raised my heavy eyelids with a huge effort. The thudding had reduced to a bearable tick, tick, ticking. I struggled to sit upright, but found I could not move. Then I noticed in the dim light that my body was tied to the bed. A feeling of sheer panic arose within me, and a piercing howl came from somewhere deep within me. Powerless, I thrust my head from side to side, as the terrified wailing and howling came from my throat.

Before long, I could hear heavy footsteps approaching, clump, clump, clump, followed by the clunking sound of heavy metal keys, and the turning of a key in a lock. The figure of a burly woman rolled in, and with it an improbably soft voice. 'Quieten down now, dearie, keep calm,' it said. 'You must rest. If you don't quieten down, one of the turnkeys will come and he won't treat you so kindly, most certainly!' said the shape as I continued my wailing. 'Once you're quiet, I'll ask the superintendent if you can be released.'

Hearing the word 'released', I decided in an instant to make a huge effort and press down the feeling of panic as my body continued its shuddering.

'Please, I will be quiet,' I pleaded. My words were thick; my tongue seemed too big for my mouth. 'Please, I need to go to the privy,' but it was too late anyway, I realised, as I became aware of the sour smell of old urine. 'Please, I need the privy,' I begged.

'All right,' said my keeper, 'I'll see if I can find Mr Gale. Just lie quietly.'

'Where am I?' I wondered, gradually becoming more alert as the minutes passed in measureless time.

Footsteps again. Keys jangling. Clunking of the lock. Two silhouettes.

A man's voice. 'Now, madam, we need you to tell us your name.'

I kept silent.

'If you don't tell us your name, you will remain where you are. Do you want to get up off that bed or not?'

'Eliza Agnes Merritt,' I said solemnly.

'Is that a Mrs or a Miss?'

'Mrs,' I replied.

'All right, Mrs Symons, you can get a turnkey to untie her now, but keep her in this cell where we can keep an eye on her. She'll need to be put in a jacket too, at least until Dr McCrea visits her,' he said.

I continued to lie still, suppressing the scream that fought to release itself from my distressed mind, lest he change his mind.

After they left, I tried to take in all that I'd learnt from the superintendent's words. 'So I'm not to be released. And the doctor's to visit me. I must be ill, but this can't be a hospital, surely.'

Mrs Symons returned with a heavily built woman who proceeded to unbuckle the straps from my wrists and ankles; the chains that attached the straps to the bed clattered to the floor. The bands of grubby cloth that bound my body to the bed were removed and I was able to manoeuvre my aching body into a sitting position with the assistance of the strong woman.

'Can I go to the privy?' I asked, genuinely needing it now.

'Not yet,' said Mrs Symons as she turned to her assistant.

'Hold out your arms, Mrs Merritt,' she said.

'Why?'

'Because we need to put this on you,' she said as she held something that I could not identify in the darkness. 'It's to keep you safe from harm.'

'What do you mean?' I demanded, afraid now.

'Well, you might hurt yourself or something. Now, please cooperate,' she said as I shrank from her clutch.

'You'll be tied to the bed again, and you don't want that, do you?'

I continued my resistance.

'Well, what shall it be – this jacket or tied to the bed? It's up to you, Mrs Merritt.'

I held my arms out reluctantly. The shuddering receded to a tremble. I was too weak to put up a fight. My arms were fed into the sleeves that were secured in deep pockets at the sides of the canvas garment. The heavy jacket was dragged up over my gown, and the leather straps were buckled securely at the back. I was immobilised, my arms held tightly against the sides of my body.

The two women, each grasping one of my arms firmly, propelled me out through a gravel yard where, with difficulty and lack of privacy, my body was relieved of its excretions.

My keepers then returned me to the tiny cell, where I was left perched on the edge of the stinking mattress. What could I do? Surely I would go mad in here with nothing but these four walls and a bed. I'd forgotten to ask where I was, until it suddenly dawned upon me that this must be a gaol.

I remembered passing the gaols many times in my walks around the town; there was one at each end of Collins Street. But what was I doing here? I forced my mind to remember the time before. The last thing I could remember before finding myself in this place was setting out for town. Yes, it was to get Eliza's birthday present. I'd left in a hurry. After work. Still in my work clothes. No bonnet. Hair left loose. What then? I coached my mind to recall, but it wouldn't budge, stubborn mind.

The day passed interrupted by visits from a turnkey; the delivery of a can – my own personal privy, what a privilege; a tin dish of food that looked and smelt so revolting I tipped it in the privy; a tin mug of water that I skulled down my parched throat with difficulty due to the restrictive clothing; and every other hour a head would be thrust around the door, sneaking a peek at me through the gloom.

On one of these occasions, I ventured to ask, 'Where am I?'

A hasty response. 'In the Western Gaol.'

This confirmed that I was in the gaol at the western end of Collins Street. Now I knew where I was, but the next question that bothered me even more than the where was the why. I still couldn't remember anything beyond setting out to buy Eliza a parasol. Did I get the parasol? She will be so disappointed if I don't keep my promise; my agitation began to increase. With my body so restricted, I tried at first to punch the wall of the cell. When that produced no effect, I kicked at the stone wall. The sudden pain brought the new realisation that my feet were bare and cold, but the relief I felt at the self-inflicted pain satisfied a need within me.

As darkness descended, I was becoming hungry, and when a tin dish was placed on the floor containing some sort of mushy food, I wolfed the tasteless meal. With my arms held against my body, and my hands encased in the canvas mittens, all I could manage was to tip the plate up and slurp the contents, some of the mush sliding down the canvas beneath my chin. I was so tired, and with my hunger satisfied, I climbed upon the bed with difficulty and, pulling a heavy blanket awkwardly over my canvas-clad body, I fell asleep.

I was jolted awake by the same clunking sound of a key turning in the lock and a voice.

'Get up, Mrs Merritt. We need to vacate this cell. You're being moved to the wards.'

I was pulled roughly to a standing position and steered through the cell door. I was relieved to be out of the darkness of the tiny cell.

I was led across an unpaved yard into a big shed where breakfast was being served to the women prisoners. I guessed there to be about fifty women – of all ages and sizes. Some were shouting, others were pushing to get their share of the food, and others were gorging on the unappealing fare on offer. Seeing another woman wearing an outfit that matched mine, I approached and asked the woman how she managed to eat. The woman hissed and spat at me so I backed away hastily. I found a bench to sit on and decided I didn't need breakfast.

A young woman came and sat next to me. 'You're new in 'ere, aren't you. I don't think I ever seen you afore.'

I didn't answer, afraid of another response similar to the previous encounter.

The young woman continued, 'Want a cup of tea? I'll get you one if you like. It must be 'ard with them gloves on, I reckon.'

'Thank you,' I said, appreciating the kindness shown.

Shortly after, she returned with a cup of tea with more milk and sugar than I would have liked, but I was grateful and sipped from the tin mug as my young companion continued to speak.

'I expect to be outa here today. I was drunk yesterd'y, y'see. Naughty, eh? I been in 'ere afore. There's all sorts in 'ere – some of us for being drunk and disorderly and others for serious crimes. What did you do to find yerself in 'ere?'

'I really don't know,' I ventured.

''Ere comes Mrs Symons. She's the gaoler's wife.'

'Mrs Merritt, I see you're behaving now. You'll find your bed in ward three over there. Wait in there and a turnkey will come and take you to be cleaned up. Within the next few days, you'll come before the police court. Is there anyone we should notify of your whereabouts – your husband perhaps?'

'No.'

'You've nothing on your feet,' said Mrs Symons, as she looked down at my feet, noticing my big toe bruised and swollen. 'What have you done to your foot?'

I remained silent.

'I think we better put some boots on those feet. I'll ask the turnkey to see to that after you're cleaned up. Dr McCrea will be visiting you in the next few days and I'll get him to have a look at your toe.'

I was taken to a wash house, where I was stripped, scrubbed and splashed with cold water and then dressed in rough flannel clothing. The stained canvas jacket was placed back over the top and the buckles fastened firmly at the back. Now I wore grubby canvas boots on my feet, completing my new outfit. Nothing of my personal clothing remained. I'd been stripped of my own identity and given a new one.

After breakfast the following day, Mrs Symons approached me. 'Dr McCrea is here to see you. Come this way, please.'

I was led to a room, where a man of about my own age was seated behind a table.

He pushed his chair back and crossed his long legs as I approached. 'Mrs Merritt, I presume,' he said, his accent obviously Irish and his tone officious.

I buttoned up my lips and determined to keep them so, watching him read the notes on the table, his thumb and forefinger rubbing his chin.

After some time, he turned to Mrs Symons. 'So Mrs Merritt has calmed down. What was it you gave her?' he asked.

'Digitalis, doctor. I think it helped to quieten her.'

'From the notes here, I do believe it would be wise that she remain in the lunacy ward.' After a pause, he peered over his glasses at me. 'And you'd better keep her in the canvas too,' he added. Then he addressed me. 'Is there someone we can notify, Mrs Merritt – a family member perhaps?'

Mrs Symons spoke. 'She says not, doctor.'

A few days later, I was led to the police court, where I heard the verdict.

'Eliza Agnes Merritt, you are charged with lunacy,' was the accusation.

I struggled to take in the account I was hearing from the policeman who arrested me. I was horrified. Surely that couldn't be me.

The police magistrate peered at me over his spectacles. 'On the evidence of Dr McCrea and the police, you have been unsafely lunatic. You are therefore found guilty of lunacy and will be transferred to the Yarra Bend Lunatic Asylum.'

Jasey

I was a little surprised when Lizzie failed to turn up for Eliza's birthday tea. When the children arrived home from school, Monica had the table set for a special meal, including a birthday cake complete with fourteen candles.

'It would have been thoughtful of Lizzie to come early to help you with the preparations, Monica,' I said.

'Don't worry, Mr Merritt, she'll be along shortly, I imagine.'

We waited for about half an hour, but Jesse was persistently asking when we were going to eat, observing the enticing fare on offer, so I suggested we start without their mother.

After the children had gone to bed, I was in my chair reading when Monica approached me.

'Mr Merritt,' she ventured, and waited until she had my attention. 'I'm concerned about Lizzie. I'm surprised she didn't come to the party. She knows how important it is for Eliza.'

'Don't worry, Monica. She was probably out gallivanting – distracted by one of her latest frivolities.'

'Oh, no, Mr Merritt, I'm sure she wouldn't forget Eliza's birthday. I'm worried something's happened to her.'

'All right then. I'll go and check on her tomorrow,' I replied.

I really thought Monica was unnecessarily anxious, but felt I must do as promised, so I rode round to Gertrude Street the following morning. The landlady seemed quite concerned, telling me she hadn't seen Lizzie since Monday last.

'I'm worried that she may have been arrested,' she said.

'Really,' I replied, perplexed. 'Why do you say that?'

'Well, one of her friends called to see why Lizzie hadn't shown up at work on Tuesday. She was afraid that your wife may have been locked up. She said Lizzie had been arrested some months ago.'

I was shocked. 'Surely not.'

'I'm so sorry, sir. According to Jane, she was given a warning and set free. But Jane was worried at the way Lizzie has been behaving lately, and that it may have happened again.'

I thanked her for the information, telling her I would keep in touch and let her know the outcome of my investigations.

I went first to the gaol at the eastern end of Collins Street, but there was no one named Eliza Merritt there. Reaching the Western Gaol, I tied my horse to the rail provided and after I explained my purpose, a guard unlocked the heavy iron gate to allow me to enter.

'I wish to see the superintendent, please. I am here to enquire about Mrs Eliza Merritt,' I said, mustering a confident tone and stature.

'Yes, sir, I'll see if I can locate him,' said the attendant. 'Just wait here.'

I had never been inside a gaol before, and was horrified to see the dirty yard with its clutter of neglected humanity. People were shouting and arguing, presenting a frightening scene. Surely Lizzie could not be among them.

At last, a man approached me with outstretched hand. 'Mr Merritt, I believe. I'm the superintendent – Mr Gale. You're looking for Mrs Merritt?' he asked. 'Your wife, I presume?'

I nodded to both questions.

'Yes, she is here.'

'There must be some mistake, Mr Gale. My wife is a good, respectable woman. She gets a little excited at times, but she's most certainly not a criminal,' I said persuasively.

'Well, I'm afraid it's out of your hands, Mr Merritt. She came before the court yesterday and was found guilty of lunacy. Dr McCrea has seen her and pronounced her unfit to be at large in the community.'

'Surely that can't be true,' I said.

'Well, wait until you hear the account the police gave of her arrest,' he said, as he proceeded to tell me the sordid details. 'Your wife imagined she was a close friend of Queen Victoria.' The superintendent paused, allowing time for his words to sink in.

'Well, that sounded like Lizzie,' I thought. I suppose he expected me to be shocked.

'Well,' he continued, 'she went into one of the shops in Victoria Arcade announcing that she was a close friend of the Queen, and asked to see their best parasols. She had no money to pay, and said she was sure the Queen would be happy to pay. Apparently, she made quite a spectacle of herself, and eventually the police were summoned. She became very loud and extremely agitated. The police struggled to restrain her. Apparently, she was quite incoherent, Bertie's name being mentioned among her jumble of words – the Queen's husband, I presume,' he said, with a glint of amusement in his expression.

I was not amused. 'Can I see her?' I asked.

'I don't think that would be possible. Your wife is still quite confused. I expect she'll be transferred to the asylum within a week or so. It would be better for you to visit her there,' he said.

I felt powerless. What could I do?

'I know,' I thought, as I rode back to Kew, 'I'll write to William. He'll be sure to have some ideas on how to proceed.'

Once the children were settled for the night, I spoke to Monica, sharing my predicament. We would need to determine what to tell the children, but surely we'd have her out of there before long, so there would be no need to tell them of this latest escapade of their mother's. That evening, I wrote to William, but failed to include the events that led to Lizzie's arrest, saying I would explain later. It was too complex to relay in writing.

When William received the letter, he wrote back immediately, telling me he would come to Melbourne as soon as he could make arrangements.

He turned up two days later, with a plan of action ready to be implemented. He had some influential contacts in Melbourne through his work with the Benevolent Society, he said, and would knock on those doors.

William first visited the chambers of a lawyer he had dealt with previously and learned that once the court had made its judgement, it would be very difficult to have Lizzie released unless the medical profession intervened. So his next move was to make arrangements to speak with Dr McCrea regarding Lizzie's condition, and see what could be achieved.

William came to see me after his visit, recounting what the doctor had said. Dr McCrea had explained to William that his sister needed special treatment. He said that it would be irresponsible of him to release Lizzie in her current condition, and that if she was admitted to the asylum, she would receive treatment that would provide a cure for her condition. There seemed to be no other option than to take the doctor's advice. I reluctantly agreed with my brother-in-law that there was really no other avenue. William returned to Ballarat.

I visited the gaol for a second time; on this occasion, Lizzie happened to be out in the yard when I entered. I was shocked by her appearance. It wasn't just the restrictive canvas clothing, but her whole demeanour. It reminded me of the ragged urchins I'd seen in London's streets. She looked tiny, childlike, encased in the loose canvas jacket. Her hair was a tangled stringy mess and her face and the canvas clothing wore dirty smears. She was almost unrecognisable.

'Lizzie, what have they done to you?' I cried as I approached her.

She turned away. Her head hung down.

I took her shoulders gently in my hands and turned her to face me. I lifted her chin. Was it shame or fear I could detect in her eyes? Maybe both, I surmised.

'Have you been dressed like this since they brought you here?'

'I can't bear it,' she said, nodding. 'You understand, don't you, Jasey – how I hate being restricted. I've begged and begged and I've screamed and shouted, but they won't let me out. I can't wash myself. I can hardly eat. It's just unbearable. Can you at least get them to let me out of these,' she said, thrusting her hands toward me.

'I'll see what I can do, Lizzie. This is awful! William has tried to have them release you, but it's no use. The court and the doctor have made their binding decisions. You should be transferred to Yarra Bend soon. They say you'll get good treatment there. I'll go and see if I can get you out of that clothing,' I said.

I hurried off to find the superintendent. He said he would see to it. I hoped I could trust him to keep his word.

That night I discussed with Monica what to tell the children. Monica suggested that in order to avoid the fabrication of a false story, I simply tell them their mother was unwell and she was to receive treatment to make her better. I conveyed this to the children, and when Mary asked if she could see her mother, I replied, 'Not yet, Mary,' which seemed to satisfy her.

I had been to see Lizzie's landlady and her employer to convey a modified version of the truth of the matter, saying I hoped Lizzie would soon be restored to good health, and that I would keep them informed of developments. I paid the landlady what was owed, plus two weeks lodging in advance. Lizzie's employer assured me he would be pleased to have her return to work as soon as she was able.

I dreaded the thought of visiting the gaol again, and let a week go by. I expected that Lizzie would have been transferred to the asylum by now, so I visited the gaol to make sure she had left there, only to find she hadn't. I was informed that no date had been arranged for her to be moved to the asylum. Three weeks had passed since she'd been arrested, and two since she'd received the judgement of the court.

'Why hasn't she been transferred to the asylum where her treatment can begin?' I asked the superintendent.

'I'm afraid Dr McCrea is reluctant to send any more prisoners there, as the place is grossly overcrowded. I think he's holding off until they can manage to accommodate them,' said Mr Gale. 'He seems to think Mrs Merritt would be better off staying here for a little longer, anyway.'

'Better off here!' I was normally slow to anger, but found it difficult to contain my rage. 'For goodness sake. Better off here – in this hellhole among hardened, dangerous criminals and drunks?'

I wrote to William again, and his letter in response was to say he would return to Melbourne and see what he could do. On arrival a few days later, he visited the asylum, where he was able to meet with the superintendent.

William spoke with me following the visit. 'Dr Bowie seems to be a reasonable sort of fellow. I have contacts in Ballarat who knew of him. Apparently, his background is as a sanitary reformer both in the old country and on the goldfields here, but he founded benevolent asylums for the homeless in England too. I hear the asylum at Kew was mismanaged and since he's been there the place has improved a great deal. There doesn't seem to be any choice – we'll just have to follow the process. There's really nothing else we can do. Bowie says he'll keep in touch with us.'

I felt powerless now. I'd handed the reins over to William, hadn't I? So there was nothing else I could do except to visit her. The weeks straggled by with frequent visits to the gaol, but I didn't get to see Lizzie again. When she wasn't anywhere to be seen in the yard, I would ask if I could see her and the answer always came back that she wasn't able to see me. I had to admit there was some sense of relief when I heard that news, because, to be honest, I couldn't bear to see again the repelling image of my earlier encounter. I knew Lizzie would not want me to see her like that, either. I made sure I went to the gaol on her birthday, taking with me gifts from the children.

'She'll be thirty-nine,' I answered, when Jesse asked how old his mother would be.

Lizzie had been in the gaol for more than five long weeks when I finally received the news that she was to be moved to Yarra Bend Lunatic Asylum on 26 November 1856 – a date I would remember for the rest of my life. At that time, I was hopeful this would provide the cure that was promised and Lizzie would soon be released. I was already beginning to wonder where she would live when she left the asylum.

Lizzie

The horses were drawn to a halt as the other women and I craned our necks to see what lay ahead. We were confronted by huge iron gates that hung from giant stone pillars. An attendant unlocked the heavy padlocks, and the carriage entered the extensive grounds of what proved to be the Lunatic Asylum. The gates swung shut again with a clanging sound that announced my destiny.

The carriage progressed through bushland at a slow pace, until an odd assortment of buildings came into view. They ranged from a couple of substantial stone constructions, gaol-like with their high barred windows; some larger low wooden buildings without any windows; and a couple of tents; all confined within high bluestone walls blocking the view of the natural beauty of the heavily treed extensive parklands beyond.

We came before Dr Bowie, who was obviously disgusted by the condition of his latest batch of inmates. We were all clad in dirty ragged garments; the exposed parts of our bodies wore bruises and scratches. Our bodies and hair were swarming with vermin and a repugnant smell emanated from our filthy bodies.

We were placed in the charge of the matron, who led us to the bathroom, where I was ordered to remove my clothing. I shivered at the coldness of the water on my shrunken body as a young attendant scrubbed me from head to toe. I winced as the coarse cloth was pressed roughly against my bruised shoulder. Handed a skimpy towel, I was left trembling with just the towel to hide my naked body and waited fearfully while the other women received the same procedure. Eventually, we were each handed a pile of standard asylum clothing and left to dress ourselves. I hurriedly climbed into the rough calico bloomers and petticoat. I pulled the chemise over my head, completing the outfit with a drab grey heavy cotton dress that hung loosely on my small frame. Every garment seemed to be huge.

I was led through a doorway into a room that was spotlessly clean compared to the dirty condition of the gaol. I was seated on a wooden chair and instructed to wait. The same attendant who'd carried out the scrubbing returned with some scissors and began to hack at my hair murmuring, 'Agh, disgustin', absolutely disgustin',' as she continued her brutal mission to remove my tangled mess.

I watched as my hair drifted into soft piles on the harsh cold floor. The silver scissors flashed with rapid movement, at one stage snipping the tip of my ear, producing blood that made the attendant swear with annoyance. My hair was now reduced to uneven stubble, exposing patches of scalp that bore a few nicks where the scissors had gone off their path due to my flinching. I looked down at my hair piled on the bare boards surrounding the chair. Another part of my identity had been removed. The dim light fell on the scattered remains, irretrievable like the person I used to be.

I was taken to a small room, where I was ordered to sit on a wooden chair close to a table, and left to wait and wonder what would happen next.

An elderly man wearing a long black coat over a white shirt that reminded me of pictures I'd seen of penguins, entered the room. He shambled around to the other side of the table, sat and pulled the chair forward making a grating sound as it scraped the rough surface of the scrubbed floor.

I found myself facing the gaze of two dark, piercing eyes framed by bushy eyebrows and baggy pouches. The eyes were set in an age-worn face with greying side whiskers and a balding, receding hairline. The face was finished off with a sharply pointing nose. Yes, I observed, the penguin has a beak.

The mouth with its downward creases opened, and the words came forth. 'I'm Dr Bowie, the superintendent here. Now, Mrs Merritt, can you tell me how you have found yourself here at Yarra Bend?'

I stared back at the imposing figure, surprised that the penguin could talk, but I kept silent.

'Your brother tells me your behaviour is normally very acceptable.'

'Does he now?' I thought. 'That's hard to believe.'

'I informed Mr Dimsey that we will be able to treat you here and make you well again,' the doctor continued.

'Well?' I asked. 'Am I ill then?'

'Not exactly, although I have to admit, you've spent – six weeks, isn't it – in the gaol? I can see you're definitely worse for wear after that ordeal.'

'So you might as well tell me why I'm here. I'm a lunatic – that's it, isn't it! You believe what the police said – I know!' I said, rising to my feet.

'Now, Mrs Merritt, quieten down. There's no need to get excited.'

'Excited! You can't keep me here for being excited! What treatment can you give for excitement, I'd like to know! Cutting off all my hair – is that part of your treatment?'

'Now, Mrs Merritt, I'm going to leave you here until you quieten down,' said Mr Penguin, as he rose to his feet and approached the door.

I heard him turn a key in the lock. I was now free from the wretched questioning, but was locked in this room until further notice.

I heard footsteps and a key turning in the lock.

Matron turned up with a male attendant. 'Doctor says you've been misbehaving,' she said, her tone matter-of-fact. 'I'm to take you to a seclusion cell until you behave yourself. This way,' she said, as she grasped one of my arms and the man the other, as they steered me towards the door.

I fought to be released from their clutches, to no avail, as I was led down a long corridor lined with foul-smelling stained mattresses.

'We're full up in 'ere, as y'can see,' said the man as we passed along the corridor. 'You're lucky you'll 'ave yer own private room, I reckon,' he chuckled gleefully.

I found myself in a small cell, much like the one where I'd spent my first night in gaol, the lack of light being the most difficult for me to bear. The only light available found its way through a small barred window above the heavy iron door. However, at least this cell was clean, with its whitewashed walls, unlike the one in the gaol.

The hours that followed caused me to feel like a caged lioness. At regular intervals, I heard the sounds that were becoming a monotonous routine – footsteps, the door squeaking open, a face peering in at me, the door squeaking shut, click, the door knob turning. Locked in.

The only break in this routine was when an attendant – a young girl – entered carrying a tin plate with a piece of buttered bread and a mug of lukewarm tea to wash down some medicine she handed to me. 'You're to take this,' she said in a soft voice.

Appreciating the girl's gentle approach, I obediently swallowed the unidentified contents of the glass.

'There's a good girl,' she said encouragingly. 'It will help you sleep.'

I sank into a restless sleep, out of bed at times when I needed to use the can, groping my way groggily in the darkness, almost knocking over and spilling the contents.

In the morning, Dr Bowie visited again and I managed to keep calm, knowing that if I showed any signs of being excited, I would surely remain incarcerated. So I coaxed myself into a sedated state.

It worked, as I heard the doctor say, 'I see you've settled down, Mrs Merritt. I hope you had a good night's sleep. I'll have an attendant come and take you to the ward.'

I was relieved to find the attendant was the same young girl who had treated me with kindness the previous day.

'This way ma'am,' she said. 'By the way, my name's Grace.' She led me down the corridor past the stinking mattresses that had already been lined up against the wall now their occupants had risen for the day.

I was ushered into a large room filled with women of all ages, pain in their eyes. I was shocked by the sights and sounds that emanated from the fearsome women. Guttural sounds were punctuated by the intermittent piercing scream of a terrified woman. All were dressed in similar clothing to the outfit I had been given the previous day. It was obvious there was a one-size-fits-all policy. One woman was pacing around the room like a caged panther; others sat motionless, staring into space. A woman stood with her head turning fearfully from side to side as though looking for something she was unable to locate. Another sang tunelessly, the same song over and over. I became aware that although the room was clinically clean, it could not disguise the cumulative stench of stale bodies. I was unsure of my place among this human misery. Was I really one of them?

I sat on the bed and wondered how I would be able to sleep in here; the beds were so close there was barely room to stand between them. How could I possibly dress and undress in this tiny space?

I approached a young woman, who responded with a blank look when I asked, 'Can you tell me where the privy is?' My voice was thick as clotted cream; my tongue would not allow me to pronounce the words clearly.

I felt a hand rest gently on my shoulder. The hand remained there, reassuringly. I turned to see the owner of the hand and met a pair of blue eyes that dominated the elongated face of a tall woman. I could see in her eyes the kindness that was evident in the touch of the woman's hand.

Her face creased into a smile. 'I can show you where the privy is. They call it a water closet here. Would you like me to take you there?' she asked softly.

'Yes, please,' I said, as the gentle woman removed her hand and led me down a dark corridor to a large open area that contained a number of baths and doorless water closets.

'This is the bathroom,' said the woman, 'and here are the water closets. As you can see, there are no doors in here at all. I'll wait for you here so you can have some privacy.'

I rejoined the woman. 'Thank you. I do appreciate your kindness. My name is Lizzie.'

'And mine is Agatha,' said the woman.

I guessed she was only a few years older than me.

As we walked back to the day room, Agatha explained about the bath. 'We have a bath once a week. I suggest you try to be one of the first, because if you're the tenth one, you'll find the water disgustingly dirty. The smell is revolting, as you can imagine after nine dirty people bathing in it before you, not to mention the grimy colour of the water and the dirty ring of scum around the edge – I simply dread bath day!'

I was beginning to wonder if there would be any dignity in life here, and yet my new friend Agatha seemed to have been able to retain her self-respect.

'Would you like to come and sit with me?' asked Agatha.

'Yes,' I said. 'Yes, I really don't know what to expect. It's all very confusing.'

'I know. I found the same when I got here. People are here for all manner of reasons. I suffer from fits. Others are in here for melancholia. Some are in here because they tried to take their own life and others have succeeded once they were placed in here. Last week, one of the men drowned himself in the river. There are some patients who will be in here forever. There's a woman who murdered her husband. Some have problems with alcohol – they're not usually in here long. There are even children in here – they call them idiots, but I think they're just suffering from delayed development. I've only been here a few weeks. If they can find a way to stop my fits, I'll be able to go home,' said Agatha. 'How about you, Lizzie?'

'I really don't know,' I said. 'They actually labelled me a lunatic but I'm not really mad. I just can't control my moods. At times, it feels as though the earth is shifting beneath my feet. At those times, I'm not on an even keel – like a ship tossed about on the ocean. My mind just seems to take over my body. It prances like a young gelding that can't be reined in.'

'Well, I hope they can help you in here, although I'm not too sure they have the answers we need.'

'Can we go for walks in the grounds?' I longed to be out in the open air. I had an urge to run and run; to find a place where my mind could roam free.

'Not while we're in the wards,' said Agatha. 'We only have a yard we can walk around, but patients who are considered harmless are to be housed in the new cottages that are being built. Perhaps there will be more freedom then. But I'm expecting to be released soon, so I won't find out. I suppose you'll be released before long too.'

'Mmm,' I responded. 'I hope so.'

'There's a bench I sit on out in the yard. We can find a shady spot and wait until they come to round us up for dinner. Meat and potatoes again, I expect,' she said with a grimace.

I was greatly relieved to discover there was at least one patient here I would be able to communicate with.

Time passed quickly while I got to know my new friend. Then a bell announced dinner time, and an attendant stepped into the yard. I was reminded of the cows on farms where I grew up.

'We're like a herd of milch cows,' I said to Agatha as we were channelled into the corridor toward where the meals were served; like cows being herded along a familiar path to the milking shed.

One woman resisted, causing upset and confusion among the other patients. I remembered seeing cows in a similar situation in the paddocks at Hitchin when a cow suddenly began to race, bellowing, setting the whole herd gambolling in circles of confusion.

Joining the hustling crowd, I was shocked to see huge plates of potatoes and meat. People were diving in to get their share, confirming for me the comparison to a herd of cows. The greedy scoffed the food that was already half cold, the fat congealing on the surface of the huge tin trays. I stood back and surveyed the scene. Not cows, I thought. More like the starving children I'd seen in London's streets when someone threw out some leftover food scraps. Tin plates were available, but no knives or forks were provided.

I decided I wasn't hungry enough to join the unruly pack.

Agatha waited until the rush was over and managed to place a little of the unappetising food on a plate, which she ate with her fingers. 'We have to eat, you know, Lizzie,' she said. 'I know it's primitive, but you'll starve if you don't eat. They won't allow knives and forks because they're afraid we'll stab someone – or that we'll be stabbed by someone else.'

The afternoon passed in a monotonous blur. By the time supper was served, I was ravenous and was relieved to find that dry bread and cheese was on offer. Joining Agatha and the others at the table, we scrambled for our share. I managed to get more than my share, scoffing down several helpings.

I followed Agatha out into the corridor.

'They'll bring round the medicines next. They'll be mixing them up in the apothecary now. We have to go to the day room and wait there,' explained Agatha.

A trolley laden with an assortment of wine bottles was wheeled into the room. I was surprised to learn that the bottles contained the medicines we were to be given. How can they know which medicine is for which person, I wondered as I looked around the room at what appeared to be about one hundred women and girls.

'Mrs Merritt,' called an attendant.

I moved forward. A concoction was poured from one of the bottles and handed to me.

'No, thank you.' I pushed away the attendant's hand.

'You should take it,' urged Agatha, appearing at my side. 'If you refuse, they'll force you anyway, and they'll report you as being a troublesome patient.'

Taking my friend's advice, I gulped down the nauseating brew. Within an hour, I was beginning to feel the effects. I could not make sense of the world around me. Agatha's words were a jumble of nonsense, and the voices of others were garbled.

Agatha must have noticed I was having difficulty and called for help. My legs refused to cooperate and I was pushed and shoved along the corridor to the ward, where I was thrust upon the waiting bed.

Slipping into and out of sleep, I heard snippets of conversation I imagined were about my condition. On hearing my name, I tried to speak, but found the words trapped in my throat.

When a bell sounded, signalling that all patients were to get up and get dressed, I managed to drag myself from my drug-induced slumber. Finding myself clad in a loose cotton chemise, I wondered where my clothes could be. I asked the woman in the next bed where I would find them.

'Hanging on a hook in the corridor,' she said, but the clothing I'd been wearing the previous day was nowhere to be seen.

'Where are my clothes?' I asked of anyone within earshot.

'Well,' said one of the other women, 'someone else must have put them on. When that happens, we just put on whatever we can find.'

I was repelled at the thought of wearing underclothing someone else had been wearing. I soon discovered there was no such thing as personal possessions when it came to anything in here. When the washing was dumped in our room in a pile, people just grabbed what they could. I was horrified to learn I would not have any personal underclothing. Everything was shared.

As the days passed, my only comforts were my friend Agatha and the hope that soon I would be allowed to leave the asylum.

One morning I was sitting in the day room, lost in my thoughts, when suddenly I heard a familiar voice speak my name. I turned to see Jasey sitting on a chair beside me.

'How are you, Lizzie?' he asked.

I didn't answer – didn't know what to say. How was I? I wondered.

Jasey talked on – something about meeting with Dr Bowie, that I was much better. Was I? It didn't feel like it. Each day drifted into another. No joy in living. I couldn't imagine a life beyond these walls. Jasey said something about a house at St Kilda – that I could live there by the beach.

I recall saying something like 'That would be nice.'

He talked about the children. I remembered that I'd written a letter to them at some stage. I asked Jasey to wait while I went to find it. I returned with the letter. He took it, saying he expected I'd be home for Christmas.

It hadn't taken long for me to become accustomed to the highly regulated gaol-like routine of the asylum. However, I would often awake feeling drained, my head heavy from a drugged sleep. I wondered about leaving this place. I tried to imagine living in the cottage at St Kilda that Jasey had spoken about. But I was well aware that despite the medicine that had been making me feel like a zombie, it didn't stop the familiar scrambled-head feeling. I could feel it building like gases in a volcano. 'When will the volcano's contents be released?' I asked myself. 'Or will it eventually explode with a bang?'

And then it hit! I was locked in a cell, tied to the bed and dressed in restrictive canvas clothing once more.

Jasey

I carried a deep sadness within me as I left the Asylum. To see Lizzie's lively temperament diminished – her vivacious personality muted – it left me bereft. I had found her sitting quietly, her eyes glazed – vacant really. I sat next to her in the day room. I spoke her name. She turned to look at me. She seemed pleased to see me, but it was hard to tell. I tried to talk to her, telling her about the St Kilda cottage, but I don't know if she was really taking it in. Oh, the times I wished she would be like this, the times when we were living together with the children and I was at my wits end to try to calm her, but not like this. No, this was not the Lizzie I knew and had once loved with a passion. Not a sliver of emotion was evident. There were times when she had been in a low mood for weeks at a time, but it was never like this. She would be irritable, angry even, but never this empty shell. I almost wished she'd show some anger.

On reaching home, I took out the letter Lizzie had written to the children. It lifted my spirits to realise that she must have some days when she was close to her old self. I smiled as I read the glowing account of her situation. She wrote how kind the people were at the place she was staying, leading the children to believe she was being well looked after. She even added that she'd had baked plum pudding and black-berry cordial with her dinner the previous day. Deciding to give the let-ter to the children, I chuckled to myself, remembering how Lizzie had always been a good storyteller, with her vivid imagination.

Christmas came and went, and my enquiries at the asylum always resulted in the same answer: 'Mrs Merritt is still under treatment, and no date has been set for her release.'

My requests to see Lizzie were refused as the weeks stretched into months. One day, I received a letter that had obviously been sent to William and readdressed in William's familiar hand to me. My hopes were dashed when I read the enclosed letter from the superintendent.

30 April 1857

To Mr Merritt,
C/o Mr Dimsey
Lydiard St
Ballarat

Mrs Merritt has improved so much lately that I was in hope she would soon be able to leave the Asylum – but she has experienced a relapse which will cause her further detention.

It is probable this attack will soon be over. She is in good health. I forward enclosed a letter written a few days ago. It may enable you to judge what progress she is making.

R. Bowie, S.S.

I unfolded the letter from Lizzie. The writing was barely recognisable, her hand so unsteady due to the drugs. She explained this, saying she had difficulty forming the letters in the way her father had taught her. 'Father would be disappointed in me,' she wrote, her words on the page encapsulating her feelings about her father's high expectations of her. Her letter went on to tell me I should return to England – she knew I had business there to attend to, she said. She was sure Monica would stay on and look after the children. Or if not, William would take them to Ballarat, where he now had a 'proper house'. It seemed to me that she was trying to let me off the hook, trying to get across the message she no longer needed me, saying I'd done more than could be expected. Her letter had a reassuring tone, leading me to imagine that going home to England might be an option. I did indeed need to return to the old country to attend to issues relating to Father's will, and my properties.

Finally, I decided to wait in the hope Lizzie would soon be released, so I could see her safely settled in the St Kilda cottage before returning to England. I even toyed briefly with the idea of Lizzie and the children accompanying me, but no, I quickly decided. A future for Lizzie and me could never be a permanent solution for either of us.

Winter had just descended on Melbourne when I received a further letter per William, asking that arrangements be made to collect Lizzie from the institution, she having been cured.

I hoped the seven months spent in the asylum had indeed cured Lizzie of her affliction, but history warned me this was just wishful thinking.

Lizzie was subdued when I arrived to collect her. I gave her the clothes Eliza had sent with me. She went off to change into them. She returned, looking somewhat like her former self, but it was evident that she had lost much weight. I felt a little awkward, unsure of how she might be feeling. I hoped she'd be in an agreeable mood. I made a tentative attempt at conversation on the journey to St Kilda, trying to sound cheerful and relaxed, but I gave up when my questions were either ignored or answered with a brief response.

'Are you looking forward to seeing the cottage?' I ventured.

'I don't know,' she said in a flat voice.

I stayed with Lizzie in the cottage at St Kilda, realising she would need support and someone to keep an eye on her lest she have another episode. Leaving the children did not pose a problem, as Monica was quite capable, and I could see the children loved her. Monica brought the children to see their mother regularly, and Lizzie seemed to enjoy their visits. However, as the weeks passed, the relationship between the children and their mother became strained – Lizzie became irritable, often losing patience with them. I observed her spirits beginning to rise; I tried to believe that her unrestrained energy was due to her relief at being free again, but gradually I had to admit the extremes in her behaviour were a disturbing sign.

On one occasion I came home from work in the middle of the day to find Lizzie was not home. My heart sank when on her return I observed her overexcited mood.

'Look,' she cried. 'I've remembered Eliza's birthday,' as she waved five pretty parasols above her head. 'Won't Eliza be pleased – I kept my promise,' she said with elevated enthusiasm, as she popped one of the parasols up and swung around in a circle.

I was becoming concerned about Lizzie's excessive spending. I'd warned her, but it seemed she didn't really hear what I was saying. She was in such a buoyant mood, any warning words seemed to be brushed aside. Creditors had begun to approach me at my work.

I wrote to William and he wrote back promptly stressing the importance of not letting Lizzie go out alone. He was right of course. That way, if she did behave oddly, there would be someone to speak for her, and guide her back to safety.

Each morning when I set out for work, I reminded Lizzie that she was not to go out alone under any circumstances.

I wrote to William letting him know of my concerns. As expected, William travelled down from Ballarat with haste and said he believed returning Lizzie to the asylum might be our only option.

'Oh, no, surely there's another way,' I said. I hadn't really expected this to be William's advice.

'If we don't take her, she'll end up in gaol again, and we don't want that do we,' he said when I began to protest at the idea. 'Where is she now, by the way?'

'In town, I expect – probably making more outlandish purchases, I imagine. She's been buying inappropriate clothes and multiples of other useless items, I'm afraid. I told you about the parasols, didn't I?'

My brother-in-law had a further piece of advice for me. 'You must place a notice in the newspaper – I suggest *The Argus* – stating that you won't be responsible for any more of Lizzie's debts.'

'I'll wait for her to come home,' said William, 'then I'll take her to the asylum.'

My emotions were churning inside me. I couldn't let William see. I knew he had judged me long ago as being too soft. Surely he could come up with a solution that would avoid her having to go back to that dreadful place. I knew William had a high opinion of the superintendant at Yarra Bend, but I'd met with Dr McCrea, who'd said he wouldn't trust Bowie, believing him to be old-fashioned in his treatment. The only compliment he could give regarding the superintendent was that he kept the place clean and orderly.

'Isn't there anywhere else we can take her? A hospital, perhaps?' I pleaded with William.

I was never strong enough to stand up to William and, afraid of being unable to control my emotions, I reluctantly gave in. I felt disloyal to Lizzie. I knew she'd blame me as well as William for depositing her back into the hands of Bowie.

Lizzie returned late in the afternoon, laden with parcels. She seemed surprised to see her brother. 'Oh, William, I didn't know you were in town! I hope you didn't come to check that I was behaving myself.'

'No, Lizzie, I had business in town,' said William.

I stayed out of sight. I didn't want to be involved – didn't want to be identified as an accomplice.

'There's something I want you to see,' said William. 'Jasey said I can borrow his jinker to take you there.'

'What is it?' she asked.

'It's a surprise,' he said.

Lizzie agreed without further questions – probably excited by the prospect of a mysterious outing. She followed William outside and they set off for Yarra Bend.

My emotions were tugging at my gut. It had taken immense strength of will to contain myself. Remorse simmered. A feeling of paralysing powerlessness engulfed me.

William returned, telling me how Lizzie had almost escaped when they stopped at the gates to the asylum.

'I had to get help from the gatekeeper,' he said.

In response to my worried frown, William defended his action.

'She had her chance, Jasey. You set her up here, even stayed with her. She'd only continue with her reckless spending and who knows what else. If she couldn't manage to control herself, you can't be blamed.'

William made me an offer. 'Why don't you return to England? I know you have business to attend to. The children could come to live with Mary and me. Mary and Jesse could go back to the Methodist School, and Eliza may be able to gain work there after her experience at Collingwood. Besides, she's clever with her hands too. There are many opportunities for seamstresses and milliners in Ballarat,' said William.

'That's a generous offer, William, but you don't have room at your place, do you?'

'The owner of our cottage has given permission for me to extend the building and I've been planning to add another room, so we could accommodate your three then. Besides, the older ones will soon be independent.'

'I'll think about it,' I replied, not wanting to commit myself before discussing the idea with the children and Monica. 'I would pay you for their keep, of course,' I added.

Over the following days, my thoughts roamed. I examined myself, wondering if there was some point in years past when I could have made a change to prevent this happening to Lizzie.

I'd first got to know her when she was in her teens. I used to attend the nonconformist church with my family. It was next door to the British School where Lizzie lived with her family. When her mother and grandmother died within two days of each other, she moved with her father to Biggin Lane, close to the market place. I began to visit her there and her father allowed me to take her to spend time with my family at Preston Hamlet.

William was already living in the village of Chelsea, on the outskirts of London, and when her father died, Lizzie moved to live with him. Soon after, when I completed my qualification as an artist, it was convenient to move to Chelsea, which was closer to London, where there were opportunities to employ my newly acquired skills. Lizzie and I married at St Luke's. William and Mary married there the following year. At first, we had a wonderful life at Chelsea, where we had many interesting friends and acquaintances: painters, poets, writers and creative types.

I realise now that it was after the birth of Tom that our relationship began to unravel. Lizzie's moods became unpredictable. Before the birth of our second son, she agreed a separation might be good for us both, so she moved to live with my father and sisters at Preston. Some months later, she said she found it too quiet in the hamlet and wanted to return to live with me at Chelsea. I was prepared to give it another try, so she came back. It was not easy. Three more births didn't help much, and Lizzie would return to Preston for extended visits. Soon after the birth of Jesse, Lizzie made the decision to leave again. This had to be the end of it, I insisted. I organised the lease on a house in Luton where she could keep boarders. She had developed a skill for straw bonnet making, so she felt confident she could manage to take over the lease once she became established. What else could I do? She would do what she wished. I had no control over her actions.

I made inquiries as to Lizzie's progress, and received the same response – there was no change. So after two months had passed, I decided to take up William's offer. I had talked with the children and Monica about the idea. The girls wanted to stay with Monica but, as I explained to them, I would need to sell the Cotham Road house, as it would be too difficult to manage from England. I had given some thought to Monica's future, and had made enquiries in advance, and found friends who would be pleased to offer her a position as housekeeper. I had already explained this to Monica the previous evening, once the children had gone to bed. She had seemed a little apprehensive at first, but once I assured her that this family would treat her well, she accepted the proposal quite happily.

Jesse was torn; he wanted to come with me to England – I'd learnt how much he'd enjoyed the journey out, so perhaps it was the idea of another voyage that attracted him. I didn't tell him of my plans for his future. I'd wait until the time came. I knew he had great potential. I envisioned that he might have a future as a botanist – he spent hours engrossed in my natural history books, often seeking my help to read the caption beneath one of the pictures.

William came to collect the children before I set sail for England. As planned, Mary and Jesse would attend the Methodist School at Ballarat with their cousins. William had secured a position at the school for Eliza, the headmaster at Collingwood having provided her with an excellent reference.

I wrote to Lizzie, telling her of the arrangements I'd made for the children and Monica, saying I hoped she would agree this was for the best. I told her the children and Monica all seemed to be happy with the move, hoping that Lizzie would be able to put concerns for the children out of her mind.

Lizzie

'Now settle down, Mrs Merritt! You'll be put in a jacket if you don't cooperate,' said my keeper as she struggled to hold me down. I was now distraught; anger and feelings of powerlessness engulfed me as I fought against the attendant's firm grasp of my body. How could William do this to me? Why didn't Jasey stop him? A male attendant appeared. Each of my captors grasped an arm tightly as I was propelled to the interview room.

'I think you'll need to tie her to the chair, doctor,' I heard a male voice say, as I was forced to sit upon the wooden chair.

I found myself facing the familiar countenance of the superintendent.

'How are you, Mrs Merritt?' he asked in his calm voice.

'How am I? What a stupid question,' I thought.

'Well, I must say I'm not happy to see you back here.' Disappointment was evident in his tone. 'Do you know why you have come back to us, Mrs Merritt?'

My eyes met those of my captor with a silent stare. 'If you don't know, how can you expect me to,' I thought.

The doctor rose to his feet with a sigh, instructing the attendants to place me in a seclusion cell. 'Oh, no!' I thought. 'Not the cell again.'

When I'd been in here before, I'd found the heat of the closed cell stifling, but now it was winter and the cold of the tiny stone enclosure caused me to shiver. I curled up on the bed and shrank myself deep into the sagging mattress, tugging at the rough grey blanket tightly tucked in at the bottom the bed, until suddenly it gave way. I drew it up to cover my head.

I cried, first with frustration that faded to a sobbing sadness until eventually I became lost in a deep, drenching sleep. Morning broke through the darkness, signalled by a shaft of light that pierced my eyes open. I closed them in protest at the unwelcome brightness.

I became aware of the familiar sounds that preceded the arrival of an attendant, and was relieved to hear the familiar voice of Judith, one of the young attendants who had been kind to me on a previous occasion.

'What is you doin' back in here, Mrs Merritt? I thought you was cured,' she said, sympathy in her voice. 'Deary me!' she exclaimed. 'I never thought I'd see you again. Now, up you get. Oh, just look at you, dressed any old how. Your lovely dress has had a rough time by the looks of it. I'll get it cleaned and put away for you. We'll need to get you some fresh clothes and matron said if you're quiet, you can join the others for breakfast.'

I was dressed once more in the drab regulation clothing. Here I was again, back in this dreary costume and stuck in this boring regimental place that I thought I'd managed to escape just a few weeks ago. Anger bubbled beneath the surface as I recalled the events of the previous days, the betrayal of William and Jasey.

'I'm not mad!' I cried aloud, forgetting that Judith was still present.

'Indeed not!' exclaimed the attendant. 'I'll take you to the necessaries first, if you like. They're all at breakfast, so you'll have the place to yourself,' she continued as she led me down the long corridor to the bathroom. Judith moved away discreetly so I could have some privacy in the doorless water closet and waited patiently for me to relieve myself.

'Now come along,' said Judith softly, when I emerged. She ushered me down the corridor to where the other patients had devoured almost all the breakfast. Judith found me a seat and managed to round up a slice of bread and butter and a steaming cup of tea.

I was allocated a bed in the same ward I'd occupied some weeks ago with its odd assortment of occupants. Occasionally, loud guttural laughter or an unrestrained scream would rise above the nerve-jangling sounds that broke the silence. Some of the women paced up and down among the beds as though they were oblivious to their surroundings. One woman was patting the covers of the bed continually without pausing, just the constant steady unbroken rhythm.

Later, when I met up with my friend Agatha, I was tempted to say I was relieved to see she was still here, but knowing she had been hoping to be released, I said instead, 'Oh, Agatha, you didn't get released yet. I'm so sorry, and yet I am so pleased to see you.'

'I'm afraid I had another bad fit, and now the doctor has said they'll have to wait to see if I have another. Goodness knows how long they'll wait. Probably until I do have another turn, which I feel is inevitable,' she said wryly.

I found the nights testing my endurance as I drifted in and out of a restless sleep. The long hours were punctuated by sounds of women talking to themselves or some imaginary person and attendants checking the patients. One night, long past midnight, the woman in the next bed sang over and over the same song:

> Lavender's blue, diddle diddle
> Lavender's green
> When I am king, diddle diddle
> You shall be queen

I loved the words of the familiar song, and would have liked to join in, but the tune was unrecognisable as the singer continued in a flat tuneless tone.

I settled back into the regulated routine of asylum life and the weeks dragged by in a monotone. The cooler weather had blown in bleak and depressing. Agatha and I found a new place in the yard that drew the warmth of the sun like a magnet. The yard was sheltered from the blighting winds and our keepers; we would engage in conversation about what was happening within and without the walls of the asylum. Newspapers in the asylum were always out of date. We had heard this was deliberate; the reasoning was that if we heard some of the news it would add to our anxiety. 'How ridiculous!' I thought.

'I read in *The Argus* that they're building a new asylum across the river,' said Agatha as we sat beneath a sun-infused pale blue sky.

'Do you think they'll close this one then?'

'Apparently that's the plan, but I hear from someone who's just recently been admitted that work has actually stopped. Apparently, there's some controversy over the actual project. There's been a lot of criticism about how this place is run.'

Each day, I woke with a leaden feeling; my head felt heavy, my hands and arms felt heavy; in fact, my whole body felt like a lump of lead. I wondered if I might find a way to avoid taking the medication each evening. There was no way I could know what the medicine was, because no labels were adhered to the odd assortment of bottles. When I asked what I was being given, I was informed that it was what the doctor had ordered and it was to do me good.

I was relieved when the long nights ended and I could escape the sickly stench that pervaded every corner of the building, retreating into the fresh air to join Agatha at our place in the yard.

I had been back in the asylum a week when matron approached me. 'Now, Mrs Merritt, doctor tells me you have sewing skills. You will be put to work in the sewing room – you can sew, can't you?' When I didn't answer her question, she continued, 'And if you don't agree to that, you'll find yourself cleaning or whitewashing the yard.'

I had seen other patients with the bucket of white mixture, painting the timber walls of the yard with a long-handled brush, covering up the faeces that some patient had smeared there. I felt repulsed at the thought, so remained silent, signalling my non-resistance to the order given.

I was led to the sewing room, where other women were already engaged, working with pieces of drab flannel or cotton cloth, making clothing for the asylum patients. A few items of clothing were handed to me from a huge grey pile and I was instructed to repair the torn and damaged garments. I sewed on buttons that were missing from a flannel vest. Picking up a petticoat, I discovered a tear near the hem of the garment.

On the second day spent mending, I saw what I hoped would be an opportunity regarding the shared clothing. I decided I would add a fancy stitch in a hidden place on some garments, so when I retrieved items of clothing from the pile brought to the ward, I might be able to find the same clothes each time. I particularly hoped this would work for the bloomers.

The weather heralded that spring had burst in, bringing with it warmer nights that I found oppressive. No cooling air was able to find its way into the windowless building and I would toss aside the bedclothing to give myself some relief. Dr Bowie inflicted punishment on patients when they threw off their bedclothes. Who could understand his strange reasoning? I tried hard to avoid being caught. At the sound of footsteps, I would quickly grab at the blanket and sheet and draw them over my body, avoiding detection.

One night I must have been in a deep sleep, and didn't hear the attendant coming to do the nightly round. Tonight, it happened to be Nettie. Everyone in the asylum knew this young attendant by the nickname Nasty Nettie.

I woke with a start.

'Out you get,' said the impatient attendant crossly. 'Off with your nightclothes,' she demanded as she whipped off my chemise and threw a blanket-lined canvas bag over my head.

'It's ridiculous. It's such a hot night! I bet you don't have a blanket on your bed on nights like this.' I cried, angry that I'd allowed myself to get caught like this.

'Dr Bowie's orders,' responded the attendant harshly. 'Anyone who refuses to keep themselves covered at night is to wear the bag for a week.'

Nettie laced the bag up from behind and I had to bear the night out enclosed in this heavy encumbrance, the rough surface of the blanket lining prickling my bare skin. Now the heat was unbearable. It took huge effort to turn in the bed, as the bag came up to my chin, and with my arms and hands contained within the bag, I could not scratch an itch that arose on my cheek.

I woke frequently after intermittent drugged sleep, my body raw from scratching the heat rash that covered my body. I was relieved my hands were free inside the bag, but I was unable to drive away the mosquitoes that buzzed around my head. At one stage, I thought I could hear a rat running about the room and was terrified lest it should come near my head. I desperately needed to go to the water closet, and held off for as long as I could. Unable to hold on any longer, I could feel the warmth of my urine as it soaked into the lining of the bag. Fortunately, Nettie had finished her shift in the early hours of the morning, and one of the kinder attendants found me still restrained in the bag.

'Deary me, let's get you out of this,' she said as she struggled to assist me in the removal of the heavy canvas. 'You'll need a wash and some clean clothes too, I can see that. Come along, Mrs Merritt. I'll take you to the bathroom.'

Eliza

In the spring of 1857, Uncle William received a letter from Dr Bowie informing him that Mother had now been restored to full health for three months and was ready for release.

Uncle went to collect her. We had all gathered at his home to welcome her back. I was feeling rather apprehensive; the last time I'd seen Mother she'd become enraged, saying how she never could please me. I had to admit, I could have handled the issue of the parasols more diplomatically, but I couldn't believe she'd purchase five of them. I know I should have been grateful, but I was exasperated.

I didn't know if she'd be pleased to see me or not. However, it was a relief when she greeted us with warm hugs. I had been feeling anxious on Mary's behalf, but when Mother complimented her on her appearance, Mary's face beamed with pleasure. Jesse was bursting to tell Mother about all his exciting discoveries since he'd last seen her. She commented on how his front teeth had grown strong and straight. It was as though nothing had changed. And indeed it felt like that, for Mother engaged with each of us, just as she had in better days throughout our childhood.

Uncle kept a tight rein on Mother; I often heard her arguing with him. I wondered if he needed to be so controlling, as Mother never did like anyone telling her what she should and shouldn't do. He had arranged for her to see Dr James, who continued to prescribe the drugs that had been administered at the asylum. This meant she woke late and filled in the days helping my aunt with the housework. Aunt was under strict instructions from Uncle not to let Mother out of her sight. Her only outings were to go with Aunt Mary to do the shopping in the town and to attend women's meetings and Sunday services at the church.

At the end of the year, I was informed my position at the school would not continue the following year, and Uncle William suggested I could obtain a position as a dressmaker. He'd heard that a woman who lived in Sturt Street was looking for someone she could train to help her in her dressmaking business. Accommodation would be provided as well.

'What do you think, Eliza?' Mother asked. I know she thought Uncle was trying to control my life too.

'Yes, I like the sound of that,' I replied.

And so all was arranged and within a few days I was living with Mrs Marshall. I had a room to myself, and appreciated the privacy and space compared to the cramped conditions at the home of my uncle and aunt. I enjoyed my work, learning new techniques from my employer. Some of our clients were interesting to observe, and I loved sewing garments in the latest fashions. With my earnings, I was able to purchase materials from Mrs Marshall that were not available in the shops, and in the evenings I could work on my own creations.

I had reached my sixteenth birthday when I met Tom Gardiner. Each Sunday I attended the Primitive Methodist Church with Mrs Marshall. Apparently, Tom noticed me first.

After church one day, my employer said she thought I had an admirer. She said a man she knew had commented on how pretty I looked. 'And you certainly do, dear, in that new frock,' she said.

'Who is he?' I asked.

'He's the nephew of my friends Jane and Eli Forth. They are more like his parents really, because they took him and his siblings in when their parents died. I believe Tom was quite young. Five children under the age of eleven years – imagine that! They're fine people, the Forths.'

They say love begins with sympathy, and that's what set me thinking about Tom. My heart went out to him – to lose his parents at such a young age. At church the following Sunday, I asked Mrs Marshall to point Tom out to me. My first thought was, he's a man. I'd pictured someone my own age. Too old for me, I decided, dismissing the possibility of befriending him.

As we walked home from church, Mrs Marshall asked what I'd thought of Tom.

'He looks too old for me,' I said.

'Perhaps,' she said. 'But I think you'd like him. He's a good man, I can vouch for that.'

I began to observe him. I noticed the way he waited respectfully for Mr and Mrs Forth to take their places in the pew, his arm encircling Mrs Forth's shoulder protectively. He always looked so solemn. I waited in vain for him to smile.

Over the following weeks, I looked forward to Sundays, becoming intrigued to know more about Tom, until one day, talking after the service with Mrs Marshall and her friends, the Forths approached. Tom was with them. Mrs Marshall was quick to introduce us. He took my hand in his. His eyes smiled a warm-hearted greeting.

We began to talk with one another after church, then started sitting together during the service. I loved to see a smile light up his face when we met. Mrs Marshall asked if I'd like to invite Tom to tea during the week. He began to visit each Wednesday evening, so I was able to see him twice each week.

Mrs Marshall had asked on numerous occasions if I'd like to ask Mother round to meet her, but I'd always managed to find an excuse. I didn't feel I could trust Mother to behave. I'd felt embarrassed by her behaviour on so many important occasions. I hadn't shared much about my family with Mrs Marshall, especially about my mother. I knew I'd have to introduce Tom to her eventually, so when my employer suggested I invite Mother to meet Tom one Wednesday, I reluctantly agreed. I realised I couldn't keep putting Mrs Marshall off for ever.

When I was next visiting Mother at Uncle's, I ventured. 'There's something I need to tell you, Mother.'

'Yes, Eliza, what is it?'

'I've met a lovely man. I'd like you to meet him.'

'That's nice, dear. What's his name?'

'Tom Gardiner. I met him at church. He's very kind – a good man.

I think you'll like him. Uncle William might approve too – he's signed the pledge. Uncle has probably met him at the meetings.'

'Oh,' said Mother.

I could guess what she would think of that. 'He's older than me,' I added. 'Best to get this bit out in the open,' I thought. I knew what the next question would be.

'How old is he?'

'He's twenty-four.'

After a brief silence, I was surprised when she responded. 'Well, I'd better meet him then. When can we do that?'

'He's been coming to tea at Mrs Marshall's on Wednesday evenings, and she said I could invite you too, so that you can meet him.'

'That would be lovely,' said Mother. She sounded genuinely pleased. 'I'd like to meet your Mrs Marshall, too. It sounds as though she's good to you.'

'She treats me like a daughter, really,' I said. Immediately after the words were spoken, I regretted them, hoping Mother wouldn't feel hurt.

'Don't worry, Eliza, I'll be on my best behaviour,' she said.

I certainly hoped she would.

The meeting date was arranged for the following Wednesday. Mother was dressed untypically in a conservative dress. My aunt may have lent it to her for the occasion.

On her arrival, Mrs Marshall greeted her warmly, and asked if she'd like to see some of the work I'd been engaged in. 'You can be proud of your daughter, Mrs Merritt. She's a fine seamstress. Just a moment. I've something to show you.' She returned with some lace I'd been making. 'Look at this lace Eliza's making for a client, as a special request. It's exquisite, is it not?'

The hint of a smile showed at the corners of Mother's mouth as she nodded in pride.

The meal proceeded without any mishaps, Mother putting on a persona that I recognised as contrived.

Mother addressed Tom. She had a knack of knowing just the right questions to ask, drawing information from people. 'How long have you been in the new country?'

'About two years now,' he said.

'I suppose you came to Australia for its opportunities, just like most of us.'

'Yes, I guess you could say that. I was born at North Pitt Head.'

'Where on earth is that?' asked Mother.

'It's a coal mining area in County Durham,' he said.

'I thought I detected a Durham accent. Where are you living now?'

'In Wendouree Street – down by the swamp. I live next door to my aunt and uncle.'

'So I guess you're a miner, Tom,' said Mother.

I knew she was making an effort to keep the conversation alive.

'I've done some gold seeking, and have been finding enough to cover my expenses. I'm saving to buy a horse and cart so I can start my own business carting goods between Ballarat and Geelong.'

I was glad Tom wasn't an inquisitive type, so he didn't quiz Mother about her life. I had been prepared to steer Mother off topics I'd rather avoid, but found this was not needed.

Mother left soon after the meal had been consumed. I was relieved that all had gone smoothly and I could now put aside my fear that these two newly important people in my life would find out about Mother.

Lizzie

I was becoming frustrated, irritated by William's strict control of my life; I could cope on my own, I decided. After all, eighteen months had passed since William had collected me from the asylum and brought me to Ballarat.

I had met a woman of around my age with similar interests to mine. Abby lived in a house she shared with a married couple. They had a spare room available and Abby suggested I might like to take it. I had received another payment from Uncle Ralph's estate, so I could afford to pay for the board.

I knew William would be furious when he found out.

Mary recounted that he had indeed been mortified. He'd blamed her for letting me go.

I stopped taking my medication; it made me feel lifeless. I stopped my visits to the doctor as well. It was not long before my enthusiasm for living returned. My days were now filled with fresh energy and new experiences. Life was wonderful. I was so absorbed in my new-found freedom that I failed to notice the warning signs as my feelings began to escalate. I convinced myself that I could coach my mind to behave. I knew I should seek help, because my behaviour could lead me back to Yarra Bend again. I couldn't tell William, because the answer would be that he'd force me back to the asylum. The same would probably apply to the doctor. Besides, in the chaos of the mining town, I would be less noticeable than in Melbourne.

One night when sleep could not be summoned, I remembered nothing beyond setting out for a midnight walk. I learnt later that I'd been found running aimlessly among the mine shafts at the gravel pits lead, waving my arms and shouting incoherently, wearing only my nightdress. As the troopers approached, I had almost tripped on a mullock heap; I was in great danger of slipping down the gaping hole that had been dug by the gold diggers, they said. I was arrested by the troopers, who had been patrolling for drunken revellers.

When I awoke in a Ballarat Gaol cell, my first thought was 'OH, NO, not again. My poor children – and William. I can't put them all through this again,' I agonised as I struck my head against the stone wall of the cell. The physical pain gave only a little relief to my mental torment. I chastised myself. 'How can I avoid bringing them more shame?' Finally, I resolved on a plan, hoping the news of my arrest would be hidden from the still small community of Ballarat.

In the watch house, the interrogation began.

'Name, please. What's your name?' asked a gruff voice when I hesitated.

Unable to pronounce the words that were trapped in my throat, I made an attempt. 'Eliza Stowan.'

'Pardon?'

'Eliza Stowan! Like a stowan. I should be thrown down one of those shafts – or in the Yarra – sink to the bottom, never to be seen again,' my words tripping over each other as I tried to shape them, but all that came out was a nonsensical babble.

'Pardon, what's that?'

'I can't do this any more!' I cried.

'What?'

'Life in this hellhole! I want to go home.'

'Where's home?'

'Hitchin…' I began to sob uncontrollably.

'Take her back to the cell,' said the policeman with a sigh. 'We'll need to get Dr Allison to see her later.'

The following day, I was led to the police court, where I sat quietly diminished; I longed for the boards of the floor beneath me to open and swallow me into oblivion.

I heard as though from a distance, 'Please present evidence on the prisoner, Eliza Stone – or is it Stoward? There appears to be some confusion as to the woman's name,' said Mr Taylor, the police magistrate.

'Stone, I believe, your honour,' said the doctor.

'Proceed please,' said the magistrate.

'This middle-aged woman – Eliza Stone – has been unsafely lunatic. I've been informed that she is usually of a quiet demeanour, but last night she was found behaving in an extremely dangerous manner near the mines at the gravel pits.'

It only took a few minutes. I heard the proclamation.

'Eliza Stone, you are to be remanded to Melbourne Gaol, found guilty of dangerous lunacy.'

Two weeks would pass before I was received back into the asylum at Yarra Bend. My life was progressing, but I wished it would unravel like a ball of string and I could stop and rewind it, eliminating the erroneous strands of my life.

On my first night back at Yarra Bend, I wrapped my shivering body in the blanket-lined canvas coverlet, sank to the bed in despair, curled up and cried myself to sleep.

Drifting in and out of a restless sleep, I heard the familiar sounds – I was being observed. At one stage, bread and tea were delivered, but I was too despondent to eat.

Eventually, faint light drifted through the bars above the cell door, signalling that another day was rolling in like an approaching storm.

A voice that I recognised ran through me like a lightning strike. 'Oh no, not the spiteful one!'

'Come along, old girl,' said Nettie, 'I'm to take you to the water closet. What are you doing back here then?'

I stayed silent, my lips closed tightly.

Nettie continued, 'Too proud to talk to the likes of me, I suppose.'

Too worn out to argue, I continued to follow the obnoxious attendant to the water closet. I had hated going to the privy, always trying to find a way to go when there was no one else about.

'Right, here we are,' said Nettie.

I waited in the hope that she would leave me alone, but the fierce attendant stood with her hands on her hips, glaring at me.

'Well now, we're too proud, are we, your ladyship?' Nettie sneered, and grasping my arm, forced me to be seated on the privy. 'Go on, lady muck,' she continued.

I sat there stubbornly, refusing to pull down my bloomers in front of the bullying attendant.

Finally, Nettie gave up. 'Don't go then. See if I care,' she said as she stormed off.

I hastily got to my feet, pulled down my bloomers, and was able to relieve myself before the attendant returned carrying a pile of regulation clothing. She threw it on the floor at my feet, and retreated without saying a word. I was dressed once again in the clothing of the institution, my individuality extinguished.

I had noticed a number of women with shaved and bandaged heads when I'd been in the asylum previously, and had learnt that it was some sort of treatment thought to cure many conditions concerned with the brain.

One morning, I was taken to the bathroom, where I was seated on a chair.

'Doctor has ordered blistering for you, Mrs Merritt,' announced the attendant.

'Blistering!' I was alarmed. 'What's that?'

'It's part of your treatment,' said the attendant. 'You'll have to ask the doctor to explain.'

My head was shaved and the doctor entered.

'Please, doctor,' I demanded, 'please tell me what this treatment is for.'

'It's a treatment called blistering. It will help to rid your body of toxic substances. You should soon be feeling better once the procedure is carried out,' he said.

I felt some cold liquid applied to my shaven head. Before long, a burning feeling on my scalp caused me to cry out in pain. I raised my hand and gently touched the spot with my fingertips; a large blister had arisen. The doctor left me with an attendant who did her best to comfort me while we waited for the doctor to return.

Dr Bowie returned. 'Sit still,' he said, as he picked up a large syringe and pierced the blister. 'Right now, that should help,' he said as he left the attendant to dress my wounded head.

As time ambled by, I could hear my disloyal mind mocking me; self-doubt crept in and became a constant chaperon. It was my own fault. Why hadn't I listened to William's and Jasey's words of caution. How could I bring this shame on my family? Oh, my poor, poor children, having a lunatic for a mother.

I began to look for ways to punish myself, depriving myself of food, or hurting myself physically, such as banging my head against a wall. The pain I inflicted made me feel better. It was what I deserved. It made me feel more alive. I could feel my heart beating in my chest and the blood throbbing in my temples.

Following Jesse's twelfth birthday, Jasey wrote to tell me that he had enrolled our son in a good boarding school in Bedfordshire. The school year would begin in the English autumn, so he had sent the money to pay for the passage and William had booked a berth on a ship bound for Liverpool.

It seemed that all decision-making regarding the children had been taken from my hands. However, I felt I no longer deserved a say in their futures, having forfeited that right through my own actions. I doubted that neither Jesse's father nor Uncle had considered how the young boy would feel about the idea. I knew how much Jesse had enjoyed the passage out, so I clung to the hope he would have fun on the voyage and reach England safely. There was no opportunity to say goodbye, which caused a yearning ache of loss.

I waited anxiously to hear word from Jasey of Jesse's arrival, being well aware of the risks involved with the long sea voyage. Half a year passed before I received a letter from Jasey. He said he had gone to meet the ship as soon as he heard it had docked at Liverpool Wharf, but there was no Jesse Merritt on the ship. Jasey explained that he had gone to great effort to find out what had happened to our son, to no avail.

I was distraught! What could have happened to Jesse? My greatest concern was that he was safe and well. Surely he wouldn't just run off without letting the family know.

I had found a way to shut my mind down regarding Jesse. Now all my fears surfaced in a volcanic eruption. I tried and tried and tried to lock my fears away once more, but now my mind amplified the worst scenarios. What if he fell overboard? What if he died of a contagious illness? What if he was captured by pirates? What if? What if?

Doris sometimes managed to get hold of recent editions of newspapers that had been left lying about by a careless attendant, despite the fact that Dr Bowie did not allow his patients to read current newspapers.

There had been rumours spreading among both staff and patients about the Bowie versus Wilson case in the Supreme Court. Dr Bowie had taken libel action against *The Argus* for printing articles about the asylum that he believed were damaging to his reputation as superintendent. Some of the asylum community were sympathetic to the doctor, but most were pleased that much of what went on in the asylum was made public during the nine-day trial before a jury.

On a winter morning in 1862, I was sitting in the yard with a few others in a secluded spot hidden from the attendants.

'Listen to what Bowie said about us. How offensive is this?' said Doris as she read from a copy of the *Ballarat Star*.

When a witness remarked that patients lay about in the yards like wild animals, Bowie responded, 'They are like wild animals.'

'He's the animal, I reckon!' exclaimed Doris.

Finding a copy of *The Argus* a week later, Doris read aloud to us.

The roof has been off the Yarra Bend Asylum for nearly a fortnight, and the public have been so sickened by the ghastly spectacle there revealed, that nothing will now suffice but a thorough and immediate reform of our whole system of lunatic treatment. No language could adequately depict the horrors of that terrible place, as sworn to by reliable witnesses. For the crime of having been deprived of reason, the poor creatures imprisoned there have been subjected to the most cruel punishment, sometimes inflicted by Dr Bowie and his assistants as punishments, but more frequently through the ignorance or indifference of their keepers.

'I'm glad freedom of speech won the day. I hear Bowie's been asked to stand down. I wonder what we'll get in his place. However, I reckon the devil you know is often better than the one you don't,' concluded Doris.

'Gawdelpus if we get another one o' the likes of 'im!' said Gilda, becoming distressed. 'I had to endure the punishment of the shower bath. I already told you about it, didn't I?' Before any of her listeners could answer, she continued, 'Locked in that wooden box, strapped in with the water pouring down on top o' me.'

'Shower no, shower no, shower no…' began Ellen, whining fearfully as her ears picked up mention of the dreaded shower bath.

Doris intervened. 'It's okay, Ellen,' as she tried to soothe the disturbed young woman, at the same time raising her arm with its open palm held up in the direction of Gilda as a signal to drop the subject.

'Not to worry. I imagine they'll be more careful this time. After all these enquiries, surely they'll appoint someone who won't draw any more negative attention to the place,' concluded Doris.

I often searched through the pile of old newspapers that were kept on a table in the reading room, for copies of Ballarat editions. From time to time, I was able to find news of William and his family. Leafing through a copy of the *Ballarat Star* one morning, my eyes caught upon a headline 'DEATH FROM A FALL DOWN A SHAFT' as I learned of the death of William's and Mary's son Davey. Why had no one told me? I read of the tragic mine accident where David John Dimsey, a young man of twenty four years of age had been wheeling a truck of mullock into a cage at the Wheatsheaf Mine at the Ballarat diggings, when the truck fell down the mine shaft and the young man with it. The paper reported that he was brought to the surface, and asked to be rolled onto his back; a few minutes later, he was dead.

Poor Mary, I thought. She must wish she'd never set foot on this land. It was supposed to be the land of promise. First her baby girl dying soon after arrival and now her eldest son – both gone. And a tragic loss for William too. I recalled the excitement surrounding my nephew's birth. William had been so proud of his firstborn son, but I doubted the young man had lived up to his father's high expectations. Davey had been named after his paternal grandfather. I sometimes wished I'd known my grandparents, and wished I could have grown up in the the Three Horseshoes Inn, which had been Father's childhood home. Growing up in the inn close to the marketplace would have been much more fun than living in the schoolhouse where the school board members kept an eagle eye on our family.

'You're lucky, Mrs Merritt. You're to be moved to one of the new cottages. I'm to take you there directly,' said the attendant. 'I'm sure you'll be much more comfortable there than you've been in the old building – just a dozen or so of you in the cottage.'

I had seen the cottages that lay beyond the high stone walls. They were all built in the same style with neatly tended flower gardens and were more like a home than any of the wards I'd been housed in previously. I was led through an arbour where a climbing rose was being encouraged to creep, and along the path onto the veranda of my new home. I turned to survey the scene. It seemed like a street in a country town with its views of paddocks and trees. Cows grazed in the distant paddock and I could see some male patients working in the gardens where vegetables were grown to feed the hundreds who lived and worked within the asylum. In the distance, I could see the meandering course of the Yarra River, identified by dense native vegetation that grew along its banks, marking the southern boundary of the property.

On the veranda sat a woman in a stiff pose. Staring into the distance, she constantly tugged at the long sleeve of her dress, as though the sleeve was too short.

'Come along, Mrs Merritt,' said the attendant as she opened the door of the brick cottage.

She led me into an expansive room where a bounteous fire crackled, cheerily shedding its warmth to every corner of the room. Tables were set with knives and forks, awaiting the midday meal, creating an impression of normalcy. Colourful pictures hung from the walls and a birdcage at one end was found to house a canary. I felt sorry for the little yellow bird. I'd always hated to see any creature caged.

A buxom woman bustled into the room, wiping her wet hands on the floral apron that was tied around her ample waist. 'I'm your attendant in the cottage here. I'm sure you'll find it better than the wards,' she said warmly, the creases of a smile on her generous face conveying a motherly impression. 'I'm Mrs Blyton,' she said as she took my slender hand in her pudgy one. Your bed is through here, Mrs Merritt,' she said as she led me into a dormitory with about a half dozen beds, all lined up in a row.

My heart sank; I'd been dreaming of a place like a normal home where I'd have a room of my own.

When Mrs Blyton spoke again, she must have read my thoughts. 'We're a mixed bunch in here, but mostly we get along somehow. I'm sure you'll fit in.'

Seated at the table, a china plate bearing an appetising meal was set before me. I was relieved to be able to sit at a table and eat my meal in a civilised manner, despite some of the others at the table dribbling and consuming their food with odd mannerisms and utterances.

I soon became accustomed to the routine of cottage life, finding the order a comfort to some degree. Now I had more freedom and was able to walk about the grounds and visit women in the other cottages.

On one of my walks, I discovered the stone wall that surrounded the asylum. 'I could easily climb the wall and walk out of here,' I thought, but arriving at the wall I was disappointed to find a deep ditch dipping down to the base of the towering bluestone wall. What a clever trick! I soon learnt that the walls surrounding the asylum were called ha ha walls – as though the walls were sayin,g 'Ha Ha, I tricked you, didn't I!'

I had little desire to escape from the place now, but I knew many others did and many that had succeeded, although I wondered how – certainly not over the walls. Perhaps they swam across the river.

My manic attacks were becoming less frequent, and during those long intervals, I managed to cope with the monotony of the daily routine.

On Sundays, I went to church, not because I chose to, but because it was regarded by the superintendent as essential moral treatment. Occasionally, a ball would be held, and on one occasion I was persuaded to attend. The old me would have revelled in such an opportunity, but even the lively music of the jigs could not tempt me to join in. I didn't go again.

Eliza

Tom removed his glasses and lowered the newspaper as I appeared through the kitchen door. 'There's an article here about the Bend. Dr Bowie has been replaced by a management board under the direction of…let's see,' he raised the newspaper and put his glasses on again, '…a Mr James Harcourt, who has a good knowledge of the latest English methods of asylum care. The article says he's recommended that the asylum at Yarra Bend be closed and replaced with a new one just a few hundred yards across the river.'

'Oh, dear,' I said. 'Mother has become accustomed to living at Yarra Bend. She seems to have settled into the routine. I don't know what might happen if she's moved.'

'Don't worry, it may not happen, and surely under the circumstances, a new place should be better managed, now they've someone in charge who has a good understanding of the latest methods of treatment,' said Tom, as always trying to reassure me. 'I expect there'll be a new superintendent appointed, and he'll be in touch to let us know what's happening.'

Communication from the asylum regarding Mother's care now came to us. Uncle William's life was very full; he had enough worries of his own, what with Davey's death and his many commitments.

Some months later, we did indeed receive a letter from the asylum. Mrs Merritt was now cured, or so wrote the new superintendent, requesting that we come to collect her. So, a few days later, Tom travelled to Melbourne by train. I was busy with young Robbie. I'd been feeling ill in the mornings, so joining Tom on the journey was not even considered.

I felt apprehensive about Mother coming to live with us, but at the same time, I looked forward to spending time with her. I was unsure about how much help she could contribute to the household, including the care of Robbie, now that another baby was on the way, but it would be good to have company when Tom was away for long days on his trips carting goods to and from Geelong.

As expected, Mother was tired from the journey, and asked to be shown straight to her room. Tom spoke softly of his concerns about her. He'd found it impossible to gauge how she was feeling, as she'd said little during the long journey. We decided it would be best to tread carefully, so as not to disturb her. Three and a half years in the asylum was a large chunk of time and we understood it would take some adjustment for her. The asylum had worked its wizardry on Mother and sent her out an altogether different person. Her personality was shrunken, diminished, she looked much older too; the sparks had been stamped out and replaced by smouldering embers.

She had been with us a few weeks when one evening we were seated at the tea table.

'It's your birthday next week, Mother. What would you like to do?' I asked, once grace had been said and we'd begun to eat the cold lamb and salad.

I shrank from her reaction. Hostile!

'Nothing! Please don't organise anything, Eliza. I don't want a birthday. Just forget about it – please!'

I glanced at Tom, who wore a concerned look on his face and we sat quietly, our silence an unspoken acceptance of her wishes. Gone was the vibrant personality I remembered. I had begun making a dress for Mother while I was in the employ of Mrs Marshall. I had admired a dress I'd been making for one of my employer's stylish clients at the time. It was a new design; I had been sure she would love the colour of the new printed muslin fabric, but now I wasn't so sure. The light fabric would be suitable for the warmer days that were on the horizon. I had finished off the dress while I had long days to fill while waiting for Robbie's birth. My plan was to send the gift to Mother on her forty-fifth birthday. Now she was here, I would be able to deliver it directly to her on the day.

The day arrived, and, respecting her wishes, I invited no people to help celebrate the occasion. However, my sister, and Uncle and his wife, called around with gifts. In the morning, I had presented Mother with the dress; I had ironed it and wrapped it carefully in tissue paper. I watched her face as she tore off the wrapping, hoping to see a look of pleasure. My hopes were dashed to pieces and the familiar hurt feelings visited me once more.

Her expression revealed a look of disgust. 'You can't expect me to wear this, Eliza. It's not my style at all,' she said.

Tears welled up.

Mother must have noticed. 'I'm sorry, Eliza. You've done a lovely job – and it's very thoughtful of you, but I just don't deserve to wear something as splendid as this. You wear it – or give it to Mary,' she said, handing it back to me.

I found Mother increasingly angry and argumentative. I didn't know how to handle her when she was in this state. She would often storm out of the room in a rage when she was upset, and that was happening almost every day now. She had only left the asylum weeks earlier and I feared she was heading on the road back there once more, so I tried my hardest to avoid any upheaval.

The only signal that her old self was buried somewhere deep within her was when she played with Robbie. When first placed in his grandmother's lap, he was unsure, screwing up his little face, and about to cry. But it wasn't long before he began to smile at his grandma, and she was even able to draw a chuckle from him when the bonnie boy dived in and retrieved her hidden personality.

She had missed out on so much. I had written regularly to tell her about the happenings in our lives over those years. First, there'd been the news that I was to marry Tom. Now, my name was Eliza Gardiner; no longer did I have to bear the same name as my mother. Then a year later, I was able to tell her the news of the birth of our son, Robert – her grandson.

Six weeks had passed since Mother's care had been placed in my hands, when the fateful day intervened just before Christmas. Once again, she stood before the police magistrate. Under the heading 'LUNACY', the *Star* reported that Eliza Merritt and a younger woman had been charged with lunacy, and on the evidence of Drs Bunce and Richardson, the pair was remanded to Melbourne.

Lizzie

Here I was once again, locked up, restrained and medicated. For the first few days in Ballarat Gaol, I found myself slipping and sliding, trying to hold on, longing for an unending sleep, eventually slithering back into a fitful slumber. I heard garbled voices in hushed tones; picking up scraps of the conversation – old lunatic, mad, maniac, were the words that jumped out of the garbled voices.

A few days later, Cathy and I were cuffed together like a pair of horses as we were ushered along the platform of the newly constructed Ballarat railway station. Two policemen guarded us closely as we waited for the train to be ready for boarding. The steam was puff, puff, puffing, as hundreds gathered to board the train that would take us on the new steel road to Geelong; we would continue to Melbourne.

Cathy is really just a girl, I thought, as I observed my fellow prisoner struggling against her captors. Terror was evident in the young Irish woman's eyes. I could imagine how Cathy felt. These events were becoming routine for me; I was resigned to the fact that resistance was futile.

Cathy and I struggled to remain steady on our feet, so heavy with the large dose of opiate medicine we'd each been given. I had learnt from others at the asylum that it was standard practice to give the powerful drug to manic or violent patients. Cathy had continually begged the policemen to get in touch with her mother and sister. The two officers were becoming impatient with the tedious repetitive plea. 'I want my ma. I want my sister.' They would come and take her and look after her, she pleaded. But Cathy was repeatedly told that the sentence had been given by the court. There was no way out.

On the train, I dozed, my muddled mind muted. Snippets of

Cathy's story floated through the fog to my brain. 'Should have let me drown… Why did he rescue me? My little baby… I want my ma, I want my sister, tell my ma to come an' get me.' The next time my foggy brain cleared, I could hear young Cathy sobbing inconsolably.

'When she gets to the gaol, they'll probably keep her dosed up on laudanum,' said one of the policemen knowingly. 'Melancholia, I suspect.'

The journey took the most part of the day, due to the long stop at Geelong where passengers disembarked or joined the train for the onward trip to Melbourne. It was late afternoon when the train drew into the Melbourne station. The effect of the medicine we'd been given was beginning to wear off. What with Cathy's continual struggle to be free and me trying to persuade her that it was no use, our foursome drew much attention as we scrambled our way along busy Collins Street to the gaol. Cathy tried to kick at the policemen as her hands were not free. I tried to calm her, at the same time cursing the policemen for their lack of understanding.

On arrival, we were shoved into separate cells. The days passed in a nightmarish blur. Later, I would try to remember those weeks spent in the Western Gaol, but all I could recall was a terrifying dream that came over and over again, like a never-ending Shakespearian tragedy. The images of one scene in the dream rose to the surface incessantly. The bed I lay in was made of sand; I would wiggle my small body into its depths, sinking beneath the sand and disappear forever. The worst part of the nightmare was to discover on waking that I was still alive. I wanted to dive back into my dream, make a change to the ending, facing death like a welcome suitor.

Once I was moved out of the cell into the lunatic ward, I was constantly under attack from the other inmates. There was nowhere to hide. When I eventually reached the Bend six weeks later, my legs were covered in blue, black and yellow bruises. My body was covered in lacerations and I bore a huge lump above my right eye that had been inflicted by another 'lunatic'. As on previous occasions, I was in a filthy state, my clothes in tatters. I was again under observation, back in a high bed, beneath drum-tight sheets.

I recognised the voice of Nasty Nettie as I felt hands grasping my shoulders.

'Come on, Lizzie,' said Nettie crossly, 'this won't do,' as she continued to shake me, becoming increasingly agitated.

I forced back the sheet that was trapping my body, throwing it off with an abrupt snarl. The startled attendant jumped back in fright, as though a wild cat was about to pounce.

'Ha! Scared you, didn't I!'

'Well,' said Nettie once she'd regained her composure, 'you're behaving like a wild animal.'

At that, I picked up the tin plate that contained my half eaten dinner, and threw it at Nettie with all the force my weak body could muster. Bits of potato and meat stuck to Nettie's neat uniform.

'You're off your trolley — well and truly,' muttered the attendant, making a hurried retreat.

I slipped in and out of a rational state. Anger was always just below the surface, and at times bubbled up until it overflowed. When in an agitated state, I would tear at my clothes as my mind insisted that I didn't deserve to be clothed this way. I tugged and tugged with my right hand until the stitches began to stretch and eventually gave way to reveal a gaping hole in the side of my bodice. So I was once again dressed in canvas. 'Yes, this is more suitable for someone like me,' I thought. But I was surprised to find the clothing was less restrictive.

'Dr Paley doesn't believe in restraints,' said an attendant when I showed my surprise that I was not clad in one of those straitjackets again.

One day, an attendant entered the day room carrying a tray of medicines, which she placed carefully on the table. Shards of mischief prickled my veins as I smiled inwardly at the thought of what I was about to do. I sidled up to the table as the attendant began to pour medicine into a glass. Suddenly, the tray had slid off the table sending its contents clattering to the floor, bottles splashing their contents onto the two of us.

'Oh!' Her cry so loud that another attendant came running.

'Look what she's done!' 'You're a horrid woman!' she cried, shouting at me.

I simply gave her a sullen look. 'It was an accident. I must have just bumped it.'

'You're lucky we've got Paley and not Bowie, otherwise you'd be in for it, I can tell you!'

At the end of the week, Dr Paley visited. 'How is she now, Ruth?' he asked the attendant.

The sympathetic attendant wrapped an arm around me supportively. 'She's much quieter, less destructive and much more rational.'

I looked up at the doctor and a pair of kindly eyes met my troubled gaze.

'You can take Mrs Merritt to a ward now, Ruth,' he said.

'Come along, now,' said Ruth in a reassuring voice, as she gave me a gentle squeeze.

I was placed in a ward where I soon discovered that most of those I'd got to know before my release were still here. After all, it was less than three months since I'd been discharged the last time.

'Back again, Lizzie,' said Rose, stating the obvious. 'We've just been having a conversation here about our various conditions. They say Daphne's mania is chronic. That probably means she'll never get out of here, poor thing. Mine's recurrent. What do you think that means?'

'Well, I'm recurrent, too,' I said. 'Recurrent visits to this place, it seems,' as I considered the implications of what I'd just said. The thought of the arrests and the weeks in prison filled me with dread.

My mind trawled back through the events that had deposited me back at Yarra Bend. I wondered how Cathy had fared. I asked around if anyone knew the young Irish woman. I learnt that while I was suffering in those long weeks after my last admission, Cathy too had suffered immensely. She had tried to end her life, cutting herself with a broken bottle, tearing off her bandages and throwing herself about, so that she had to be locked in a padded cell. I knew Cathy had tried to drown herself in a goldfields dam, and now she'd tried to end her life again. She must have been desperate in her wish to die. I often felt that way too, but I just couldn't bring myself to do it. Perhaps I lacked the courage.

Where was Cathy now, I wondered. Some weeks later, I heard she had been discharged. Cured, I guessed. I did hope so. I hoped too she had been released into the care of her mother and sister.

I could never get used to sleeping in a bed surrounded by others like me. My first night back in the ward was spent tossing and turning in the oppressive heat of mid-summer. I thought about the conversation I'd joined during the day. What was the future for me? 'I can't keep on like this,' I thought. Exhaustion eventually took over. I couldn't even summon the energy to cry. I had reached my conclusion. There was no hope for me. I might as well die in here.

Sinking into a deep depression, I refused to do anything at all — willing my life to end. I refused to eat, hoping I might die of starvation; it wasn't hard as there was nothing on the menu to beguile my tastebuds into action.

I managed to get away without eating on the first day, but on the second day the attendants tried to force me. One attendant attempted to coax me to open my mouth and eat breakfast – an unappetising sludgy porridge, but I kept my mouth firmly shut, clenching my teeth. At dinner time, they tried again. This time, one attendant held my hands down by my sides while the other tried to force the spoon into my mouth; with determined effort, I clamped my teeth and lips into a locked position.

Soon after, I was led to the treatment room, where a doctor awaited, clad in his white coat. I was forced onto the bed by two strong male attendants. It felt as though I was surrounded by an army as my arms and legs were held down tightly. Later, I could see the prints of their fingers on my bruised arms. The doctor had in his hands the end of a long rubber tube that he forced up my nostril. I screamed in pain as the tube invaded my body. The doctor held the tube in place while a nurse poured liquid into the funnel at the end of the tube.

I still refused to eat and the next day I faced the procedure again. My right nostril was so red raw from the previous day that the doctor pushed the tube up my other nostril. As the liquid ran down my throat, I began coughing violently, almost choking.

Ruth was one of the attendants present on this occasion. She was so upset that she bravely protested until the doctor relented.

'All right, we'll try another way,' he conceded.

Sitting me on a chair, and held down once again, the doctor grasped my cheeks with his thumb and forefinger, creating a sort of pouch, while an attendant forced the spout of a metal feeding cup into my mouth. I wanted to spit the liquid back in the doctor's face, but it was impossible due to the painful pressure of his grasp, and I had no option but to gulp the concoction that filled my mouth.

My fear of further attempts at force feeding led me to abandon my goal of death by starvation.

I had stumbled on this secluded spot one day in mid-spring when I was searching for a quiet unpeopled place. As I stopped to catch my breath at the peak of a hill, I was overwhelmed by the abundance of nature that met my gaze. Mauve and blue wildflowers sparkling with dewdrops were scattered on the hillside as it sloped down to the Yarra. The river bank was dressed in shades of greens and greys. Wattles nearby were in full bloom, their branches weighed down by the fluffy yellow balls that clothed them. The heavy fragrance of pollen produced by the abundant floral boughs reminded me of a tree that flowered in spring in Hitchin's churchyard. The scent from the blossom was powerful enough to drive away the sickening smell that followed me whenever I moved beyond the yards. On returning, I would again be confronted by the ever-present stench of poor reviled humanity. Hidden from the asylum buildings, it became my private refuge. Here, I could almost pretend I was no longer a prisoner. Retreats to my private hideaway became more frequent as the years limped along.

I often received letters from family members, but one day a letter arrived inside another envelope addressed to me in William's writing. I was relieved William's inquisitive eyes had not perused it. I know he'd have been tempted. I was not surprised. I would expect that of him, because no matter how he wanted to manage my life, he had scrupulous integrity.

The smudged writing on the envelope, 'Mrs L Merritt, C/o William Dimsey', brought a flood of emotion and I struggled to tamp down my thumping heart. I opened the tattered envelope and took a peek inside. 'Can it be true? Am I thinking in a lucid manner or is this one of my crazy confused spells?' I needed some space to get my thoughts in order. I needed to get away from my constant companions. Reaching my secluded sanctuary and panting from the effort on this warm summer morning, I clutched the letter tightly in my hand. A raven squawked a warning of my arrival, but no human ears would heed the giveaway message.

Plopping down on the grass, I lifted the heavy canvas of my dress, and settled into a comfortable position. I had been wearing these canvas dresses for years now. They said it was to stop me from destroying my clothes. Apparently, I'd tug at the cloth when I was in a distressed state in one of my manic attacks – although I could never remember doing it. They said I was dirty too. Well, what could be dirtier than this stained canvas garment? An odour of stale urine clung to it; it never paid a visit to the laundry. But I didn't care any more. In fact, I didn't feel worthy of anything better than the drab canvas dress with its brown stains, shapeless and sack-like.

My attention moved to the letter. I disengaged the folded pages from their envelope, unfolded them carefully and looked again at the signature on the last page, 'your son Jesse'. Yes, it had to be real. Jesse was really alive. I had to believe it. How old would he be now? I could still remember his birth date, despite the loss of important fragments of my memory. His eighteenth birthday would have been on 13 February.

I began to read Jesse's letter. He explained that when his father had sent for him, he could not face the future life that had been mapped out for him. The thought of years spent in the boarding school in England was something he couldn't go through with. So when Uncle William had deposited him at the ship dock, he boarded, but once his uncle was out of sight, he left the ship. Jesse said he'd asked sailors on the dock if they knew of any opportunities to work as a ship hand. He continued his account.

> As you know, lots of sailors were jumping ship at Melbourne and at Geelong it was the same. The lads saw the chance of finding riches and took off for the goldfields. So I've spent these six years as a sailor on many ships and have seen lots of different countries too. I hope you understand why I did this, Mother. I just could not follow Father's wishes come hell or high water.

I chuckled when I read the phrase Jesse must have picked up from his sailor mates. He said he was sorry he'd not written sooner, and it wasn't until recently, when an older sailor asked him about his family, that he realised his mother might be worried about his whereabouts.

It was reassuring to see Jesse's enthusiasm for living spill from the pages as he entertained me with his experiences of sailing the seas and visiting places I'd never heard of. Suddenly, I burst into laughter. I couldn't remember the last time I'd laughed. My laughter pealed like the bells of St Mary's in my home village. I enjoyed it so much I forced myself to continue for as long as I could, puncturing the ending with an abrupt sound that came from deep in my throat. To know my youngest son was alive and still the Jesse I'd loved as a little boy made me glad I wasn't as dead as I often wished. I reclaimed the images of Jesse on the *Oliver Lang*. He'd been so engaged with the operations of the ship as though he'd been born a sailor. I should have realised this was what had happened to my little boy. A man now. Fancy that. A sailor!

A willy wagtail circled around me on the grass repeatedly chirping 'sweet pretty creature.' I began to laugh again. 'Pretty? Me? Just look at me little bird!' I said as my jubilation receded. 'No one could possibly call me pretty,' I said, shaking my head and admonishing the little black and white bird as it flicked its tail back and forth. I raised my hands to the nape of my neck, where my hair was tied back now it had grown long again. This morning I untied it and let the stringy tendrils hang over my shoulders, no longer the lively colour of the corn straw I used to sew into bonnets. It needed a wash. One day, Jesse might come to see me. But there was no mention in Jesse's letter of a visit, and it sounded as though he still had further adventures to pursue.

$$\Omega$$

Eliza's visits to see her mother became infrequent as time strode by. On Lizzie's first spells in the asylum, requests to see her were often refused, so Eliza was often disappointed when she'd mustered the courage to organise a visit to her mother, only to be told at the last minute that Lizzie was unable to see her. She wondered whose decision it had been – was it the superintendent's or her mother's? Eliza continued to write letters, never expecting a response, feeling it was the only thing she could do for her mother now.

Tom moved to the front of the hall, hoping to get a chance to speak to his wife's uncle, the Temperance Union meeting having reached its conclusion. He waited patiently while William engaged in post-meeting discussion with the chairman.

Finishing his conversation, William strode over to Tom, his hand extended in greeting. 'How are things, Tom?' he asked. 'We're making good progress here, don't you think?'

'Yes, a good meeting,' responded Tom. 'But I wanted to talk to you about something. In private,' he added, glancing around.

'Come over by the fire,' said William, as those who had been at the meeting moved toward the door. 'I'll lock up,' he called to the chairman, with a wave of his hand.

Standing with their backs to the dying embers, Tom explained that Eliza had recently received a letter from the asylum suggesting her mother should come on leave. 'We're concerned there may be more to it. We know Yarra Bend is still overcrowded, despite the new asylums that have opened at Beechworth and Ararat.'

'Yes, and the new asylum across the river is due to open in a few months. Maybe they want to get rid of her!' said William, his eyes wide with alarm. 'Look, Tom, it's getting late. I'll come round in the morning and we'll talk about it then.'

'Thanks, Uncle,' replied Tom. 'I know Eliza would value your advice.'

'Around nine, then?'

'Good,' said Tom, satisfied.

Arriving just before nine next morning, William was greeted at the door by Eliza, her brow creviced with lines of concern.

'I'll put the kettle on, make a cup of tea,' she said.

'No, it's much too early for that,' said William as he launched into his purpose for the visit. 'Tom tells me you have a letter about your mother. Can I see it?'

Eliza retrieved the letter from the mantelpiece, and handed it to her uncle.

Muttering to himself as he finished reading, he addressed his niece. 'I really doubt that it would work. We couldn't take her, I do know that! You know how hard I tried, and she was never comfortable staying with me – would never listen to any of my warnings. Besides, I doubt that she'd want to leave the place now. I don't think she'd cope with living outside.'

'I know,' Eliza agonised, clasping her hands to her breast. 'But somehow I feel I must offer her the choice. Every time I visit that place, I come away feeling so sad to see Mother living among all those other tormented creatures. I know she's just as bad, but she's still my mother. I should be able to help her!'

'Now, Eliza, you expect too much of yourself. You took the role of carer through those years when you were only a child. No child should be expected to do what you did. You have your husband and children to care for now. I imagine Robert consumes much of your energy. By the way, how are the boys doing?'

'Robbie's much the same. He's ten now, and the doctor gives us little hope that he'll ever improve. He says he's seen other children recover fully from this illness, but Robbie just seems to get worse. He has diffi-culty walking even now.'

'And Ernie, how's he?'

'He's doing well at school. Ernie's a good lad – doesn't complain when so much of our attention is focused on Robbie.'

'So, have you responded to the letter from the superintendent?' asked William, returning to the matter of his sister's future.

'Not yet. I thought I'd speak with you first. I'll need to send an answer soon though because a date has been set – 26 June. That's only three weeks from now.'

'How about suggesting a week? Surely we can manage that, and it will give us a better idea of how it's going to work.'

'Yes, Uncle,' replied Eliza realising this might be a solution. 'What do you think, Tom?' she asked of her husband, who'd sat quietly through the conversation.

'Whatever you decide will be fine with me,' he said.

'I can't help but think that maybe the asylum wants to get rid of her – less patients to move from Yarra Bend to the new asylum.' William paused, and then had another thought. 'But then again, I hear the chronic patients are to be kept at the Bend. I doubt that she'd want to be moved, and I know the superintendent believes she's better kept to her familiar surrounds and routine. I guess we'll just have to see how it unfolds. I'm very busy with meetings and so forth, but I'll try to make time to come and see her –26 June, is it?' he asked, taking a notebook and pencil from his coat pocket.

Noting the date and returning the book and pencil to his pocket, he clasped his hands together in a confirming gesture. 'How about that cup of tea now, Eliza?'

Eliza was consumed by anxious feelings as she waited for Tom's return from Melbourne. Her mother appeared, enveloped in an old woollen cloak, her shrunken form further shriven from the frosty journey to Ballarat.

At Eliza's insistence, Tom had taken an extra rug to wrap around his mother-in-law's legs on the long train journey.

Clasping her mother in an awkward embrace, Eliza received little emotional response. It seemed that her mother was further morphing to an unrecognisable form – both in stature and personality. The word 'decay' came to her. Yes, that was it. Mother was disintegrating. What a repelling thought. It had been more than a year since she'd seen her mother, and each time she saw her, she felt the distance increase.

Eliza busied herself with settling her mother into the comfy chair by the fire she'd organised in preparation for her arrival. Carefully positioning another log on the fire, she addressed her mother. 'I hope you'll be comfortable here. The boys have been looking forward to seeing you,' she said, as she turned toward the kitchen.

Lizzie continued to stare blankly into the leaping flames as she held her icy hands out to scoop up the warmth from the fire.

Eliza called to the boys. 'What are you two up to? Come and see your grandma.'

Ernie and Robbie entered the room, Ernie standing behind the sofa while Robbie's twisted frame ambled toward his grandma.

Their grandmother looked up, her lips parted, a flash of horror in her eyes as she observed the older boy's crippled body.

'This is Robbie, Mother. You must remember meeting him when you stayed with us last time. He would have been a toddler then.'

Lizzie looked confused and simply nodded in an unknowing manner.

Eliza moved over to Ernie and drew him forth. 'And this is Ernie. He'd not been born when you were here last. He's recently turned eight.'

Recognising efforts to engage her mother's attention were in vain, Eliza spoke to the boys. 'Come and help me in the kitchen with supper.'

The boys jumped at the opportunity to escape the awkward atmosphere in the parlour.

Later, after the boys and their grandmother had been settled for the night, Eliza shared her concerns with Tom. 'I can't seem to reach her.

It's as though she's an empty shell. I don't even know if she's hearing anything I say to her. I haven't mentioned the news about little William yet. I know I told her the news of his birth in one of my letters, but maybe she's forgotten.'

'Perhaps it's better not to mention him at all. I fear this week is going to be difficult – so much for her to take in.'

Eliza knew also that she would be unable to contain her emotions if she spoke about the loss of her baby son, the grief so raw and ever-present. Tom and Eliza's third son had been named William Dimsey Gardiner. He was a healthy happy baby until he died suddenly as a one-year-old from an attack of dysentery.

'She'll need to see Mary and Jesse, at least. I know Mary feels she must see her. I'm not so sure about Jesse. Whenever I raise the subject of Mother, he fobs me off. I think he had such a bad experience when he visited her, he's afraid to go to Yarra Bend again. I don't think he'd risk bringing his new girlfriend to meet her, either. He said he was horrified by what he saw at the place, too.'

Jesse had returned to the colony in the new year, his sailing days behind him. Unaware of the full extent of his mother's descent – despite the warnings from his sisters as to what he might find – he visited the asylum. He was shocked to find Lizzie was no longer the mother he remembered. She was unfamiliar and unrecognisable. As she approached, Jesse caught a glimpse of her old self, as a spark of recognition and pleasure flickered in her tired eyes, confirming that it was indeed his mother. All colour had been bleached from her personality – an emaciated ashen remnant was all that remained. He had gone expecting a welcoming gesture – if not an embrace, at least a warm-hearted smile. It was a harrowing ordeal – he felt weak in the knees. It demanded strong control to hide his emotions at the repelling sight.

Lizzie didn't surface till mid-morning, and when Eliza encouraged her to take the medication the asylum attendant had sent with Tom, sparks arose instantly, as Lizzie became aroused. 'I'm not taking that stuff. It just makes me want to sleep all the time. You can't make me, Eliza,' she announced.

Eliza, shocked by the sudden outburst, recoiled hastily, parking the bottle back on the dresser shelf. 'Jesse and Mary will be here to see you today, Mother,' she said softly, in an effort to diffuse the situation.

Her mother failed to respond.

Jesse dropped in immediately after dinner, wearing a tentative smile. 'Hello, Mother,' he said with outstretched arms.

Lizzie responded with a weak smile, but remained seated in her chair next to the fire. In the old days, she'd have jumped to her feet and given him a huge hug, but the bright and lively motherly warmth was now gone. Somehow, Jesse managed to get through the visit laden with vacant pauses; it took great effort to shuffle the conversation along. In the end, he resorted to talking to Eliza. He'd been there less than an hour when his sister Mary arrived with baby Edith, so he took the opportunity to retreat, telling his mother he would return to see her again later in the week.

Mary approached her mother tentatively. 'Would you like to hold her, Mother?' she asked, turning the baby to face her grandmother.

Lizzie shook her head. 'No,' she said.

Mary hid her disappointment and drew a chair closer to her mother. With Edith in her lap, she made great effort to engage her mother in conversation. She was more successful than Jesse had been, finding topics she thought might gain her mother's interest. She talked about her husband Jack, and of how he was such a good husband to her. They had a cosy home in Buninyong, where Jack was a cooper making barrels and buckets for the miners. She told her mother how her husband's father had been a ship captain, reminding Lizzie of the journey on the *Oliver Lang*. Mary wasn't sure if her mother was taking all this in, but at times Lizzie murmured acknowledgement, so Mary continued her chattering.

Eliza made afternoon tea and the trio sat sipping their tea and eating the teacake Mary had brought with her. Anyone watching would have observed a mother and her daughters enjoying an intimate reunion, but Eliza and Mary were unsure what to say, and the conversation was stilted.

On the second day of Lizzie's visit, after returning from school, Ernie was sitting on the sofa in the parlour, when he looked up to see his grandmother gazing at him intently. Perhaps he reminded Lizzie of her son Jesse at a similar age. In fact, Ernie was not at all like his lively outgoing uncle. He was a quiet young boy, small in both stature and personality.

Suddenly she spoke – her request gentle. 'Come over here', she beckoned with a hand gesture.

The obedient child sidled up to stand beside her chair. She began to tell him about the voyage to Australia and the terrifying storms they'd encountered. Ernie listened attentively, as a sliver of Lizzie's old story-telling prowess returned. Eliza, listening at the door, was surprised to hear them engaged in discussion about whether it would be better to live in Australia than England.

'I prefer England,' said Mother, as she began to tell Ernie about her childhood experiences. 'Don't you think that sounds better than here?' she asked the boy.

'Yes,' he said, hesitant, 'but I don't think I'd like to go on a ship like you did, with all those storms at sea.'

A bond grew between the pair, as Ernie began to open up and ask intelligent questions of his grandma.

Later in the week, Mary returned.

Meeting her at the door, Eliza was in a distressed state. 'I can't cope with her,' she cried to Mary. 'Nothing I do seems to please her.'

Mary carried her sleeping baby to the bedroom, and placed her on the bed, returning to the parlour, where Lizzie was in an agitated state. The two women tried to calm their agitated mother with soothing words, with no success. Finally, Lizzie stormed off to the bedroom, leaving her daughters frustrated.

'I can't see how she can possibly live with us, Mary. It's just too hard! I feel so guilty. I should have done more to prevent all this. I can't help but feel I might have been able to avoid her being sent to the asylum the first time. If only we hadn't left Luton. Things weren't too bad back then, don't you think? I should have been able to stop her from bringing us out to Australia.'

'Now, Eliza! You always took responsibility for us all. Yes, maybe Mother wouldn't have gone off the rails if we'd stayed in Luton, but how could we possibly have stopped her? I carry guilt too, you know. I've often felt I should have done more to help. When I was a child, I used to try so hard to make her happy when she was feeling sad.'

'I've been afraid I'll turn out like Mother,' admitted Eliza. 'You know how they say it's inherited – a family trait, they call it.'

'I know, but I think we're okay. You've a completely different personality to Mother's.'

'How do you think Jesse's coping?' asked Eliza. ' I think that's part of the reason he stayed away at sea – out of sight, out of mind sort of thing. I know he feels ashamed and is afraid someone will find out he's the son of a lunatic. Oh, how I hate that word. I never use the word lunatic, but now I've said it – twice in fact. It's what the doctors have called her, so that must be what she is.'

When Jesse heard from his sisters that Lizzie was becoming difficult to manage, he decided against another visit. He'd been about to invite Polly to come with him next time, but was relieved he'd not done so.

William had made a brief visit earlier in the week, shaking his head in a resigned gesture to Eliza as he left. On the day before Lizzie's return to Yarra Bend, he had been invited to dinner by Eliza.

At the conclusion of the meal when all the dishes had been cleared from the table, Lizzie took the opportunity to announce her plan that this would be her final visit. She said her home was now at Yarra Bend and they should forget about her. She knew she'd told them that on previous occasions, but she insisted that this was what she wanted. 'You don't want people to know your sister is a lunatic, William, what with your standing in the community, do you? I want you all to forget about me. I cause you all too much anguish.'

Eliza began to protest, but her mother cut her off. 'No, Eliza, I really mean it! Tomorrow I'll return to Yarra Bend and you can get on with your lives. I'm of no use to you, only a burden. I know you don't really want me here.'

Eliza burst into tears.

Lizzie

It was a huge relief to be back in familiar surroundings. I accepted the fact that the Bend would be my home for the rest of my life. After all, three score years and ten would soon be on the horizon, and with the life I'd led, I'd not expected to make it this far. I'd heard staff refer to me as 'old Lizzie', so surely I didn't have too many years left.

I was glad I'd finally carried through my resolve to be exorcised from my family. They'd suffered so much on my account, and I felt certain they would be better off without the constant burden of responsibility and unpredictability that my actions brought them. By cutting myself out of their lives, I could unburden them from the stigma they would carry forth to future generations as the descendent of a lunatic.

Following that week of leave at Eliza's, I realised I would be unable to cope outside. That week had seemed like one of the longest weeks of my life. The effort it would take trying to live a normal life, although surrounded by loving family, was incomprehensible. The world outside seemed utterly chaotic, as though there was no pattern, just a jumble of unfamiliar happenings. I couldn't make sense of it all. But uppermost in my mind was the fear that should I be released again, I would face the inevitable path to arrest, be judged guilty of lunacy, imprisoned and sent back to the asylum. What was the point of being released if you had to keep returning? I was relieved I'd never revealed to my family the full horror of my life in the institution. Perhaps if I had, they'd have made a greater effort to keep me out of there.

At Yarra Bend, I had a life I'd become accustomed too. I didn't have to make decisions. I didn't have to bother to be polite or pleasant. At least in the institution I had reached a stage where I was left to myself most of the time. I had reached a point where the rituals and order of life provided me with a sense of security. I'd become accustomed to the strange wailing and animalistic sounds of some of my fellow inmates, especially during long sleepless nights. The odd behaviour of some now seemed almost normal.

Placed once again on a heavy dose of chloral hydrate, my days were flat and emotionless with little colour to life. I felt I'd become an empty shell, my days filled with nothingness as the years slid by in a monotone of sameness. I kept to my resolve, refusing to see any members of my family who sought a visit. However, there was no escaping the visitors the asylum organised. The middle-aged ladies would file in, dressed up in their smart outfits, high heels with matching handbags, hat and gloves completing the prim spectacle. I was still wearing the drab, shapeless institutional garments, several sizes too big for me.

On one occasion, I'd not been aware that visitors had arrived, and when I burst into the day room and surveyed the spectacle of colourful visitors mingling among the greyness of my fellow detainees, the stark contrast was obvious. The ladies were hesitant, unsure of what to say to the patients. Their faces wore sickly smiles of condescension. They often spoke with raised voices. They brought gifts of fruit and sweets, and asked questions that indicated they were eager for gratitude – most likely for their kindness in visiting the lowest of society.

Alice, a young patient, would tell the visitors the same story each time they came. The ladies would listen politely, nodding, as though what Alice was telling them was perfectly normal.

'I've got free angels,' she'd say proudly. 'See – one on each shoulder and the uvver one 'ere in me 'and.'

'Oh,' a lady would respond, 'I imagine they are looking after you.'

'Yeah, they are, specially this one 'ere in me 'and,' she'd say, pointing her right index finger at her open left palm. 'Ain't she beeoootiful?'

'Yes indeed,' the ladies would murmur, gazing at the invisible creature.

On every visit, the same scene would be played out in similar style. Those of us who were 'lucid' – a term used by the staff – wondered if they'd been trained to courteously accept all behaviour as normal.

We – the lucid – were relieved when the visitors had gone and we could unashamedly make fun of the poor ladies, who'd no doubt left feeling they'd done their good deed for another month.

'One lady actually said to me, "I expect you'll be going home soon, dear.". What made her say that, do you think?' I asked the others.

'Well,' said Daphne, 'she was probably just trying to cheer you up. You look so glum today, Lizzie. The woman who spoke to me was so loud. Perhaps she thought I was deaf.'

On days when the official visitors from the asylum board came for their quarterly inspection, we were spruced up and seated tidily along wooden benches, lined up so the visitors could peruse us as though we were merchandise presented for purchase. A large rotund man, his waistcoat buttoned so tightly across his bulging stomach that is seemed the buttons could pop at any moment, picked up his eyeglass and focused his attention on the lump on my forehead. His enquiry as to how I had come by the yellowing bruise was met by a defiant stare, my mouth clamped shut.

In the spring of 1876, an attendant handed me a letter. It had been addressed to me c/o Eliza Gardiner, initially; I could see that the Ballarat address had been crossed out and the asylum address inserted. I moved to the veranda of my cottage and sat on the wooden bench, tearing open the envelope that bore an English postmark. It was from Jasey's sister Mary Ann. My mind spread its wings and carried me back across the ocean.

'My dear Lizzie,' wrote Mary Ann. 'I'm so sorry I'm unable to meet you in person to deliver the news that we laid Jasey to rest last week. Ten months ago, he suffered from apoplexy which left him paralysed. He was bedridden from that time. It had affected his speech, so communicating with him was extremely difficult. On 16 September last, he passed away.'

The letter fluttered to the floor at my feet as I gazed blankly into the distance, unseeing. An unfamiliar numb feeling encompassed me.

For some minutes, I sat in the feeble sunlight of the fading day, the shadows slowly creeping, my stomach clenching. It would take great effort to comprehend the mixed emotions that gripped me like a vice. My mind journeyed back across the years to the cobbled streets of Hitchin. Where had life taken me?

Eventually, I reached down and retrieved the pages of the letter and continued to read.

Jasey's sister went on to tell me how Jasey had returned to his cottage in Wimbush Lane in Hitchin before his illness and had been cared for by a live-in nurse over those months when his health continued to deteriorate. Mary Ann had spent many hours with him, travelling the two and a half miles in her jinker from her home in Preston, and had been with him when he died.

She said Jasey often felt as though he'd deserted his family. He'd given up writing to me when he received no replies. He had intentions of returning to Australia at first, but when he learned that Eliza had married, Mary was happy with William's family and Jesse was missing, he decided to stay in England. Eliza had kept in touch, the two corresponding regularly. On his return from Australia, he'd been lost, and didn't return to his profession. He'd lived with his cousins, Mary and Jane Watson, in his house at Weston, and lived off the rental of his properties.

'He left a will,' wrote Mary Ann, 'and when he was writing it, he asked me whether I'd like to have his opossum rug or his scotch plaid. I was unable to decide which I'd prefer, and when the will was read I found he'd left me both. That was typical of Jasey, don't you think? He left me thirty pounds as well.'

A small part of my former self was still reserved for Jasey, but my emotions had been muted by the medications and treatments that had been forced upon me.

Less than two years after Jasey's death, I received further tragic news in a letter from Eliza. She said she wished she could convey the news in person, but since visits were no longer possible, she had no other way to deliver the sad news that Mary, at the age of thirty-two, had become ill with tuberculosis. Eliza said she had persuaded Tom to have her sister come to stay with her so she could nurse her despite their fears of contracting the contagious disease. Mary was pregnant with her third child and, after the birth, her health deteriorated further.

Eliza said she had nursed her sister through the last months of her pregnancy. Mary had given birth to a healthy baby boy but, weakened by the birth, she had died two weeks later. Eliza had promised Mary she would care for the baby, named John after his father, as Jack had the two older children to raise. 'You met Edith, Mary's eldest when she was a baby,' she wrote. 'She's eight now, and her little sister Ellen is three. Jack says he will manage to keep the two girls with the help of his family.'

John, Mary had named her son – after his father, she wrote – not the baby I had lost in another life, then. Eliza, carrying the burden, ever the carer. The memory triggered an emotion buried deep within me. An unbearable ache pressed into the roof of my mouth. The sorrow I had escaped on the loss of Jasey now bubbled to the surface as the tears began to slide down my cheeks and the pent-up grief for all that was lost poured forth in an effervescent stream. 'What sort of a mother am I? I should have been there for the girls.'

I realised now that when I left Eliza's place following that last visit with family, I had walked out of their lives. As I left on that day to return to the asylum, I had walked away from my family. I'd never see them, ever again. It was my own fault, I knew that; there was no one else to blame. This sorrowful path was the one I had chosen.

Ω

For Eliza, an undercurrent of grief, silent, invisible, flowing on and on beneath her life, ran like an endless underground stream searching for an outlet, rising and receding as each loss punctured her life. Her intermittent grief, peppered with guilt, was not only for her sister and her mother, but for baby William's death and son Robert's afflictions. 'What did I do wrong?' she asked herself. Her sister had really been the only one with whom she could share her feelings about their mother. The two women had remained close to each other as they reached adulthood, Eliza continuing in her mothering role.

After Mary died, she had no one to talk to about her mother. The only time she could laugh about her mother was when she was with her sister. They would look back to times when their mother's odd behaviour, although causing them acute embarrassment at the time, was in hindsight, amusing.

'Remember the time she was convinced that the Queen was coming to Luton for a visit?' Mary had said with a giggle.

Eliza chuckled. 'I do! We knew, didn't we, that it wasn't true. She got us all dressed up and we went to the centre of town. When she realised the Queen wasn't coming, and I said I knew, she was very angry with me. I was so embarrassed by all the fuss she was making.'

'Yes, and when we were children – those amazing stories she'd tell us about her childhood. I think a lot of it was made up, don't you?'

'Yes, I think so too. She was a great storyteller, though, wasn't she?'

Contact between the Gardiner, Dimsey and Merritt families decreased over the years, and when they gathered for special occasions, Lizzie was absent from all conversation. Eliza and Tom had moved further south, where Tom had taken on a farming venture. The geographic distance between Eliza and the other members of the family enabled the secret to be kept. William was busy overseeing his successful horticultural enterprise and involved in mining pursuits, often travelling to Melbourne on business, so his family was unaware when he was occupied by issues involving his sister. It seemed that Lizzie's wish to be wiped from the family story had been realised; however, she was never far from the mind of her daughter Eliza, no matter how hard she tried to shut her out.

When he reached adulthood, Ern questioned his mother. Where was his grandmother? Why didn't they visit her?

She managed to avoid answering his questions by responding with vague dismissive answers until on one occasion, her guard down, she became exasperated by his persistent questioning. 'At Yarra Bend,' she blurted.

'Where's that?' asked Ern.

'Kew – Melbourne. Now let that be the end of it,' she snapped, disappointed she'd given him this much information.

It didn't take Ern long to discover what was meant by 'Yarra Bend'. When he asked an acquaintance if he knew what it was, the answer came, 'That's the loony bin.'

'Loony bin!' exclaimed Ern. 'So people are thrown in there because they're regarded as rubbish, it seems.'

Jesse, in one of his infrequent letters to Eliza, wrote that he had told his family his mother had returned to England with his father because she couldn't stand the heat of the Melbourne summers. 'After all,' he reasoned, 'they're now saying that sunstroke can cause madness, so there could be some truth to it.'

Eliza feared also that further grief and misfortune would be visited upon her family. She worried about young Ern, his lack of physical strength suggesting he would not be suited to work of a physical nature. William's son Will had established a school at Creswick North. He suggested a teaching role could be a possibility for his cousin, so when Ern reached the age of seventeen, he took up a position as a pupil teacher at the Broomfield school in the Creswick district. He was able to live with Uncle Jesse and Aunt Polly and their growing family. Some of his cousins were pupils at the school.

On completion of his three years of teacher training at Broomfield, Ern was posted to part-time schools in the north-east of Victoria, far from his family. He was the headmaster and sole teacher of remote schools at Laceby South and Greta West, where he taught the children of Kelly sympathisers. The rural community was still reeling from the hanging of one of their own – Ned Kelly – at the conclusion to the saga of the notorious bushranging Kelly Gang.

Eliza wrote to her son every week, expressing her concerns about how he was coping. This was not only his first move away from the security of family, but his first role as a qualified teacher. Being in full charge of children connected to the families of the bushrangers involved could prove too much for the quiet young man. Eliza felt her fears were well-founded, but she tried to hide her concerns, writing words of encouragement instead. Ern, in turn, responded to his mother's letters, doing his best to reassure her he was coping.

However, he was relieved after eight months to have his request for a move closer to family accepted. Much to Eliza and Tom's relief, Ern was posted to schools at Princetown and Peterborough on the south coast, not far from his parents' farm at Nirranda. His brother Rob was with them, his cousin John having returned to live with his father when he reached his early teens.

Small parcels of land had become available in the Heytesbury Forest in the south-west of Victoria. Large stations had been subdivided by the government to provide opportunities for individual mixed farming pursuits. Tom leased a small acreage, taking over a dairy farming enterprise vacated by an earlier selector. The land was partially cleared of the tall messmate and stringybark trees and scrub that grew along the Curdies River flats. There was little financial reward to compensate for the back-breaking work. Keeping up the lease agreement terms was a burden, and a severe financial depression was approaching.

Tom sat the billy of milk on the veranda of the farmhouse, careful not to slosh any milk on the timber surface, swept clean by Eliza. It was more a shack than a house complained Eliza when they'd first moved here. Tom kicked off his rubber boots, standing them neatly to the side of the back door. Eliza would scold him if he left them lying haphazardly, as was his natural inclination. He stood in his darned hand-knitted woollen socks, noticing the soles of his crackle-worn rubber boots would soon wear through, and wondered how he would afford a new pair. He padded to the end of the veranda, where Eliza had set out a basin of water, soap and a towel on a wooden stool, rolled up his sleeves and lathered his hands and arms up to the elbows to remove the cow manure that had accumulated during the morning milking. He dried his arms and opened the screen door, its whining announcing his return from the milking shed.

As always, the table was set with a clean tablecloth, the fold marks showing on its crinkle-free surface. Eliza was fastidious in her housekeeping and Tom often wished she'd be a little less particular. She often complained when he left things lying about, and on most occasions he silently retrieved the offending item. Today, as usual, she had the porridge ready, and the table set for father and son.

Eliza busied herself at the stove, taking pride in its gleaming surface as she cooked eggs and bacon in the heavy pan. Each morning, she applied blacklead, scrubbing and polishing the iron stove top to a glossy shine.

Laying the appetising meal before the two men waiting at the table, she sat heavily with a deep sigh. 'How did you manage with the new heifer this morning?' she asked Tom.

'She's a flighty beast,' he replied. 'It took all my effort to get the leg rope on her, but I managed in the end. She didn't give much milk, though.'

'I wish I could help you, Father,' said Rob wistfully.

'Don't worry, son, we know you can't help it,' replied Tom. It had taken him years to accept the fact that his eldest son was a cripple.

That evening, once Rob had been helped to his bed, Eliza raised the issue that was constantly on her mind. Lines of worry creased her forehead. 'Oh dear! I really don't know how we're going to make the next payment. I've been thinking, and wonder if Uncle William could help us. He sounds to be doing well with his mining ventures.'

'Mmm,' Tom mumbled as he mulled over the idea. 'I'm not sure. If he lent us money, how could I commit to paying him back?'

'I could tell him we're struggling, but not directly ask for a loan. He may have a suggestion,' argued Eliza, persuasively.

'All right,' said Tom with resignation. 'Write to him if you like, but I don't think there's much point. I heard rumours that the banks are closing their doors. The decision might be made for us. I had hopes that the potato crop would save us, but the caterpillars and locusts put an end to that, and the price has dropped right down, anyway. They're saying that the government is encouraging fruit-growing now! But it's too late for us.'

Eliza was on her way back to the house from the clothesline with her wind-dried basket of washing when she spotted Ern riding down the driveway on his horse. She could not hide her delight at the sight, and sat the basket on the veranda as she hurried out to meet him. Ern was now living in the schoolhouse in Nirranda township.

'Hello, dear. It's so good to see you. You're just in time for dinner,' she said as they walked toward the house. She was glad she had a lamb roast in the oven that would stretch to an extra serving.

'How's Rob?' asked Ern.

'Well, I'm afraid he has a lot of aches and pains at the moment. He's finding it difficult to walk without the aid of the walking sticks.'

They found Rob sitting by the kitchen stove. He was startled when he looked up from the magazine he was reading. A smile of pleasure infused his tired face when his eyes lit upon his younger brother.

'What's that you're reading, Rob?' asked Ern.

'It's a farming magazine a neighbour lent Father. He doesn't seem to find time for reading, so I'm checking to see if it has anything that might be of use to him. It's about the only way I can help him.'

Ern turned to his mother. 'Has Father found any solution to his financial problems?'

His mother signalled to Ern with a shake of her head and waving hands that she didn't want to discuss it now.

'I suppose he's down the paddock. What's he doing? Perhaps I could go and help him,' said Ern, concerned now.

'Well, he'll be doing a bit more clearing, I suppose. He says we need more land cleared so we can grow pasture for the herd, but I can't see the point. Perhaps you could have a talk to him. He'll be coming up for dinner soon, so you could go and meet him. He's down the bottom of the paddock where the herd is.'

'Yes, I'll do that,' said Ern, turning to go.

He found his father grubbing out some scrub. Tom looked up to see his son approaching. Ern noticed how his father rose from his stooped position, wincing as he tried to straighten his back.

The pair wandered up to the farmhouse.

'This work is too hard for you, Father. It's time you were slowing down.'

'You sound just like your mother. I'm all right, really,' he said in response to his son's worried expression.

'It's time you gave all this away,' Ern said, spreading his arms wide as though to demonstrate the capacity of the farming project. 'You and Mother and Rob could come to live with me in the schoolhouse. I'm sure I could get approval from the department. The house is much too big for me, and it would be good for us to be together as a family again.'

'That does sound inviting, Ern. Let me think about it, but don't tell Mother yet, will you.'

'No, of course not,' said Ern as they reached the house, where the family of four shared a hearty meal.

A few weeks later, Eliza received a letter from William. As a man who guarded his emotions like a warrior, his words could not hide his pain of life without Mary. It was now six years since her death, but he said he was still missing her dear presence. He said he understood how difficult it must be for Tom on the farm, but failed to make any suggestions on what could be done about it.

'He sounds as though he's given up – not the old William at all,' said Eliza. 'His letters used to be full of his various interests and engagements – such a busy life, but it sounds as though he's lost interest. He has all the family there, of course. I'm sure the girls visit him often.'

That evening, after Rob had retired to his room, Eliza closed the kitchen door, untied her apron and folded it neatly before placing it in a kitchen drawer. She joined her husband where he sat staring into the flames of the stove's firebox.

She raised the issue of their future. 'What are we to do then, Tom? We can't make the next payment on the farm, let alone the one that's still owing. If we have to leave the farm, where would we live?'

'I didn't tell you before, Eliza, but when Ern was here a few weeks ago, he suggested we might go to live with him in the schoolhouse in the township.'

'Yes, it did cross my mind, too. It seems the only real solution to our problem, don't you think?'

'Yes, it's not really ideal, but I suppose it could work.'

Ern's parents and brother moved from the farm to the township of Nirranda, where they lived with Ern in the schoolhouse. After teaching at Nirranda for two years, Ern moved schools again, this time to Nirranda East, while continuing with his position at Peterborough. The schoolhouse at Nirranda East proved to be even more accommodating for the family than the one in Nirranda, and Eliza was happy to make the move with her husband and sons.

One day at the height of summer, Ern's friend Jack invited him to come to a singalong on a Sunday evening. Jack said the evenings were great social occasions and provided an opportunity to meet girls. Ern hadn't had much to do with young women and now, well into his twenties, he doubted he'd ever get married. He knew his mother longed for grandchildren, and he appeared to be her only hope. Ern decided to take up Jack's offer and the pair arranged a time to meet on the following Sunday evening.

Riding their horses along the narrow paths through the Heytesbury Forest, Jack filled Ern in on who he could expect to meet. There were the Becketts, he said, the singalong being held at their home. 'Pat Beckett, their daughter, has an organ and provides the music,' he said.

'I've two of the Beckett children at my school. Pat must be one of the older ones.'

'Mmm, she'd be about seventeen, I imagine,' said Jack.

On arrival, Ern was introduced to some of those he'd not yet met. He and Jack found seats, and were handed Sankey's hymn books. The book was familiar to Ern, so he imagined he'd know some of the songs they'd be singing tonight. Ern looked across to the organ, and there he saw seated on the stool a young woman, her eyes intent on the music book before her. 'What a delight,' he thought instantly.

The following Sunday, Ern was eagerly waiting astride his horse to ride with Jack to the Beckett home. During a prayer, Ern took the opportunity to open his eyes and get a better look at the young organist, only to discover she was doing the same. He blinked his eyes shut, embarrassed at being caught out. Dared he hope something might come of this? 'I'm much too old for her,' he said to himself. 'She must be at least ten years younger than me.' But he could not let go of the feeling that stirred within him whenever he thought about her.

Ern discovered he could row his boat down to the Beckett home more easily than riding. After several weeks of attending the singalongs, when there was a pause in the singing, Ern looked across at the young organist and his eyes met the smiling eyes of Pat Beckett. It felt to him as though they shared a special moment.

When Pat had finished her playing, Ern spoke to his pupil Maude, asking if that was her sister who played the organ.

'Yes,' replied Maude. 'Do you want to meet Pattie?'

At last, Ern and Pattie were introduced formally.

Not one to engage in small talk as a rule, Ern struggled to make conversation. 'You play the organ very well,' he said. 'Where did you learn? It must be difficult to find a teacher around here.'

'I learned to play when I lived with the couple who raised me – the Robilliards,' she said nodding to a couple across the room.'

Ern's questioning eyes followed the direction of her nod as he asked, 'That's them over there, is it?'

'Oh, no,' said Pat, shaking her head solemnly. 'They're relatives of theirs – their name's Robilliard too – but the couple that raised me died, so I came back to my family here a few years ago.'

They were interrupted by Pat's father, Alfred, making some announcements. He said next Sunday they would begin church services here on a Sunday night. There'd still be plenty of singing, but a more formal program for the evening was proposed.

Pat's father, a learned man, became the eloquent preacher, with others sharing in the service. Pat continued to provide musical accompaniment. Ern had persuaded his parents to attend the church services. At first, his mother used the excuse that they couldn't take Rob, so she must stay with him, until Rob insisted he could manage on his own for a couple of hours. He had reached a stage where he needed help with most everyday tasks.

Eliza immediately noticed the friendship that was developing between her son and the young organist. Once they'd climbed into the boat and Ern had begun to row back to the schoolhouse one evening, Eliza questioned Ern. 'I notice you've become friendly with Pat Beckett.'

'Yes, Mother. She's such a lovely young woman – but Pattie's much too young for me,' he added.

'I don't think that matters, Ern,' she said. 'Remember, I'm eight years younger than your father.'

'Do you really think I might have a chance with her? How would I know?' he asked hopefully.

'I can see she likes you. Her sister Maude is a pupil of yours, isn't she? Perhaps you could write her a letter – get her sister to deliver it. See how she responds.'

Ern followed his mother's advice and a romance began to blossom. Pat's father strictly adhered to the moral code of the time, and Pat's sister Belle became chaperon, accompanying Pat to the river, where Ern would tether his boat.

One Saturday, Ern arranged to take Pat for a picnic at the beach at Peterborough. Belle had woken up with a bad cough and was not able to accompany the pair, so on this rare occasion, Pat's father relented and Ern and Pat had several hours alone in each other's company. Alfred had come to hold the schoolteacher in the highest regard, confirmed by his youngest children, who had great respect for their headmaster. Alfred had been enjoying getting to know Ern, as they shared a similar interest in affairs of the world. However, he was very strict when it came to the matter of his nine daughters. He made it clear to Ern that Pattie would need to wait until her twenty-first birthday to marry. His wife, Selina, felt this was a bit excessive, and when in August 1894 Ern learnt that he would be relieved of his duties at Peterborough and become full-time at Nirranda East School, Alfred relented.

The marriage ceremony was arranged for Christmas Day of that year. The practicality of having all the family together for the double occasion was accepted by Ern and his bride. Alfred told Ern he was welcome to invite other relatives as well as his parents and brother. Eliza still carried her fear that her mother's condition would be discovered, so counselled Ern that he should explain to the Becketts that the travelling distance was too prohibitive. No one had asked Ern if he had grandparents, assuming they had all died or were still in the old country, so it was not hard to hide his only surviving grandparent. Ern would never reveal the fact his grandmother was in a lunatic asylum.

Ern and his new wife lived in the schoolhouse with Ern's parents.

Ω

Time slithered by as one year snaked into another. With little change in her condition, Lizzie would often retreat to her hide-away by the river. It seemed to be the only place she could salvage parts of her memory. On these occasions, she would try to delve into her store of memories. Whole chunks of her life seemed to be missing – it was as though so many events in her life had been deleted, never to be retrieved. She carried no memories of her eldest son Tom's adulthood, and her hopes of seeing Tom again and meeting his wife and children had been discarded long ago. All that survived was the notion of the little boy who'd pressed a bunch of bluebells into her hands in Wain Wood.

She struggled to remember what had been happening beyond the high stone walls that kept her safe or imprisoned her, depending on your viewpoint. How could she begin to unpick the knots in her tangled life? Sometimes she was at peace, and able to sit in silence as her grandmother had tried to teach her as a child by taking her to the Quaker meetings in the village.

The Yarra below seemed to tell the story of her life as she watched it in the seasons that came and went over the years. At times, it flowed swiftly, threatening to overflow after heavy rains upstream, carrying rubbish gathered along the way. It had already stolen her last sliver of self-respect, but she wished it had carried away all the other tawdry components of her life. When it was low and stagnant in the summer, it matched her depressive moods. Her manic episodes had been muted by the heavy doses of the sedative, chloral hydrate, on which she had become dependent.

Sometimes, Lizzie thought about all the strange behaviours and ramblings of her fellow inmates and came to realise she was one of them. It was a great relief when she finally reached the point where she concluded she was indeed mad. Despite this admission, she still felt burdensome guilt at what she had inflicted on her family, and she continued to punish herself.

On that last visit to her family, she'd made a plea that the truth about her history be kept secret because she wanted to protect future generations from hearing her story, wishing to be wiped out like chalk from a slate. And yet the lonely life she had chosen found her longing for the loving embrace of those dear to her. She was so ashamed and determined to prevent her grandchildren from knowing about her, for fear of the stigma that might be attached to them having a grandmother like her. She'd heard it was believed by some in the medical profession to be a 'hereditary taint'. 'Have I tainted the lives of my descendants?' she agonised.

Once, when one of the malicious attendants recounted Lizzie's actions during one of her manic episodes, she was mortified, and resorted, as she often had, to banging her head against one of the stone walls in the yard. When the doctor asked her why she continually inflicted this damage on herself, she said it was because she believed she deserved punishment.

As she became increasingly frail, she was unable to climb the hill to reach her retreat.

Dignity had deserted Lizzie long ago; left, never to return. She often wished her life would end, but the end obstinately refused to come. Death would not visit, although it had a welcome invitation. Sometimes, she thought she was already dead, or a large part of her was, and the fragments that were left continued through the bleak years that dragged onwards, decade after decade.

She developed a reputation – 'mad Lizzie', they called her. The old mischievous part of her emerged at times, and she would find ways to keep her reputation intact. Some of the young attendants were afraid of her, although most of the staff knew the little old lady was harmless.

Yarra Bend was always under threat of closure. On Lizzie's first visit, makeshift wooden buildings had been added to the original bluestone one in order to accommodate the swelling number of new arrivals. The extensive gardens now provided fresh fruit, vegetables, eggs and dairy produce for the patients; pigs were farmed and there was a brewery where beer for the asylum community was manufactured.

Although, just a few years after the opening of Yarra Bend Lunatic Asylum, a decision had been made to replace it with a new asylum barely three hundred yards across the Yarra River, it was not until 1871 that the first patients were moved to the new Kew Asylum. Lizzie was not one of those to make the move. Although new asylums had been established in Victoria at Beechworth and Ararat, there were still more than one thousand patients housed at Kew. In 1886 the Victorian government accepted the report of a Royal Commission to review mental health in the state. The chairman of the enquiry deemed Victoria to be the 'maddest place in the world'. The report recommended closure of both Yarra Bend and Kew asylums, the land being too valuable for the purpose of housing the mentally ill. With an economic recession descending, the cash-strapped government recognised the land as a valuable asset. However, both institutions at Kew continued to operate well into the twentieth century.

As Lizzie's life gradually expired over the following decades, so did the old Yarra Bend institution. Resources were funnelled into the new asylum that stood imposingly on the hill opposite, leaving Yarra Bend hidden away as the poor relative it had become, dilapidated and abandoned.

Together with others who had become permanent residents, never to be released, Lizzie lived out her days forgotten and neglected.

When she reached her seventies, the manic episodes departed, but the effect of the long years in the asylum had taken their toll. The years slunk by relentlessly, until her life finally ended a few months before her eighty-third birthday. She had begun to die little by little once she entered the gaol at the western end of Collins Street – a gradual death that took more than forty years.

The superintendent sent telegrams to Lizzie's children, notifying them of her death and requiring a family member to identify the body. Tom asked Jesse to go, as he knew his wife would find it distressing. When asked where the inquisition report should be sent, Jesse nominated his sister. He felt it fitting that Eliza be the one to take charge of the report, not only as the eldest, but because she'd unceasingly carried the responsibility for their mother's welfare. He'd always admired his older sister's strength of character. The loathsome sight of his mother's mouldering body would revisit him on uninvited occasions for the rest of his days. He didn't need to see any words written on paper. Nor did he want the responsibility of dealing with the documents.

One afternoon, some weeks after Lizzie's death, Ern collected the family's mail from Nirranda Post Office. An official envelope addressed to Eliza A. Gardiner was the only mail today. Ern handed the letter to his mother, guessing it contained the awaited documentation concerning his grandmother's death. Eliza grasped the letter, hastily stowing it away in a drawer of the dresser.

Days crawled by as Eliza waited for the opportunity to examine the contents of the envelope. She dreaded the thought, fearful of its unknown contents. She'd never seen an inquisition report before, imagining that her mother's life would be under judgement.

One afternoon when Tom was working in his vegetable garden, Ern was at school and Pattie having a lie-down while the children had their afternoon nap, she prised open the envelope. A short letter from the superintendent wrote that he had included with the post-mortem report the only remaining personal effect belonging to her mother – a gold wedding band – despite more than half a century having passed since the death of her marriage to Jasey. Eliza placed the ring, wire-thin, in the palm of her hand, pondering its future. Slipping the ring back into the envelope, she drew out the pages and began to read.

It was as she'd suspected. 'Maniacal outbursts, destructive and dirty, knocking herself about, refusing food.' The phrases leapt off the page, confronting Eliza as she read from the coronial enquiry.

The brief history of her mother's four decades in the asylum was followed by the reports by staff who witnessed the horror of her mother's last days. So clinical. So impersonal. The familiar ache somewhere beyond the roof of her mouth came without an invitation. She would not cry.

The account from Nurse Susan at the coronial inquest recorded that on the first day of September Lizzie was in her care.

She was in bed. I was in the room. She rose to get up and fell against the wall. She was not violent but very feeble. She was partly standing when she fell over. It is a wooden wall. She fell with great force against the wall. A small red lump arose.

Nurse Emily said,

A week last Saturday she fell down and knocked her head against a wall. Last Thursday 6th instant she commenced vomiting and appeared to be faint – she was placed in bed and I sent for the doctor. She never rallied and sunk and died at 12.30 on 7th instant. Her son saw the body yesterday.

The surgeon reported,

There was slight contusion on the legs. There was extensive contusion with much swelling on the left forehead orbit and cheek and nose. There was much blood beneath the scalp on the left side. The brain was gangrenous at the base. There was an old fracture at the base and necrosis of the bone.

The surgeon concluded,

The cause of death was old disease and injury of the brain, and disease of the lungs and heart.

How could she have let her mother die in that place, surrounded by strangers? 'I should have been there at the end,' she agonised as guilt grasped her stomach and became the dominant emotion. 'I can't let anyone else see this,' she decided. This had to be the end of it. She took the pages, deposited them back in their envelope' where they joined her mother's wedding band, opened the door of the stove, and gently tucked the envelope with its contents into the fire. Eliza bent over and watched until all traces of her mother's disreputable history were consumed by the flames. As she straightened her back, she failed to hear the smouldering remains' invitation to her shame and guilt. 'Come with us,' they whispered.

Kew, Melbourne, 1921

$$\Omega$$

The little man stands on the wide veranda of the homestead, its timber rails longing for a coat of paint, twiddling his greying beard as he watches the jersey cows straggling along the path beside the Yarra River on their way to the far paddock, where the cows will spend the day grazing on fresh pasture.

He is wearing a freshly laundered shirt, originally white, but now a dull bluey-grey from Pattie's efforts with the blue bag. The shirt sleeves are too long for Ern's short arms, so they are hitched above his elbows by silver armbands. He has inherited an obsession with cleanliness from his mother that takes precedence over the condition of his clothes. Pattie always sees to it that a freshly laundered set of clothing is laid out for her husband each morning.

The shirt is showing the signs of wear, and the cuffs, fastened at the end of the sleeves with silver cufflinks, are now fraying. He wonders if perhaps Pattie could repair the cuffs. He has a habit of twirling the buttons on his waistcoat, so Pattie often has buttons to sew on. A frugal man, his clothes often wear patches. He is reluctant to throw anything away or to spend money on what he regards as unnecessary. However, he is abundantly generous when a human need is brought to his notice.

The phosphorescent sun hangs low in the cloudless sky. Its warmth signals summer days ahead. Across to his right he can just see the grandiose buildings of the Kew Asylum, standing steadfastly with the sky as a backdrop. The sandstone walls on the eastern side are illuminated by the sun's rays. The asylum stands as a constant reminder of the other institution, the one just across the river where Ern's grandmother had spent half her life. Ern has heard there are still a few patients remaining at the Yarra Bend Asylum, hidden from view by the gums and silver wattles that grow along the banks of the Yarra. The word 'lunatic' has been removed from the institution's name.

Ern had begun his working life as a schoolteacher, until his hearing and poor health forced his retirement. He had then purchased the newsagency and fancy goods store in the seaside town of Queenscliffe, before taking up farming. He purchased the farm from Colonel Wills, who had given the property the name Willsmere Park. Ern had taken a huge risk, some thought, purchasing the place with its rich alluvial soils and old homestead for fifteen thousand pounds, with a deposit of just one thousand pounds.

Ern could see the potential that is already proving to be well founded. There is great demand for the fresh milk produced to supply the growing population of Melbourne nearby. His sons Tom and Stan are still at the milking shed, stripping the last of the herd, as the milk fills the buckets with frothy warm milk that is then tipped into the waiting cans. After breakfast, the boys will load the cans onto the cart that will be harnessed to two horses. Then they'll set out to deliver the milk to the Model Dairy.

As he stands surveying the scene, Ern remembers the occasions during the last two decades when he's stood by the grave in the Boroondara Cemetery; first his grandmother, then the following year his mother, and his father another ten years after that. All three share a grave in the Presbyterian section.

Word had come yesterday that the addition to the gravestone had been completed. Today, Ern is eager to have a look at the result.

The older boys are still cleaning up at the dairy. Des has gone to school. Isla and Gwen, the two red heads, have caught the cable tram that trundles along Belford Road and delivers them to their respective training institutions in the city: Isla to the Kindergarten Training College and Gwen to a milliner's in Little Bourke Street. It will be just Pattie and his eldest daughter Dorrie who may ask where he is going.

If they ask where he's heading, he'll manage to avoid telling them if he can. He's worked so hard at keeping the secret. They don't need to know about their great-grandma.

Attitudes are changing, reflects Ern. Lunacy is no longer a crime. There are those in the medical profession who now recognise that people with mental problems are suffering from an illness. Even his own brother, who had been crippled with polio, had been hidden from view. It's as though it was their fault, Ern often thought.

Ern had been disappointed to see the disgust on the faces of some of his own children when occasionally a patient from the Kew Asylum wandered onto the property. There had been one incident since they'd moved here, when the boys reported with great excitement how they'd seen a man down near the river wearing a big overcoat. The boys had hidden in long grass near a fence and watched mesmerised as the man peeled off layers of clothing one after another until he stood naked. The boys laughingly repeated the story whenever they had the chance. Ern admonished his sons, telling them they were not to repeat the story. He just felt very sad. However, he realised the boys just didn't understand.

Ern opens the screen door that whines itself shut, keeping out the odd blowfly that is eager to explore the rambling old homestead. Inside the vestibule, the shimmering sun splashes colours from the stained-glass windows that border each side of the entry. The bells along the wall summon no servants these days. There are hands enough for the chores to sustain this large family. Joy, the youngest member of the Gardiner family, loves to play with the bells, but no one comes to her bidding. When the family first moved here, the children found it interesting that there were two lavatories out the back – one for the boys and one for the girls. Ern didn't bother to explain his guess that one toilet was for the family and the other for the servants.

He picks up his felt hat from the hat stand and places it on his head purposefully. Entering the breakfast room, he finds Pattie resetting the table in preparation for the boys' breakfast.

'Where are you off to now, Ern?' asks Pattie, noticing he is wearing his going-out hat.

'What's that?' enquires Ern, cupping his hands behind his ears.

'I said, where are you going?'

Ern has his head to the side, with an oft used expression on his face that is very familiar to Pattie. He either didn't hear or didn't want to answer.

Frustrated, Pattie decides it isn't worth pursuing her question, but more important to her is that she'd like a break from her young daughter. There is a busy day ahead. So she turns to face Ern, speaking clearly so he can read her lips. 'Can you take Joy with you?'

'Yes, of course,' he replies, relieved.

The thought of spending the morning with his youngest daughter is such a pleasure. He finds the little girl in the dining room; the central hub of the sprawling house. Joy is sitting on a stool next to the mirrored and shelved sideboard that stands tall, uncluttered, bearing a porcelain vase filled with roses placed on a hand embroidered doily. The roses have been cut from the bushes in the garden that Ern tends with pleasure. Joy's sister Dorrie brushes the tangles from the little girl's blonde curls.

'Ouch, that hurt, Dossie,' she says as the brush catches a tangle.

'Sorry,' says Dorrie gently. She adores her little sister and is like a second mother to the little girl.

'What are you doing today, Dorrie?' Ern asks.

'Mother and I are going to preserve the apricots you picked yesterday.'

'What's that?' asks Ern.

'Nothing,' murmurs Dorrie. It isn't worth the effort of trying to make her father hear. Ern has become quite used to not having his questions answered.

'I can take Joy with me this morning, if you like,' says Ern, as he waits for his eldest daughter to complete her task.

She nods her assent.

Joy hops down from the stool, excited at the prospect of an outing with her father. She is wearing the pretty blue smocked dress Dorrie has made for her. Dorrie kneels down and buttons up the polished leather boots that Joy has slipped onto her slim, stockinged feet.

'You'll need your sun bonnet,' says Dorrie as she follows the pair to the vestibule, where she selects the hat that belongs to her little sister. Tucking in the golden curls that frame Joy's sweet little face, she ties the ribbons loosely beneath her rounded chin.

Grasping Joy's hand in his, Ern and Joy set out along the driveway towards Belford Road, where they will catch a tram for the journey to Boroondara Cemetery. There are fewer horses on the roads now, observes Ern as an occasional motor car overtakes the tram. He guesses he'll need to buy one eventually. It would certainly save the bother of harnessing up the horses.

Father and daughter approach the ornate iron gates of the cemetery.

Ern observes the clock face that towers above them, recognising a perfect opportunity to test the child's time-telling skills. He points to the clock. 'What time is it, Joy?'

Joy turns her head upward. 'Ten o'clock,' she responds promptly.

'Correct. Well done,' he affirms. 'This is the Boroondara Cemetery,' he explains.

'What a strange name – boroodar,' says Joy, as she struggles to pronounce the word.

'Yes, I hear it means a place in the shade. It's an Aboriginal word. I've told you about the Aborigines, haven't I?'

Joy nods and Ern continues. 'The Aborigines named this place. There must have been lots more trees here then – like that big one over there,' he says, pointing to a huge gum tree that towers over the young English deciduous trees and cypresses that have been planted here.

Ern's thoughts drift to how it must have been before the invaders arrived. His mind wanders to another burial ground – on his property. The boys had been digging and loading sand from one of the low sandhills down by the river. They had come bursting into the house one day urging their father to come and see what they'd dug up. Ern followed his sons across the paddocks to see that the boys had unearthed a human skull and some other bones. Ern soon learnt it was as he suspected – an Aboriginal burial ground. He instructed the boys to fetch their shovels, and the skeletal remains of these ancient people were respectfully buried and laid to rest once more in their ancestral land.

Ern has no difficulty finding the familiar grave site. It is just past the new Syme memorial. He has read about *The Age* publisher's impressive monument. It proves to be even more spectacular than he'd imagined, with its polished granite pillars and copper fittings. It looks like an Egyptian temple with its pillars encasing the tomb.

While Joy climbs up and explores the little temple, Ern stops on the path just ahead, paying his respects to the Merritt ancestors whose names are listed on the tall headstone. It is difficult to read; the dappled shade from the waving trees nearby splays across the stone. The inscribed slab towers tall, as though guarding the one behind, lest anyone should discover its secret.

Joy appears at his side. 'These are some of my mother's relatives,' he says, 'the Merritts.'

Moving around to the slab that lies flat on the ground directly behind the Merritt one, Ern is pleased with the simplicity of the grave's stone surface with its ornate fencelike border of iron. The additional words are inscribed on the stone just as he'd ordered.

IN LOVING MEMORY\
OF\
THOMAS GARDINER\
WHO DIED 16 AUGUST 1910\
AGED 77 YEARS\
ALSO HIS WIFE\
ELIZA AGNES\
WHO DIED 9 JUNE 1901\
AGED 58 YEARS

AND HER MOTHER
ELIZA AGNES MERRITT
WHO DIED 8 SEPTEMBER 1900
AGED 83 YEARS

'Here are your grandma and grandpa,' he says to the little girl, relieved she has not yet learned to read, otherwise she might ask for an explanation about his grandmother.

'What does it say?' asks the curious little girl.

'Ask me again. You'll need to speak up, you know,' he says as he stoops to face his daughter.

Joy repeats her question and adds, 'Can you read it to me please, Father?'

Ern proceeds to read the simple words, but stops when he comes to 'AND HER MOTHER', afraid the little girl might ask questions about her great-grandmother. He's glad he's had those words added.

Ern will carry the secret into the future as the memories of his grandmother slide into the past. He will not return to this place again. His focus will now be on the future of his seven children. There will be grandchildren and great grandchildren to follow. He will feel the need to protect them from the stigma that still remains. It won't be too difficult, due to his deafness. He can always pretend he's not heard any questions that might arise. He brings to mind his mother, and remembers his promise to her. He will keep his promise. He will not share the story of his grandmother's life.

Magpies are carolling in the gums nearby, and a pair of kookaburras suddenly burst into a joyful duet, lifting Ern's spirits. He moves his gaze to his little daughter. Her blue-grey eyes hold the promise of a bountiful future.

He smiles and says, 'Let's go home, Joy-bell. Let's go home.'

Author's Note

The facts upon which this story is based emerged from my curiosity to learn more of my maternal grandfather's ancestry. I joined my local family history group to find out what I could about James Ernest Gardiner's life, wondering if there was a hidden family secret, given that my mother knew so little about her father's side of the family. My first inclinations were of convicts among our ancestors, and so I was surprised and curious to discover instead that my grandfather's grandmother Eliza (Lizzie) Agnes Merritt (née Dimsey) had suffered what is now known as bipolar disorder, and that she had spent more than forty years incarcerated in the first lunatic asylum in Victoria. Further research exposed the injustices, discrimination and maltreatment experienced by those with mental illness in the second half of the nineteenth century, which compelled me to tell her story in a way that would honour her life and give her a voice.

I followed a trail of clues from her childhood in the county of Hertfordshire, her movements as a young adult, including her marriage and the births of her children, and the passage to Australia. Clues to her movements in Victoria were found in Victorian newspapers and asylum records. While research revealed a wealth of information about the life of Lizzie, aspects of her story have been lost. Gaps were filled, however, by imaginings based on research and knowledge of her ancestors and descendants. In developing Lizzie's character, her history recorded in the asylum casebooks provided some clues. A vast collection of historical records were sourced, including the British Schools Museum in Lizzie's home town of Hitchin; British censuses; Yarra Bend Lunatic Asylum records and Victorian Public Records. Real characters from direct historical archives appear in Lizzie's story, including, for example, George

Stephen's account of the voyage on the *Oliver Lang*. All of the main characters are real, except for Lizzie's friend Monica. Cathy's story was found in the asylum casebooks, but her real name is concealed.

Two visits to Hitchin in the county of Hertfordshire in England where Lizzie grew up provided further opportunities for understanding her early life: visits to the British Schools Museum which now sits on the site of the school where Lizzie's parents taught, and the family home where she spent her childhood; walking through Wain Wood and the hamlet of Preston, where her husband Jasey spent his childhood; exploring Hitchin village and marketplace; traversing St Mary's church and its grounds and climbing the bell tower; and a visit to Luton, where Lizzie lived with her children before setting out for Australia.

Living in Victoria, I was familiar with the locations of Melbourne, Geelong and Ballarat, where Lizzie's later life was spent, and I was able to revisit those places for further research. All that remains of Yarra Bend Lunatic Asylum is a five-metre bluestone gate pillar in Yarra Bend Park, with a plaque acknowledging the history of the asylum.

Lizzie was my grandfather's grandmother. My grandfather, James Ernest Gardiner, was known to both me and Lizzie, and thus provides the linchpin connecting ancestors to descendents. He was also the carrier, in my branch of the family, of the secret of Lizzie's mental illness and incarceration. Ern, as he was affectionately known by all who knew him, was generous, kind and non-judgemental, as was his daughter (my mother), which gave me further clues as to the way I would expect my ancestors to deal with social issues.

I chose the name Lizzie for Eliza Agnes Merritt to avoid confusing her with her elder daughter who bears the same name, and also because I felt it was playful and therefore suited the character I imagined.

Sources

Agar, N. E. (1978). *Hitchin's straw plait industry*. Hitchin: Hitchin Historical Society.

Annear, R. (2005). *Bearbrass: Imagining early Melbourne*. Melbourne: Black Inc Books.

Barnard, F.G.A. (1910). *The jubilee history of Kew, Victoria, 1803–1910, E.F.G.* Melbourne: Hodges Mercury Office. https://biostats.com.au/Kew/contact.html

Barnard, F.G.A. (1920). *The Jubilee history of Kew, Victoria, 1803–1910*. Melbourne: Mayor of Kew.

Birch, J. and British Schools Museum (2008). *Educating our own: The masters of Hitchin Boys' British School 1810 to 1929*. England: British Schools Museum.

Birth, Death & Marriage certificates. Victoria, Australia & England.

Bonwick, R. (1995). *The history of Yarra Bend Lunatic Asylum*. Melbourne: Department of Psychiatry, Austin Repatriation Medical Centre.

Charlwood, D.E. (1983). *The Long Farewell*. Ringwood, Vic. Penguin.

Coroners Court of Victoria (1900). Inquisition – Eliza A Merritt.

County of Hertfordshire (1875). The last will and testament of William Merritt. England.

County of Middlesex (1844). The last will and testament of Ralph Quested Dimsey. England.

Day, C. (1998). *Magnificence, misery and madness*. Melbourne: Melbourne University.

Duruz, R. (1972). *The story of Curdies River*.

Farmer, P.W. (1900). *Three weeks in the Kew Lunatic Asylum*. Melbourne: John J. Jianlligan.

Fletcher, J. S. (1985). *The infiltrators: A history of the Heytesbury 1840–1920*. Shire of Port Campbell, Victoria: Heytesbury District Historical Society.

Foster, A.M. (1987). *Market town*. Hitchin: Hitchin Historical Society.

Frame, J. (1985). *Faces in the water*. Canada: The Women's Press.

Friends of the British Schools Museum. *School reports (Hitchin), 2007–2014*. Hitchin: Friends of the British Schools Museum.

Geelong Advertiser and Intelligencer (1855). https://trove.nla.gov.au/newspaper.

Hassam, A. (1994). *Sailing to Australia: Shipboard Diaries by nineteenth century British Emigrants*. Manchester University Press.

Hertfordshire Archives. Hertfordshire, England.

Hine, R.L. (1972). *History of Hitchin* (Vols. 1 & 2). Hitchin: Eric T. Moore.

Hornbacher, M. (2008). *Madness: A bipolar life*. United States: Houghton Mifflin Company.

International Genealogical Index (IGI) – Family Search Historical Records. Film. https://www.familysearch.org/search/collection/igi

Jonsson, P.D., Skarsater, I., Wijk, H., & Danielson, E. (2011). 'Experience of living with a family member with bipolar disorder'. *International Journal of Mental Health Nursing*, 20(1), 29–37.

Kinlock, H.W. (2004). *Ballarat and its benevolent asylum: A nineteenth-century model of Christian duty, civic progress and social reform*. Ballarat: University

of Ballarat. https://www.findandconnect.gov.au/ref/vic/bib/P00000230.htm

Merritt, A.E. (1987). Merritt family history.

Merritt, H. (1987). Merritt family tree.

National Library of Australia (1855–1870). Trove Newspapers. https://trove.nla.gov.au/help/categories/newspapers-and-gazettes-category

Northumberland and Durham Family History Society. Newcastle Upon Tyne, England.

Parks Victoria (2015). *A brief history of Yarra Bend Park*. Melbourne: Parks Victoria.

Parliament of Victoria (1857). Report of board appointed to inspect the Yarra Bend Lunatic Asylum, and to report upon the accommodation required. Melbourne: Government Printer.

Parliament of Victoria (1857). Report of the Yarra Bend Lunatic Asylum for the year 1857. Melbourne: Parliament of Victoria.

Presland, G. (2008). *The place for a village*. Melbourne: Museum Victoria Publishing.

Public Record Office Victoria (1839–1923). Immigration passenger lists, 1839–1923. https://www.familysearch.org/search/collection/2778600

Public Records Office of Victoria (1856–1872). *Yarra Bend Lunatic Asylum case books*. Melbourne: Public Records Office of Victoria.

Public Records Office, Victoria (1856–1872). Ballarat.

Richardson, H. H. (1930). *The fortunes of Richard Mahoney*. Melbourne: Penguin.

Showalter, E. (1987). *The female malady: Women, madness and English culture 1830–1980*. UK: Virago Press.

Stephen, G. (2000). Letter, May–July 1855 (Microfilm). Canberra: National Library of Australia.

The Argus. Bowie v.Wilson trial. (1862). Melbourne: *The Argus*.

The Age. Melbourne (1880). 'Hospitals for the Insane'. Castieau, J.B. Melbourne: *The Age*.

The Ballarat Star (Vic.: 1855–1865). Canberra: National Library of Australia. https://trove.nla.gov.au/newspaper/title/185

The Beckett Book Committee (1990). *The Becketts of Brucknell*. Victoria, Australia.

The Melbourne Argus (1855–1870). Canberra: National Library of Australia.

The National Archives (1841–1881). British censuses 1841–1881. UK: The National Archives.

The Vagabond Papers (1876). Melbourne: *The Argus*.

Walmsley, R. (1985). *Early education in Hitchin*. London: Hitchin Historical Society.

Walmsley, R. (1998). *Early education in Hitchin*. London: Hitchin Historical Society.

Willis, E. (1994). *Behind closed doors: A catalogue of artefacts from Victorian psychiatric institutions held at the Museum of Victoria*. Melbourne: Museum of Victoria.

Acknowledgements

First and foremost, I must acknowledge the Yorta Yorta People, traditional owners of the unceded land on which I was born and have lived for most of my life and on which the book was written. I acknowledge my own ancestors, hoping those characterised in the book would find my portrayal of them respectful.

My search for my great-great-grandmother's story began when I discovered on the internet a project of the National Library of Australia entitled 'First Families 2001'. A contributor to the project, Alwyne Merritt, was also a direct descendant of Lizzie. I was able to contact Alwyne; we met at Lizzie's grave. I thank her for generously providing me with the material she had gathered to date in her own research.

My husband, Glenn Walker, has always been my cheer leader; his faith in my ability has been a constant over more than five decades. He patiently listened to and read my early attempts at writing.

Thanks to our daughter, Shelley, without whose constant encouragement and prompting, this book would never have been published. She offered her skills in editing and assisting with submissions to publishers. Her partner, Lance, was the first person, apart from Glenn, to read the whole book; his positive feedback gave me the confidence to imagine the possibility of the book being published.

I wish to thank Terry and Rosemary Ransome, committed volunteers at the British Schools Museum in Hitchin, who introduced me to the history of Lizzie's family and village life, and shared with me their own research of the family.

Thanks to all who read part or all of early drafts for their encouraging feedback: son Ashley, daughter Natalie; my siblings Meriel, Ivan and his wife Margaret, and Maurice.

My thanks to Goulburn Valley U3A Writers Group for providing the opportunity to develop my writing skills and the courage to 'dip my toe in the water', and test my writing ability.

Thanks to my sister-in-law Pat Wheelhouse and Shepparton Family History Group for getting me started on researching my ancestors.

I express my appreciation to Ginninderra Press for publishing the book, and for a congenial approach in ushering the book seamlessly through the publishing process.

www.ingramcontent.com/pod-product-compliance
Lightning Source LLC
Chambersburg PA
CBHW021310190726
48288CB00003B/783